LIKE IT NEVER WAS

A THRILLER

FAITH GARDNER

MIЯROR
HOUSE
·PRESS·

Be the first to learn about Faith Gardner's upcoming releases by joining her newsletter!

For my mom—
who, sadly, vetoed my idea
of dedicating this book to Bigfoot.

ONE
THEN

IT WAS MID-JUNE, twilight, the sky a bruised blue above the oak-covered hills. Crickets chirped. Bats blew through the treetops with tiny screams. The highway connecting the beach to the mountains was sleepy enough that there were minute-long lulls between speeding cars.

A short straightaway unraveled into turn after turn as you started up the pass.

That's where I, Jolene Vero, waited.

Crouched behind a felled tree covered in moss and vines.

In a gorilla suit.

It was a sauna in the heavy costume, one that reeked of other people's sweat. Every so often, I pulled off the mask for a breath of fresh air. But not for too long. I needed to be ready when I heard it.

Elizabeth Smith's car, a Karmann Ghia, was a classic with shiny tangerine paint, and just like her, something was off about it. At first glance: impressive, cute, vintage. Want. But it leaked oil everywhere it went, emitted foul black clouds of smoke when it started up, and could be heard from half a mile away. It was the energy vampire of cars.

As I sat there behind the log waiting for the sound of Elizabeth's clunker, I had time to think about everything. About Elizabeth. About the misdemeanors that racked up in the past year. Her uptalky singsong voice cornering me into conversations. The random silent treatments for no reason at all. Her obsession with conspiracy theories. The clothes, the hair, the boy. And of course, the possible poisoning. Even her stupid car was something she knew I wanted and then stole for herself. And worst of all: the innocent denials she begged whenever I called her out on any of it.

The memories made me mean.

It was like a drug kicking in, my anger. I took it and I took it and I took it and then the last week of school, I heard her bragging that she saw a Sasquatch while driving home. Of course she didn't see a Sasquatch while driving home. She was unbelievably full of shit. I heard everyone laughing at her and that, right there, was the moment I hatched this plan.

I'd never pulled a prank like this on anyone before, but once I spotted the gorilla costume in our theater building recently, it was just too tempting. Elizabeth wanted to tell a tall tale about Bigfoot? Well, I'd give her Bigfoot. I was going to scare the daylights out of her and it would be hilarious. We had just graduated. I was about to leave town and start a new life and this prank on my nemesis was some version of closure.

I thought I was a good person.

But like love, goodness is never really unconditional.

Push, push, push ... at some point, somebody's going to push back.

As the cricket symphony swelled, a new sound split through it—her engine chugging closer. The tone crept higher and higher as it neared. I fluttered with a thrill, envisioning the fear on her face. She would tell everyone she saw Bigfoot—literally! She'd swear! On her life! She'd post about it with too many exclamation points on social media. People would laugh at her stupidity and I would laugh the hardest.

When the sound of Elizabeth's engine rose to a sputtering roar, I hit my cue. I popped out like a jump-scare from behind the felled tree and waved my gorilla arms at the tangerine car speeding toward me. The mask was humid from my giggling breath. Lumbering toward the shoulder of the road, I wanted to be sure she saw me.

And she did, all right.

Her lips opened wide into a silent scream. I could see the terror shining in her eyes and the way she mouthed *Oh my God* and then swerved her car in an unexpected left turn straight off the pass with a screech of burning rubber.

It happened in a blink—one moment she was barreling toward me, the next I was listening to the crunch of her car rolling down an embankment.

And then the person saying *Oh my God* was me.

The highway was deadly quiet after the sound of twisting metal and breaking glass faded. Time seemed to halt. My mind scrambled to make sense of what just occurred.

I didn't think she'd swerve across the other lane and make a left turn off the hill. I ... I didn't know what to do now. Should I run across the highway after her? Scream for help and hope someone could hear me out in this wilderness? Wait for a car to flag down?

I froze, choked by shock.

I was in a gorilla suit. I wasn't sure how to explain that to anyone who saw me. And the other side of the road was a steep embankment, there was no way to scale it in this outfit without possibly tumbling down it myself.

My stunt—my stupid, careless, idiotic, dangerous stunt —caused an accident.

My chest tightened and my feet were made of bricks.

Do something! I screamed silently to myself.

But my body didn't move.

How could I help her? What could I even do? I was eighteen years old, not a paramedic. The sound of approaching cars released a new wave of adrenaline. Help! I'd get help. I turned and ran into the trees in my gorilla suit, terrified for Elizabeth's fate and terrified someone would spot me and associate me with the accident.

It would be better for everyone if I left and called for help. There was nothing else I could do. I shouldn't have been there in the first place.

Fuck, fuck, fuck, fuck, *fuck.*

TWO

BY THE TIME I got back to my car, which was parked up a crossroad about a five-minute sprint away, I was shaking so badly that I had to take the suit off and strip down to my camisole and short shorts in the car.

My phone was dead in my purse.

Of course it was. And service was spotty here anyway.

I hyperventilated.

Should I go try to rescue Elizabeth myself? How would I, even? What a coward I turned out to be when the literal rubber hit the literal road.

But then I spotted a woman walking her German Shepherd about thirty feet away. I got out of the car and waved her down.

"Hey!" I yelled, jogging toward her. "Oh thank God. Can you call 911? There was an accident on the pass just there at the end of the street. A car drove off the side. Please, my phone is dead!"

"You're kidding me," the woman said, covering her mouth. "Yes, of course. Right down at the end of *this* street, you mean?"

I nodded.

"I live about three houses up." She gestured behind her. "Didn't bring my phone with me, but I'll go back. My goodness, that highway is so dang dangerous if you drive too fast."

A little sob escaped me. "Thank you. Thank you for calling it in. It was an orange Karmann Ghia."

"Gotcha." The woman turned and sprinted, her dog chasing after her.

Shivering from shock under the shade of the oak trees, I debated whether I was supposed to follow the woman. But back in my car, there was the gorilla suit, the evidence that this was all my fault.

Fuck was too weak a word.

I put my hand over my mouth. As I stood in the darkening road, there was nothing but the sound of the whispering leaves. I reminded myself that most people survive car accidents. My mind kept spiraling with horrid images of Elizabeth covered in blood, her car crushed, a spray of broken glass.

My fault. *Mine.* I did that to a person.

The self-hatred was paralyzing.

But I pulled my hand away from my mouth and walked toward my car. Looked back over my shoulder, where the woman had disappeared.

Inhale, exhale.

The woman had it under control. She was calling someone. Help was coming. This could be fixed. The paramedics would be here soon. Elizabeth would be rescued by the people who knew what they were doing.

I got back to my car, climbed in, and turned on the ignition. I cast one more worried glance up in the direction the woman had run. The road was all shadows, the houses set far back from the roads and shrouded with trees. I made a U-turn and then a right onto the highway, the spot where Elizabeth's car had just veered off fading in my rearview.

Eerily calm.

Looking nothing like the scene of a ghastly accident.

Trying to flush it all out of my head, I turned on the stereo and cranked up the 13th Floor Elevators, "You're Gonna Miss Me."

I shook like a human earthquake. Should I even drive in this condition? Steady, breath. Steady now.

Guilt hit me worse than the flu.

My mind fired off a paralyzing parade of possibilities: I might have just killed someone; I definitely hurt someone; her family would be devastated; my life was over.

I saw a melancholy funeral scene.

I saw the gray concrete interior of a prison cell glaring back at me.

I began to cry as I continued the drive up the hill. In my rearview, I thought I saw a plume of smoke rising above the tangled oaks—but told myself no, no, it was just a cloud.

Help was on the way.

At home, I shoved the gorilla suit in a plastic bag and stuffed it in the garbage bin. My high school theater wouldn't be getting it back now. First thing, I started checking police and highway patrol sites for any update on the crash. Nothing yet. Please make Elizabeth okay. Please make it so she wasn't hurt. I might have hated her a little, but I didn't want to injure her, and I certainly didn't want her dead. Oh man, I couldn't even fathom that thought.

I had to call my dad.

THREE

DAD WAS—AS usual—still at the office. He was a high-profile criminal defense attorney. He was also my favorite person in the world.

"Daddy," I said shakily.

"What's wrong?" His voice seemed to crawl closer, as if he could detect my horror.

I took a deep breath and chose my words carefully, the way he taught me. "Hypothetically speaking, if someone were to ... say ... cause a car accident and that car accident resulted in injury and/or—" I swallowed a lump the size of a boulder. "—death—but no one saw it happen—could that person go to prison?"

He was silent. I could hear the sound of movement, a door shutting. Finally, he murmured, "Bunny. You okay?"

Bunny has been his nickname for me since I was little, because of the way I wrinkle my nose when I smile.

"I'm fine," I said. "Hypothetical question."

He blew out a long breath. "How would this hypothetical person have caused a hypothetical accident?"

"By jump-scaring them from the shoulder and startling a driver so badly they veered off the road."

In the silence, I could almost hear him biting his tongue to stop himself from an outburst to chastise me. Hypothetically, of course.

"A pedestrian did this."

"Yes, Daddy."

"Worst case? The pedestrian could be charged with manslaughter. They could certainly be sued to high heavens for negligence."

"I thought pedestrians always had the right of way."

"Don't believe everything you Google, kid."

The blood seemed to drain from my body and I got dizzy, imagining Elizabeth dead. The weight of the guilt hit me like a rockslide. Her poor family, sobbing at their loss. Elizabeth robbed of a future, of her *life*. And then my future—my boundless future, sparkling with college and friends I hadn't met yet and starring roles in plays—all disappearing with a miserable *poof*.

"Did the driver see this pedestrian?" he asked.

I swallowed and worked hard to control the shake in my voice. "Well, yes but—not in a way they could be recognized."

"Elaborate."

"The pedestrian was ... in a gorilla suit."

The silence was so long and dreadful I was drowning in it. I closed my eyes and pushed my fingers into my forehead, hard, wondering if I could perform a lobotomy on myself.

Just carve a morsel out of my brain and make this all go away.

"In a gorilla suit, for fuck's sake," he muttered to himself. "Why the—you know what, never mind." The sigh he blew out was piercing. "Okay. Hypothetically if no one saw anything, then, well, who's to say? Tree falls in the woods, et cetera."

My mind spun this thought around and around again. I let go of my fingertips, released a little pressure from my forehead.

"Tree falls in the woods," I repeated faintly. Closing my eyes, I saw a tree falling and then vanishing into thin air.

"I mean, if no one saw it, did it really happen?"

Now it was morphing into a philosophical question. I chewed the thought, savoring it. Relaxing as the actual seemed to blur into the abstract.

I sat on the edge of my bed and eyed my wall, the reprint of Picasso's *Girl before a Mirror,* which my dad bought me at the MoMA gift shop last time we visited my grandparents in New York.

"You've been home all night tonight, right?" he asked. "You haven't gone anywhere."

The implication took its time sinking in, but then I began to feel freer. The invisible weights on my shoulders grew wings and flew away. I've always been a girl with a wild imagination, and I imagined what he was saying vividly, in color, replaying it like a movie, a memory. Yes, I was here. Right here. Look at the piles of clothes and the half-packed suitcase on my bed. Tomorrow, I was off to summer camp in the mountains of Santa Ynez Valley, to be a camp counselor for the third year in a row.

"I've been packing," I said.

"You've been packing," he agreed. "All right, let's end the hypotheticals and let you get back to it, shall we?"

"Love you, Daddy."

"Back atcha."

Beep said the phone in my ear as the call dropped. I turned to my packing and worked hard to imagine I was here for the past hour. Of course I was here, I hadn't left the house. But I couldn't help the truth from peeking in. Every few minutes, I checked the local news for updates about automobile accidents. Refresh, refresh, refresh until my index finger cramped.

When I didn't see the news anywhere, I almost started to believe it hadn't happened.

By bedtime, I stopped checking. If there had been a fatality there would have been an update by now. I started making up a story in my head that if it happened at all—which it hadn't—it had been a minor accident and Elizabeth had gone home with bumps and bruises and dents in her Karmann Ghia. Close call. Could have been so much worse.

Little did I know that Elizabeth was screaming in a burn unit thirty miles away and her left leg would be amputated at dawn.

I had no idea. I slept long and hard.

Sleep, that sweet forgetting.

FOUR
NOW

IT'S BEEN TEN YEARS, and still—sometimes I wake up and the first thing I think of is what I did to Elizabeth.

At first it happened every morning, then less and less as the years wore on, until finally, now, it's just once in a blue moon. But sometimes she pops to mind and crushes me out of nowhere. I get a nightmare stomach-churn. And then I tell myself I was never there. It's a shame and a tragedy, but not my business. Elizabeth survived. She's okay and living a fine life out there somewhere.

But when my mind trips up, when the guilt glitches and hangs on like a ghost, when I *do* really let myself think of her?

I swear she tried to poison me back in high school. Just imagine what she'd do to me now if she knew it was me who ran her off the road that day.

FIVE

I'M STARTING OVER AGAIN, déjà vu, sitting passenger in my dad's Tesla.

Central California blazes by the window, a rapid movie of greenery, fast food signs, farmland and sloping hills, gasps of small towns. It's a five-hour drive my dad fills with business calls and I fill with daydreams. Curious houses perched on hillsides, roadside stands with hand-painted signs for fresh produce. Everywhere I look, I can imagine living there.

I get a text from my best friend Alice,

> You get to Berkeley yet?

>> Still a couple hours away. I'll let you know when I get there.

> Excited for your new endeavor!

Good old Alice. "Endeavor" seems like a generous word for what I'm doing, but I'll take it.

Over the years, I've learned the art of how to sever ties.

Call it a knife-sharp gift. Where it came from, I can't say—born, learned, either way, it's mine. I can cut things and people out of my life with the ruthless precision of a surgeon.

Left California for undergrad in Chicago to pursue theater arts.

Left Chicago to try teaching English in Seoul and I couldn't stand the pollution, the lack of personal space, and the fact I couldn't find cheese anywhere.

Left Seoul to backpack through Europe and then there was my short stint trying to act in Hollywood, then art school, culinary school, cosmetology school. Somewhere in there, a pill problem and a half-assed stint at rehab. A short, sweet mental breakdown and a few flirtations with different diagnoses.

In the end, I've accepted I occupy a strange space where I'm not quite sane and not quite insane, not quite sober, not quite an addict. I'm just a professional dropout. I've got commitment issues. I'm nearly thirty years old and I'm ten miles wide and one inch deep.

And know what? That's all right. The world keeps moving and so do I.

It's fall. The air's grown teeth. And I'm about to start over once again, led by the wind of my whims.

SIX

MY DAD'S car is now in self-driving mode, hands off the wheel, as we zoom into the Bay Area.

His black hair's slicked back, he's in a shark-gray suit and plucking his unibrow in the rearview mirror. His phone's on the console with his inbox open. King of multitasking. He's also blasting AC/DC so loud my eardrums are tickling. It's okay though. It helps me tune out the advice he's spewing, a thing he does every time I take another U-turn in life.

"Maybe get your general ed done at that city college and see if you can transfer to Cal," he shouts. "Major in business. You'll hate it, but it'll give you a leg up as an entrepreneur."

"What? I'm not an—"

"Artists *are* entrepreneurs! Stop selling yourself short."

I contemplate, studying the ugly industrial buildings, graffitied billboards, and mighty warehouses as they whizz by. I grew up in the hills of luxurious, pristine Santa Barbara, but I always felt I deserved the grit of urban life. This tree-less, overpopulated metropolis is just what I need.

"I could be a nurse," I suggest.

"Jesus Christ, you want to throw your life away?"

My dad tosses the tweezers in the console between us and trades it for dental floss, starts flossing.

"I'm going to see what happens," I say. "See where the universe takes me."

He shakes his head. "Not the universe shit again."

Last week, after a nasty blackout from too many screwdrivers and a new antidepressant, I woke up in my childhood bedroom with the word *Berkeley* throbbing through me like a heartbeat. Sometimes I swear I can hear the universe talking to me. I know it's just me talking, but it feels nice, a comfort, imagining the universe cares about me and my wellbeing.

"Aye yai yai," he says, rolling down the window and letting the air suck the floss out. He rolls the window back up again. "How on earth did I father such a free spirit?"

I smile. He reaches over and squeezes my knee, right in the spot that always makes me yelp from ticklishness. He chides me, but he loves my free spirit. Every time I crash and burn, there he is with open arms. I say Berkeley and he says get in the car, I'll drive you there.

The words "free spirit" echo in my ears and a vicious, hag-like voice inside me hisses, *"Free spirit?" More like "loser." You are a loser. Every time it's the same thing with you. Pretending you're getting your shit together. Pretending this is finally the time you're going to do something worthwhile. Keep pretending, precious. That's all you're capable of doing.*

My smile melts and my eyes prickle. It hurts every time I hear that voice. But I've learned to ignore it.

Or at least, to pretend to.

SEVEN

IT'S BEEN a week now since I moved to Berkeley—a unique, chaotic little city teetering on the San Francisco Bay.

Its loud, beating heart is the oldest college in the University of California system, where a tower juts up from it like a gray middle finger in the middle of the green. Berkeley is a collision of college students, aging hippies, techies, and variegated weirdos. It's the land of free speech, of intellectualism, where Allen Ginsburg once sat in a café and wrote "Howl." It has both a laid-back, artsy vibe to it and a gritty, twitchy edge that makes you feel like someone might start randomly screaming at you or steal your wallet at any moment.

The houses in my new neighborhood are Queen Anne Victorians painted funky colors, overgrown with lush gardens and crawling with tangled vines. Unfortunately, the one-bedroom I'm subletting for the next six months is a downstairs unit in a Victorian that was clearly recently flipped—painted a stone gray, landscaped with a few trees with price tags still dangling, like a generic dollhouse that came straight from a factory. The inside of my apartment stinks of wood glue and paint.

My landlord lives upstairs, a tech bro who works from home for Google and wears Google T-shirts like a human billboard. He must get twenty deliveries a day—I hear the footsteps clomping up and down the stairs all day long. I gaze out my picture window longingly at the battered brown shingled house across the street, shaded mysteriously by a pepper tree, where a rusted VW van covered in bumper stickers is parked in the driveway, where a man sometimes sits on his porch barefoot and plays guitar.

That was what I was hoping for when I moved here.

EIGHT

MY DAD GOT me a job as a personal assistant for a former client of his. I feel stupid saying that. It's not lost on me that I'm approaching thirty years old and my daddy keeps bailing me out and trying to set me up for success, but whatever. If you've got a cow, might as well drink some milk.

The woman I'm about to start working for lives in a neighborhood a fifteen-minute walk away, where the sidewalks are sparkly clean and it's quiet enough to hear the birds' conversations in the ash trees. No one's pushing shopping carts of junk and muttering to themselves or smoking weed in the middle of the street like my neighborhood. I catch my reflection in the Mercedes parked in the driveway and that voice in my ear hisses, *You're a horrible person, you're revolting, she's going to close the door in your face.*

I bat it away like a bug and continue up the brick walkway.

The knocker on the mighty wood door is a cat with a

mouse dangling from its mouth. I use it, *knock knock,* and clear my throat, smooth my flyaways.

The door creaks open and a woman with a wild mane of silver hair aims a searing blue gaze at me. She's wearing an ankle-length flowery broomstick skirt and a teeny camisole on her thin body that makes her seem much younger than the wrinkles on her face seem to indicate. She doesn't blink and there's something almost witchlike about her stare, the poke of her cheekbones, the hard line of her mouth.

I am immediately intimidated. My inner child has turned around and run away already.

"Do you know who you are?" she asks, with the enunciation of an actor on a stage.

Obviously I do, but it's such a bizarre question my mouth drops open and I can't speak, like I've been suckerpunched in the gut.

"If you do, you are a liar," she says.

"Um," is all I manage. "I'm ... Jolene."

She studies me and it's possible that I might burst into flames under the relentless magnifying glass of her gaze. Maybe I've knocked on the wrong door.

"Suzanne Hill," she says. "And don't be alarmed. That's how I introduce myself to everyone—it's a line from one of my poems, published in the June 2012 issue of *Lyrical Horizons.* I find I'm able to see into one's aura when I surprise someone with it upon first meeting."

"You see my aura?" I ask, getting goosebumps.

"Yes, I do."

"What do you see?"

"Purple," she says. "Which is very good."

Purple?

She opens the door and spreads her arm out in a *welcome* gesture. I'm so weirded out by this introduction that it takes me a second to remember how to move one foot in front of the other.

Stepping inside, I'm struck by how both expensive and cluttered the place feels. First off, there's too much furniture —the opposite of the problem I currently have in my apartment. Every square inch of wall is hugged by a table, a chair, a settee, Tiffany lamps and glass display cases filled with knick-knacks. I've stepped into a residential antique store. Then there are the boxes of books and papers everywhere. When we touched base and she described my job, she said there would be "a melee of organizing and creative projects" and the state of this room makes it abundantly clear she truly needs the help.

"Nice to meet you," I say, unable to help the doubt in my voice.

"I'm glad you're purple, love, because the last assistant I had was a kind of grayish-green, and that didn't end well." She beckons me to follow her. "Come along, come along."

NINE

I STEP through the living room to follow her to the dining room, which is like a breath of fresh air after the space we were just in. A normal dining room, painted red, pots and pans hanging near a fern, with silver appliances shining and counters gleaming and clean.

"Are you ... moving?" I ask, glancing behind me at a stack of boxes in the next room.

"Tea?" she asks, heading to the silver stove.

"No thank you."

"Aren't we always moving? But no, no, not in the way you mean. You ask because of the living room? It feels like a violent space, doesn't it? Doesn't it seem to *harangue* you, almost?"

My dad warned me this woman was "batty," but I wasn't expecting this. Not sure yet if I can't stand her or if I adore her, but I know it's one or the other. There's no in between with this one.

"My expired husband's possessions," she says, coming to

the table with a steamy mug that says VIRGO AND PROUD. I'm interested in more details about this "expiration," but it seems too personal to ask. She points at a chair and we sit across from one another. "Detritus. Debris of a former love. I suppose your father hasn't told you much about me. *He's a character, isn't he? Talk about a smokin' white aura.*"

Is she saying my dad is hot? I can't tell.

"I owe him a favor for all he's done for me, that radiant beacon of a man," she says, sipping her tea, which smells like grass clippings. "That lionhearted prince."

I am beginning to think she does, indeed, have the hots for my dad. I breeze right over that one. "Yeah, he didn't say much, just that you needed an assistant—"

"Are you a student?" she asks.

"Not currently."

"Good. Pedantics—toss them in the heap. How old are you?"

"Twenty-nine."

"Twenty-*nine*?" Her hand, covered in rings, flies to her chest. "Good goddess, I thought you were a child. Not a day over twenty. You're a *woman*."

"Yes indeed."

I'm not sure whether to be insulted or flattered by her shock.

"Are you a poet?" she asks hopefully.

"No."

"An artist?" Just slightly less hope.

"I mean, I've dabbled."

She shakes her head. "A dabbler," she says, with sadness.

"Mainly, I'm an actress."

"An act-*tress*," she says, suddenly impressed. "Do tell."

"I majored in theater arts when I went to Northwestern. Lived in LA for a while, tried out for a few bit parts, commercials."

"Soul-sucking sex-mongering vultures down there," she says sympathetically.

"Kind of," I agree.

"What kind of acting are you doing now?"

"Not sure yet. I just enrolled in an improv class, we'll see where that takes me."

"Mmm." Her expression softens and as she studies me, I can't read what she's seeing. "Well, I hope you find what you need here in the Bay."

I smile. "Me too."

Suzanne gives me the grand tour. The rest of the house makes a lot more sense. In fact, it's a little bare, as if she's been removing pieces of furniture and boxes one by one and storing them in her living room. She tells me she's getting rid of a lot of things and she's going to need my help in organizing her house.

In her backyard, past the gazebo and browning tomato plants and wandering squash vines spilling from boxes, she shows me her "inspiration station." It's her writing studio, a tiny shed which has no windows. Inside, there are just four walls of whiteboard covered—and I mean *covered*—in all-caps handwriting with random lines like BELATED SUNRISE/ INFLATED SURPRISE and I CAN SEE CATASTROPHE BUT CAN CATASTROPHE SEE ME? In the very middle of the room, a small table that barely holds a typewriter. Of course this lady writes on a typewriter.

"I am never to be disturbed when I'm in the inspiration station," she says, aiming her intense eyes at me. "Do you understand? I don't care if Armageddon has cloaked the neighborhood. I don't care if my house is alight with fire. Nothing is more important than what happens in here."

"Understood," I say with a nod.

We shake hands. Hers is cold as a corpse, with a startling grip. I get a shiver and agree to come back tomorrow for my official first day.

Walking home, I'm smiling like I have a secret. I love this first stage when cities, jobs, and people are brand new. Like the beginning of a passionate affair—a place of pure potential, where anything can happen. Nothing will crash and burn. No, never.

TEN

I'VE LIVED in Berkeley now for two weeks. Turn the calendar page, watch the pumpkins appear on doorsteps one by one.

Here, there's something resembling seasons. Maple leaves are yellowing. One day, walking home, one falls on my head and it's like a sign from the universe—a little delicate hand reaching down to say, you made the right choice. This is it, this is where you need to be. Even if you're alone here. Even if you're spending your daylight hours running brainless errands like lugging a half-unhinged poet's tapestry to the dry cleaners and organizing her chapbook collection. Even if—

I turn a corner and stop walking.

Freeze up, stiff, upright rigor mortis.

Not ten feet away from me, parked in front of a bungalow with solar panels and a rainbow flag, is an orange Karmann Ghia.

The sight of it is horrid and familiar. That memory stabs

and thunders my pulse. The wind seems to stop along with the breath in my lungs.

Is this a heart attack?

Is this my still-young body crumbling already due to the pills I've popped and the booze I've guzzled and the poor eating habits that have stacked up over the years?

But I know it's not. It's not that.

It's panic, that monster inside me.

Elizabeth Smith, that vicious voice says in my head. *You maimed Elizabeth Smith. You can't run away from it, you pathetic worm. Lie to everyone else in your life but I won't let you lie to yourself.*

"Shut up," I whisper.

You left her for dead and didn't tell a soul. Demon girl. That's what you are. A curse. You shouldn't be allowed to walk and live and breathe after what you've done.

"You're not real," I say.

The voice is so loud, so unbearably loud. This isn't Elizabeth's car. That car is long gone. The girl I was, the girl who did that, she's long gone, too. This is ten years later and I'm standing on a street corner in an entirely different city over three hundred miles away. Still, the color orange is painful, too bright, like staring directly into summer sunshine. I shudder and keep walking.

I'm more real than you, pretender. Coward. You can stay quiet but I'll keep talking until the day you die.

Heading home, I pay careful attention to the click of my boots on the sidewalk, the tickle of the breeze on my nose, and the measured breath coming in and out of my lungs. I've learned, over the years, not to engage with the voice in my head. The more you feed it, the more it grows. If I start talking to it, that means I'm taking it seriously and I don't take it seriously. If I acknowledge it, then I believe it's real. It's a psychological tightrope, but I've been in this circus a long, long time.

Once I'm home, I put on music to fill the air with something. An upbeat playlist, girl groups from last century singing about nonsense like boys and parties. I hum along and do some dishes.

The voice gets quieter and then it's gone again. Victory. I always win.

I know hearing a voice seems alarming to an outsider. When I told a former psychologist, he was understandably concerned, and that was what started the whole downward-spiral dance with DSM-V, doctors trying out disorders on me like dresses in a dress shop. Is she borderline, is she schizoid? Schizophrenia? No, doesn't check enough boxes off the ol' checklist. Bipolar maybe? Nah, moods are too tame. They settled on trusty depression and then I went through the whole parade of antidepressants that never did much at all. What they ended up with is this: I'm not psychotic, because I know the difference between what's real and what's in my head. I don't actually hear voices. I just have a vivid imagination.

One that wants to eat me alive.

ELEVEN

IT'S ten o'clock at night. I'm sitting on my kitchen counter, eating coffee ice cream out of the carton and catching up with Alice on a video call.

"Madness," I say to my phone. "Sheer madness."

"You had to carry a medieval tapestry on a fifteen-minute walk," Alice says, as if she doesn't believe me.

"In the rain," I add. "Don't forget that minor detail."

If opposites do attract, that explains our friendship since high school, when we met at a music and arts conservatory held every summer. I was accepted as a budding actor, Alice as a gifted classical pianist. As soon as we were paired to paint each other's portrait in an art class, we knew it was kismet. There was just a chemistry there, a friendly spark that made conversation pop like popcorn. To me, Alice is a human touchstone, a steady drumbeat in a world where I can barely hold a tune. To Alice, I'm a wild child, the zany, unpredictable character in her life that feeds her entertaining stories. She's a general practitioner married to an accountant. Two roads don't fork much more in the world than ours. Alice, a gift from the universe.

She squints at me. "Doesn't this freaky woman you work for have a car?"

"Like me, this woman has no car."

Alice yawns. "Not that you drive anyway."

The way she says it is delivered with a little sting, like *not that you have your life together anyway,* but maybe it's just me. She's right. I don't drive anymore. After high school I stopped, developed a fear of it.

I put the ice cream down and clear my throat. There's something I want to say, a reason I called besides giving her the grand tour of my six hundred square feet, blank walls with nothing but my old Picasso reprint. I know she's busy and tired and has a million things to do tomorrow. So I say it, even though the words burn on the way out.

"Speaking of cars, I saw something today," I say. "The car. The car that ... that ..."

Alice waits, pokerfaced, not helping me out at all. She still looks just how she did in high school with her round face and big, expressive eyes. She even wears her hair the same—a sensible ponytail, every day.

"Remember?" I say. "That thing that happened I told you about, that I asked you not to tell anyone ...?"

"The boots you shoplifted?"

"Not that. No." Heat in my cheeks. "The other thing. From way back when."

"Starting that trash fire?"

Yikes, she makes me sound awful. Am I that awful?

Maybe I am. But anyone could sit down and write a CV of their wrongdoings and look like a horrid human being, right?

"No, the ... the car crash thing."

Alice's eyes widen and her face gets graver. "Oh. That."

She says it heavily, like it weighs on her too. Maybe it does. It's a pretty vile secret to have to carry for years for your best friend. She's the only human being in the world I've actually told about this. I confessed it to her a long time ago, maybe five or six years, and she was kind to me about it. Hugged me hard and told me it was an accident, I couldn't have known it would go so wrong. But she did urge me to come clean about it and go to therapy. Unfortunately, I'm bad at following good advice.

"It's not healthy to hold things like that inside, babes," she said at the time, as she wiped my tears. "Cortisol wreaks havoc on the system."

Since then, I haven't wanted to talk about it again. Until now.

"Wait," she asks. "*The* car? The actual car? Wasn't it totaled?"

"I mean, it wasn't the actual car. But it was one just like it."

"And you still haven't talked to someone about it?" she asks softly.

Talked to someone. She means a shrink. I would rather wrestle an alligator. "No, no."

"Oh," she says, with marked disappointment. In the background, her dog Sadie begins yipping. A chiweenie. Exactly as silly looking as it sounds. "Liam's home."

I interpret that as, *hurry up and wrap up your trauma*

dump. Should I even say that? Is it my trauma if I caused someone else's trauma? Shut up, brain.

"I just saw a car that reminded me of the whole thing. It's stupid. Not a big deal." I hop off the counter and go to my freezer, put the ice cream back inside.

"Maybe it was a sign to ... you know ... finally deal with the issue."

"From the universe?" I ask, stopping in the middle of the kitchen.

"No," she laughs. "Like, from yourself. The fact it upset you—" Her voice changes, gets higher and sweeter, and she turns her head. "Hi baby. Yeah, there's still some of that sushi from last night, want to eat that? Oh come on, it's fine." Her voice drops back to normal as she turns to me. "Liam says hi."

"Hi Liam. I'll let you guys go. I know it's late."

She smiles. "It was great talking to you though, I like your place. When you get some furniture it'll be even better."

"Yeah, that would help, wouldn't it?"

"And oh! I was thinking of coming out one of these weekends. Maybe I could visit, we could grab lunch?"

"I'd love that."

"We're not that far away now, it's like two hours with traffic. I'm excited I might get to actually see you in person and confirm you exist in real life again."

"Miss you."

"You too. Hang in there."

I wave and smile, but when the call drops, I drop my smile along with it. And I'm left alone in this apartment. Alice and Liam, having a lovely late-night dinner of leftovers and talking about their day. And here I am doing what? What am I doing?

"What do you want from me?" I ask the universe, with an edge of desperation. "What am I supposed to do with my life?"

But I get no response.

TWELVE

TELEGRAPH AVENUE IS the heart of counterculture in Berkeley. The street strikes dead center into campus and is lined with funky shops and merchants selling tie-dye and handmade jewelry on the sidewalks. The musky smell of nag champa hangs in the air outside colorful record stores. Among the power-walking, backpacked college students there are mentally ill, homeless people sparing change and wandering up and down the sidewalks. Seeing people who have, by societal standards, "lost their minds" twists me up inside. It fascinates me and stokes fear in me at once because I understand them.

Poke my head into the shops. Browse a bookstore, debate if I could pull off a sarong (verdict: no girl, please don't). People-watch, mesmerized by how young everybody seems. How confidently they carry themselves. When I was their age, I thought I knew everything. But growing up meant accepting I'm a fool. I don't dwell too long, though. All nostalgia seems to bring for me is cringing and regret.

People's Park—once a symbol of radical 1960s activism—is surrounded by police protecting the construction of student housing. The coffee shop where Allen Ginsburg wrote "Howl" is now a Japanese chain restaurant. I don't know what I was expecting to find here, but this isn't it.

There's this restless undercurrent, as if there's something I'm supposed to be doing, something more than working thirty hours a week and wandering around Berkeley to pass the time. Like the universe has a deeper mission for me here and I haven't picked up the clues yet.

THIRTEEN

"YOU DIDN'T MISS MUCH. Ginsburg was an overrated, pedophilic gremlin," Suzanne tells me as she watches me change the duvet cover on her bed.

Yes, apparently the job has morphed into part housework. The definition of "assistant" seems to be whatever Suzanne decides it is, day to day.

She sits on a chair in the corner of her bedroom, arms crossed and her many thin gold bracelets catching the sunlight. I'm not exactly sure why this task requires an audience, but I've quickly learned that Suzanne wants to watch my every move. I can't tell if it's because she's lonely or she thinks I'm incompetent, but it helps the time pass and she's interesting as hell so I can't complain.

"Yeah, I read that on Wikipedia," I tell her.

"Make sure you tie the wispy little strings in the corners."

"I am."

"And give it a proper fluff when you're done."

I fight the urge to say *yes ma'am* while I do as I'm told. I'm still wrestling that sinking feeling I got today, the letdown from visiting Telegraph Avenue. It reminds me of that summer in Seoul, that sticky regret that turned my stomach almost the moment I hopped off the plane. Something isn't right.

"Daveed used to be the one who actualized the bed," she says. "One of the only things that insufferable numbskull came in handy for."

"Oh?"

I've been waiting for the backstory of her "expired" husband. She has a section of her living room that contains boxes of *his things*—she hisses the words when she says them. Strangely, she doesn't seem ready to get rid of them. She says she may or may not need them for the memoir she may or may not write.

"Do you want children?" she asks.

She's made a violent turn in the conversation, dodging the subject of Daveed yet again. I make a note to ask my dad about Suzanne's deal later. He just told me vaguely she was "an interesting woman" with a "lotta spunk" and then reminded me of attorney-client privilege, which apparently supersedes father-daughter privilege.

"God no," I say.

I mean, I'm a grown-up child, not an adult. I'd make a garbage mother.

"I'm also childless and proud," she says, cocking her chin.

Won't lie, it's a little alarming how much I have in common with this woman.

"Do you have a significant other, love?" Suzanne asks,

nodding approvingly at my duvet cover job and reaching a hand to me. I come to help her to her feet.

"No."

Her eyes widen in blue surprise and she examines my face as if it's changed in this new light. I note we're exactly the same height. "None?"

"I mean, I date. I've just never found anyone that I care to share my life with to that degree."

In my dating life, like the rest of my life, I'm also a *dabbler* as Suzanne would say. I'm on dating apps. I try people. Just last week I had coffee with a guy who wouldn't stop talking about Pokemon, ogling my boobs the whole time; next. Then there was a woman I met up with at a bar. When I ordered a cosmo, she burst into tears and said her ex used to order the same thing; poor thing, goodbye. It's for the best anyway as when I *do* find someone I vibe with, I either lose interest in a flash or I get kind of obsessed with them.

But know what? Over the years I've found I enjoy being alone. In fact, it's not an unfortunate circumstance that's happened to me, it's a choice. This idea that people need to have another to complete them has always bewildered me. I have an excellent collection of vibrators. I'm good.

I don't tell Suzanne this, of course.

"A wise woman beyond your years/ deserts of loneliness, oceans of tears," Suzanne recites in a theatrical tone. "From one of my poems—December 2013 issue of *Celestial Stanzas Online Literary Review*."

I nod, not knowing how to respond. I finally land on, "Nice."

"Being alone is the bare-naked truth," she says, brushing a piece of my hair out of my eyes. The motherly gesture of it is comforting somehow, even if her words are not. "We're born alone and we die alone. Company is temporary."

Well, damn. That's some chilling nihilism right there. It's official: I kind of love Suzanne. She's unpredictable, yes. Sometimes she stares at me like she has x-ray vision and it gives me the willies. She recites her mediocre poetry aloud all too often. But there's a depth and strangeness to her I find compelling.

You're going to fuck this up, aren't you, you little disaster? the horrible voice whispers in my ear. I can almost feel the tickling breath of it. *You're going to do something terrible and ruin it all.*

I pretend I don't hear it.

FOURTEEN

MY IMPROV CLASS takes place at night in downtown Berkeley a few blocks from the subway station, wedged between a closed bagel shop and a packed Thai restaurant. Walking into the black box theater, beholding the rows of shadowy seats and the spotlights shining sunshine onto the stage—a smile spreads on my cheeks. I've never been to this theater before, but I've been to so many that look just like this. My high school theater, college theater, community theater. Home again.

It's been at least three years since I did any real acting. This is my first improv class, an intro workshop. I survey the other dozen or so people who are here, offer friendly smiles to strangers. An elderly dude wearing a sweatshirt that says FUCK CAPITALISM. A middle-aged woman with poodle hair ready with a fresh notebook and pen—come on, lady. You don't need to take notes in improv. A few hipsters in a row murmuring like they know each other. A handsome man with dark, messy hair and headphones on ... too handsome. I don't trust myself near him. Steer clear of that one. No college students here. Along with the hipster clique, I'm on the younger end of the spectrum.

The teacher comes in clapping, a bald man my dad's age with too-much-espresso energy. He's wearing a shirt with muppets on it and has a single dangling earring.

"Hello hello hello! All right all right all right!" he yells in a thick east coast accent—Brooklyn? Jersey? I can't tell. He takes center stage and opens his arms. "Are we ready or are we ready? Ya ready? Ya pumped?"

The room murmurs a tepid response.

"What are you doing up there?" he asks, pointing to us. "You know what this is, don't you? It's an improv class, not a one-man play. Get your butt down here on the stage where it belongs!"

I don't know about this guy. He reminds me of a sports coach and I've tried my hand at many things in life, but I've steered clear of sports. I leave my bag on the seat and join the rest of the class on stage. We sit in a circle, like a bunch of adults about to play duck duck goose. The teacher stands in the center, lording over us from the mush pot.

He introduces himself as Jerry Pinkerton and goes over his accolades: his degree in theater arts from NYU. His many classes he's taught over the years. The off-Broadway plays he's starred in and directed, some of them so far off Broadway they were actually in Newark. He proudly talks about the many times he was an extra on *Law & Order*. Listening to him, I'm reminded of how glad I am that I didn't pursue acting as a career. Because this guy's proud and that's great for him, but me? I'd be dying inside if I had slaved away at acting as long as this man and all I got out of it was some extra work to brag about.

"Improv," he says, pacing the stage. He delivers this with the passion of a monologue. "Imp-ah-*rah*-visation. Know what? I wish everyone in the world had to take this class. And not just because I'd be a billionaire." A few giggles. "Because improv doesn't just make you a better actor. It makes you a better *person*. It helps you learn to listen. To be here now. To focus on the positive. To be constructive. Supportive."

He's right. The whole concept of improv is beautiful. Someone does something in a scene and you accept it and build on it. You work with them. There's no saying "no" in improv. I love that it's a place that's all about living in the moment, accepting one another, and pretending.

We do a quick round robin of names and stand up for our first game, which will be "yes, and." Everyone's going to play together in a circle here. I love this. I shake the delightful jitters out of my arms and we all build a story together, each adding a line on.

"The sky is blue."

"Yes, and there's an airplane flying in it."

"Yes, and the airplane is crashing toward the earth."

"Yes, and I see some parachuters jumping from it."

"Yes, and one of the parachuters appears to be a horse."

That was me. I get some chuckles, which makes me sparkle with joy. I'm bubbling. I'm happier than I've been in a long time. This is where I belong, this is what I'm supposed to be doing. Should I be an improv teacher? Is this my life's purpose? Maybe that's what the universe wants. I'm wondering what kind of experience I would need to be the next Jerry when the thud of a door slamming makes everyone stop their *yes, and*-ing and a woman walks in on clicky boots, hurrying from the shadows to the stage.

Assuming she's arriving late, I don't look too hard at her at first. But then she joins Jerry in the middle of the circle. She's a bit breathless and wearing a white faux fur coat, dark blond hair parted in the middle. And then she turns her face, tucks her hair behind her ears, and I see the scars on her left cheek. Raised discolored wrinkles and tightened skin, an ear that seems to have been gnawed off. As if she can sense my staring, she whips her neck and looks straight at me. One of her eyes is bluer than the other.

My heart stops. My stomach does a horrid cartwheel.

It's Elizabeth fucking Smith.

FIFTEEN

"EVERYONE, HEY, LISTEN UP!" Jerry says, raising his hands. "This is my assistant, my protégé, the lovely and talented Liz Smith." He turns to her with a smile and says, "We've done intros and 'yes, and.'"

"Hi everyone!" Elizabeth waves. "Glad to be here. Let me tell y'all a little about myself ..."

My ears ring and my gaze glazes over. I can't hear her.

All I'm seeing is flames and all I'm smelling is smoke.

I haven't seen Elizabeth since high school, since before the accident. The last time I saw her, her mouth was in an O in horror and then she was careening off the side of the road in her car. The scars on her face, the half-eaten ear—they're all my fault. One of her legs isn't real. One of her eyes isn't real. I know this because I've looked her up on social media and followed closely the year after the accident when she posted about her recovery. And then guess what happened? I had a nervous breakdown and had to drop out of school. The guilt smothered me and I had to work hard, so hard, so very hard to get it out of my mind and move on. Stop looking her up, because it only made me writhe with guilt for what I did and irritation at her exclamation-pointy updates and then guilt that I dared to be irritated with her for exclamation-pointy updates after what I did.

It's a hellish Ferris wheel in my head.

She's telling everyone about her degree from UCLA and her work as an acting coach and the independent short film she wrote and that's great for her, really, I'm applauding her success, I won't lie and say my envy isn't piqued that she had the talent and focus to actually study acting instead of dropping out of Hollywood because she couldn't cut it but oh my God. Oh my God. Oh my *God*. As she speaks to us, her gaze moves from person to person and lingers on me and I wither under the eye contact.

Does she recognize me?

I look different now. Ten years have passed. My hair has grown out, it's a different color.

But does she remember me?

Can she tell that my cheeks are hot and that I'm standing here suppressing the urge to vomit?

Everyone else is smiling and relaxed but for me, it's as if someone pulled a fire alarm. I don't know what to do. Should I flee the room? Go grab my bag and run out of here? Why is she here? Why is this woman here, of all the places in the wide world? I can't look at her. The sight of her makes me want to implode.

You did that to her, you monster, the voice whispers.

And it's not wrong. I catch a glimpse of myself in a mirror near the curtain and it's wild how normal I look, nothing like a woman fighting a panic attack. I don't look like the truth.

Instead, I focus on Jerry. A game of freeze tag begins and while my mouth is moving and my body is going through the motions, my mind is elsewhere. All I can think is, I'm going to get through the next hour and then never come back here again.

I'm in the middle with the too-handsome guy, pretending to be a receptionist at a doctor's office. Being two people at the same time: the me who is sitting in a plastic chair and pantomiming typing on a computer and asking if I can help Mr. Handsome and the me who is a thousand miles away from here, burning up in flames of self-hatred.

"Freeze!" a voice says, touching my shoulder.

And I do freeze. Utterly, completely.

Elizabeth has touched my shoulder and she's looking right at me, not two feet away. I can smell her—jasmine, a hint of mouthwash. I flinch at the close-up of her pink scars. In this one horrible second that we meet eyes, a whole scene unfolds in my mind at intergalactic speed. She turns to the class and shrieks, *This woman tried to kill me!* And the mob roars with rage, swarms me, gives me the treatment I deserve.

Such a buck-wild imagination. No way that could happen. She never saw me, I was in a gorilla costume.

"I'm sorry, what's your name?" she asks with a smile.

Here it comes. The entire class is listening, watching, like this is part of the scene.

"Jolene," I whisper.

There's a jolt of recognition in her expression. "Jolene Vero?"

"Yes," I whisper, wishing I could jump into a hole in the ground and never return.

"Omigod!" she says, her icy blue eyes widening. "I know you!" She grabs my shoulder and turns to the class. "Jolene and I go way back. We went to high school together." Turning back to me, she grins. "It's a small world after all, isn't it? Okay, focus. I'm tagging you out now."

The relief that courses through my veins as I join the circle again is so overwhelming I think I might pass out for a second. My vision's sparkling. When she recognized me, I was expecting the world to come crashing down … but it didn't. Remorse is so powerful it feels like you're walking around spattered with red paint all over you, like you're marked, like everyone can see it. But it's invisible. In the mirror, I almost glimpse myself covered with it—but that's just my imagination.

She recognized me and it didn't matter.

I breathe a little easier. I'll be okay. I can get through this class.

After an autopilot hour, Jerry claps his hands and dismisses us, saying, "Great job, team! You did it! Bravo, bravissimo! See you next week!"

Oh, sweet baby Jesus in a manger, thank you. I make a beeline for my bag and vow to never come back here again. In fact, I'm never going to even walk within four blocks of this theater. Hell, maybe I'll change life plans and move somewhere else. I don't want to live in a city where I'm haunted by the possibility of running into Elizabeth. As I power walk toward the exit sign, a voice cuts through the air.

"Wait! Jolene!"

It's her, I'd know that shrill voice anywhere. I get a flash-back cringe from high school as I turn around. Yes indeed, it's Elizabeth. Calling out to me. Waving me down like she's waiting for me at the airport and I just got off the plane. I offer a weak smile as she hurries toward me with a very slight limp, the sight of which makes me want to crawl into the nearest Dumpster.

"This is so wild seeing you here!" she says, eyes bright. "How *are* you?"

"Oh, you know."

"Where're you headed?"

"Nowhere really, I—"

"Let's walk out together," she says, linking arms. *Linking arms.* Like we're buddies and I didn't ruin her life. "I want to know all about what you've been up to."

SIXTEEN

WHEN WE STEP OUTSIDE, the sky is starless and blue-black, a wisp of a moon over our heads. It's chilly, but I don't think that's why my teeth chatter.

We linger outside the door near a bus bench where someone has crudely carved VEGANS SHALL INHERIT THE EARTH. I can hear some deranged soul howling at the moon and a group of students on a street corner arguing about the Pythagorean theorem. A bag lady muttering to herself walks behind a group of well-dressed women with designer purses. Berkeley's a trip.

"Which way are you going?" Elizabeth asks.

"I've got to walk home," I say, apologetically—but not really, of course. "Long night ahead."

"Where's your place?"

"By the Ashby BART station."

"Same! Let's go, safety in numbers."

No consent asked. She yanks me with her and we walk in stride. What a nightmare. She lives near me? I curse the

universe as I smile and suffer through small talk with the
one person on earth I hoped never to see again.

"I was *gobsmacked* to see you in there," she says.

"Heh. You have no idea."

Elizabeth glows like someone who cheerfully eats her
vegetables and gets up early to go to Pilates. And the scent of
money just wafts off her—she was always the kind of girl
who thought everything had a price tag. An aging princess
like myself shouldn't judge, but as spoiled rotten as I am
with second chances and attention, my dad's never been one
to buy me fancy things. While I hunted for vintage treasures
at thrift stores, Elizabeth was the type to just go online and
buy them at the highest price.

She carries herself with a lightness I envy, though. She
can emanate kindness in a way that makes you feel incredibly special when you step into its spotlight. And she's cute
—freckles peppered on her nose, full lips. Like me, she still
dresses like it's 1970. She ripped my style off starting in high
school and apparently has kept it up ever since. We've both
got bell bottoms on, thick eyeliner, fake eyelashes. I'm
grateful to be on her good side so I don't have to stare at her
scars and her half-gone ear. Horrible to think, I know, but
the sight makes me sick. And it's no one's fault but my own.

"So how long have you lived in Berkeley?" she asks.

"Just moved here, actually."

"Omigod girl, same!"

Elizabeth's energy is a lot. She's a human exclamation
point. She's a soda can all shook up. Worse than that, she
was also volatile and unhinged back in the day, but maybe
she's changed. We're not in high school anymore.
Thankfully.

"You moved here from LA?" I ask, looking anywhere except her eyes.

Homeless folks have pitched tents in doorways and on street corners. The sight of it is jarring—so many encampments everywhere. I don't know if it's a reflection of how progressive this area is or how devastating the income inequality. Except for liquor stores and bars and a few deserted restaurants, most storefronts are shuttered now. Berkeley goes to bed early.

"Mmm-hmm. My fam lives around here now, it just made sense for the time being. I'm toying with the idea of going back to school, maybe become a drama therapist."

"Wow," I say. "That's awesome. I've never heard of drama therapy."

"Yes! It's a thing! Using theater for therapeutic goals. I'm actually thinking of concentrating on the use of improv, which is why I'm shadowing Jerry right now."

"That's so impressive, Elizabeth. Seriously."

Look at her and all she's been through, thriving and getting an advanced degree to help people. Meanwhile, I wander around like a lost woman-child and my daddy helps pay my rent.

"What about you?" she asks. "What's the tea? What do you do?"

"I'm an assistant for a local poet," I say.

Sounds a lot better than *I run errands for a half-madwoman.*

"Go you!" Elizabeth says. "I worked as a PA for a while for a well-known actress—don't ask, signed an NDA, can't dish, apologies."

"Damn you," I joke. "Now I *really* want to know."

"It was *fas*cinating, to say the least. A little peek into the salaciousness of Hollywood, you know what I mean?"

"Well, there's no shortage of that. I actually lived there for—"

"Anyway, the job didn't last long," she says, seemingly oblivious to the fact I was speaking. "I wanted to do more, which is how I moved into coaching, which is how I met Jerry—he was basically the coach who coached me into being a coach!" She laughs at herself. "How many times can I say coach in one sentence? LOL."

Yes, she said LOL out loud. This is punishment, isn't it? I'm being punished.

A few minutes into our walk, we gradually leave the downtown area behind. The neighborhoods darken, the ash trees hiss in the night air. Elizabeth fills me in on her life, about how much she doesn't miss traffic in LA and how she hopes she gets into the program at UC Berkeley but isn't sure and might have to settle for a state school and isn't the college debt situation so ridiculous? Oh wow, look at that dog! She loves poodles. Is that weird, to love poodles? It's probably because they're hypoallergenic. She's been thinking about getting an emotional support animal. Should she get a poodle?

I am trying hard to stop being petty, to remind myself high school was a long time ago, to give both of us some grace that we've changed. But she talks at me like this for ten minutes, every damn sentence uptalking, barely asking me anything. Then again, I should just be thankful to not have to say much. I don't have a lot to brag about and her conversation is a distraction from the guilt that is slowly inflating me and threatening to combust.

We cross Ashby and pass the BART station and I keep thinking we're going to part ways, she's going to stop for breath, something, *anything* to end this—but she doesn't. And as I make a turn up my street, she comes with me, like she's coming home with me.

Oh, what relief to behold the glow of my gentrified Victorian house. Just one more block. Just three more houses. Almost there.

I stop out front and point to my house, trying to interject while she chatters about how amazing it would be to use theater to help people and how she's always wanted to help people and how she's considered life coaching but isn't sure.

Can you imagine—this woman, going into a career based on listening? She can't stop her mouth from moving. She tagged herself into every improv game more than anyone else and she was supposed to be an assistant teacher.

There I go again. Gah. I'm trying, I'm trying *so* hard here, I swear.

"... because life coaching is so different than therapy and it ends up being a little closer to corporate coaching or executive coaching which—boy howdy, yes, pays the bills—but it's not ful*filling*, you know what I mean? I want to be ful*filled*—"

"This is my house," I blurt, interrupting her, even though it feels rude.

"Wow! Seriously? I live just around the block. One block away! Neighbors!" She turns to look at it. When she does, her face catches the light of the flickering yellow streetlamp and her scars are visible. I hold my breath. "You *live* here? Gorge!"

"Yeah, it's pretty great."

"Well, gimme your digits, let's hang." She whips out her phone. "Get a cap or a brewsky or something."

"I'll see you at improv too," I remind her.

"Oh of course we will! But we could both use a friend right now, since we're Berkeley noobs. I mean, I'm not a noob, exactly, I have lived here before. It's been a minute though, you know? What's your number?"

She looks at me expectantly, her half-lovely, half-scarred face illuminated blue by her phone. The smile she gives me is so innocent, so sweet, that it breaks my heart. She has no idea. She wants to be my *friend*. My eyes sting as I mumble my number.

"Spectacular!" she says, calling me.

My phone buzzes in my pocket.

"There, now you have my number. Wow." She reaches in and gives me a big hug, a tight one. She smells like summertime. As she pulls away, she flashes the peace sign. "So groovy seeing you. Blast from the freakin' past. We'll have to reminisce next time—take a lil stroll down memory lane! Gosh, can you believe high school was ten years ago?"

"Crazy."

As she walks away, she says, "Have a good night! Toodle-oo! Stay safe!"

"Yeah, you too."

When she finally, *finally* turns around and fades into the shadows, turning a corner, the breath I take in and out is so big it's like I grew a new set of lungs. My God. My *God*.

I rush inside my house, locking the door, and collapsing on the ground in a cross-legged position while still wearing my coat and purse. My hands are shaking. I'm fighting tears, which makes me just hate myself. Why do I deserve to cry, after what I did to her? That poor woman overcame so much and is so impressive and she's done so much with herself in the past decade. And yet I can't help it, I still find her so utterly irritating—but I make myself sick thinking that. It's all a tangled mess inside me and I wish more than anything I hadn't seen her. I want to pack my shit up and run away. I want to get so wasted I forget myself a little while. I want to be anywhere but here and anyone but me.

My phone vibrates in my pocket. Man, Elizabeth is texting me already.

Night night!!!

it says. A little goodbye, that's all. But the voice that reads it in my head isn't Elizabeth's. It's that sinister voice that's all mine.

Night night.

And it roars with cruel laughter.

SEVENTEEN

IF THERE IS an opposite to nostalgic, I am that. What point is there in ruminating on what's fixed and far behind? For the same reason I keep my eyes ahead of me when I'm walking, I keep my eyes ahead of me in time's relentless march forward. If I don't, I might trip and hurt myself.

Behind me: a mother who died of breast cancer when I was a toddler.

Behind me: a world of shame for what I did to Elizabeth.

Behind me: a trail of cities, failed careers, doomed relationships.

What is there for me back there? When I picture my past, I picture an apocalyptic wasteland, burning cars and war-torn zombies. Furthermore, my father taught me an important lesson at a young age: memories are nothing but lies we tell ourselves.

"Nearly seventy percent of wrongful conviction cases are due to eyewitness testimony," he yelled over the vacuum as he ran it back and forth across the carpet. Even when cleaning the house, he wore pressed slacks and dress shirts. "Can you imagine how many suckers have been locked up because of some bullshit story someone told themselves?"

I was in junior high then. Not exactly a looker at the time with a Supercuts bob and a mouth full of braces. I sat on the couch with my feet lifted up, a rapt audience of one. He switched off the vacuum and yanked the plug from the wall, wrapped the cord back up.

"The brain is rife with mistakes. I mean, sweet Jesus, how many times a week do you slip up and realize you misremembered something? Then imagine you put someone on the witness stand, someone who's been coached by the system, and then you have some poor schmuck behind bars for the rest of his life because someone told themselves a story." He shook his head and wheeled the vacuum cleaner into the closet, then brushed his hands off. "Remember that time I brought you to Take Your Daughter to Work Day in kindergarten, let you sit in the courtroom with me?"

I drew a blank, tilted my head.

"Come on. And you got locked in that bathroom stall during recess? We went to that place for high tea afterward?"

"Oh yeah," I said, the picture coming together in my mind. The somber courtroom, how my legs didn't touch the floor in the chair where I sat. Crying in the bathroom stall and a woman coaxing me to crawl under to get out. Scones and strawberry butter.

"That never happened," he said.

I was so taken aback I spit a laugh out. "What? Yes it did."

"Those are three memories I just conflated into one," he said. "High tea was your birthday. The bathroom stall was when we went to the zoo. You visited me in court one day, but there was never any Take Your Daughter to Work Day. I tell you this to prove my point."

His phone rang and he left the room to go yell into it and I was left on the sofa, stunned at how little I could trust myself.

I tell this story—which is what it is, a story, every memory nothing but a story—because when I sit at home tonight, hugging my knees and crying over my run-in with Elizabeth Smith, I'm haunted by a deluge of high school memories. And though I know I'm not fabricating them from nowhere, I can't be quite sure what I'm conflating, exaggerating, or seeing through a different lens.

But here's what comes back to me.

EIGHTEEN
THEN

I MET Elizabeth in Advanced Theater Arts senior year. She plopped beside me, a freckled girl in a fisherman's hat and flowery overalls and clunky hiking boots. Goofy smile and a wave like we knew each other, though I'd never seen her before—she was a transfer. You know the idea of "love bombing"? Well, Elizabeth Smith was a one-girl-sized cult.

"That outfit is so spectacular!" she said, admiring my velvet jumpsuit. I was obsessed with retro fashion, straightened my hair every morning, dyed it a bright copper red, spent more time on my makeup than my homework. "Where did you get it?"

"Found it at a thrift store," I said proudly.

She gasped. "And that hair color is so fab! Did you do it at a salon?"

"Nah, it's just box dye. Did it myself."

"Are those platform heels from a thrift store too?"

I nodded.

"Gosh, you're a freakin' model," she said, smiling. She

finger-combed her hair, as if the sight of me made her self-conscious. "My name's Elizabeth. I just transferred from Bishop."

"Oh, cool," I said.

Bishop was a private school downtown. I didn't know much about it except that it was for rich kids. My dad said he paid his goddamn taxes for public schools and private school was for chumps.

"Not that cool, actually," Elizabeth said. "My class was like ten people. I'm so glad to be swimming in a bigger pond. Hey, you have a hairbrush?"

I shook my head. I did have a hairbrush, but ... what? I just met her. I wasn't going to share my hairbrush with her. What next, my Chapstick?

When class started, the two of us were paired for a mirror exercise as a warmup activity. Everyone climbed onstage with their partners. Elizabeth and I faced each other and practiced copying one another's movements. First I was the leader and she was the follower. If I pointed and feigned surprise, so did she. If I broke into a disco dance, so did she. Then we switched. She made kissy faces at me and I made them back. Then she busted up laughing and I did, too.

After that first day, it was like Elizabeth thought we'd rolled around in glue together. She sat next to me in theater every day. At lunch, she joined me and the fluctuating group of theater and choir kids and always seemed to figure out a way to squeeze into the seat next to me. She gave me a mug she made in ceramics and a birthday card, which kind of weirded me out because I had no idea she knew when my birthday was. The day our school went home for Christmas break, she gave me a watercolor she'd been working on in art class. It was of me.

"I've been working on it since the beginning of the semester," she said, watching me as I studied it. "Since September seventh, the day we met."

It was a peculiar painting, abstract, colors bleeding into one another. I had holes for eyes and a crooked smile. I couldn't tell if the style of it was horrible or brilliant. Either way, it gave me the creeps. I rolled it back up.

"Wow, thanks," I said.

Her eyes shone expectantly.

"Sorry," I added, "but I didn't get anything for you."

Why would I? She was someone I was nice to in theater class and who ate her lunch near me. I knew barely anything about her.

"Oh," she said. "That's okay."

During Christmas break, she came to my house and knocked on my door. I didn't even realize she knew where I lived—I never told her.

"Happy holidays! I made Xmas cookies for you," she said.

Yes, she pronounced it that way, like *X-Men:* "Xmas." She handed me a cute lil tin with gingerbread men on it. I had been interrupted in couch potato mode and stood there in my pajama pants, no makeup.

"Um, thanks," I said. "Sorry for looking like a mess. I didn't know you knew where I lived?"

"I live up this way too," she said.

She gestured behind her, where a shiny Jaguar was parked on the street.

"Fancy car," I said.

"You don't drive?"

"I have my license. No car yet." I smiled. "I'm trying to convince my dad to buy me one."

"You know, you could ride home with me if you wanted, so you don't have to take the bus. I wouldn't mind carpooling. I could pick you up in the mornings, too."

"That's really nice of you," I said, wanting to wrap up the conversation.

But then my dad came up behind me. He had a spatula in hand and wore his silly apron that said *I Don't Need Recipes, I'm Italian.*

"Who's this, huh?" he asked.

"This is Elizabeth," I said.

"Her good friend from theater," Elizabeth said.

"Well, come in, good friend from theater. Don't stand out there freezing your ass off," he said. "Hungry? I'm making meat loaf."

"I'd love to!" she exclaimed. "Smells spectacular!"

Snap of the fingers and Elizabeth was in my house, marveling at everything. How gorgeous those curtains are! What a light-filled space! Love the wallpaper! Even though there was nothing fancy about it, she acted like she'd just stepped into a castle. I gave her an awkward tour of our three-bedroom house that was stamped with the same layout as every other house on the block. When she saw my room, her reaction was borderline orgasmic. She reached out and pet my duvet cover. She opened my closet and fondled my dresses.

"So this is how your room looks," she said, sitting on my bed and taking her jacket off. "I feel like you can learn everything you need to know about a person by spending a few minutes in their room."

"Mmm, yeah, definitely," I agreed, sneaking my phone out of my pocket to check the time.

"Outer space!" She ran her fingers along my constellation-printed curtains. "Do you believe in UFOs?"

"I ..." Such a left-field question I was caught off guard. "No?"

"I've seen one," she said.

"Whoa, really?"

I didn't believe her for a second, but I humored her.

Elizabeth studied my reprint of *Girl before a Mirror*.

"Picasso," she said softly. Then she turned to me, a shadow in her expression. "You didn't hang up my painting?"

"Oh—not yet."

The moment hung in the air and ballooned. I was still holding the tin of cookies. It crossed my mind that I wasn't being that friendly to her, that I wasn't making it easy to converse. Maybe I was being unfair.

"I should actually get going," she said, putting her jacket back on and giving me a quick, tight hug. "Toodle-oo."

I didn't see her again the rest of the winter break. The more I thought about it, the more I wondered if I had been cold to her, rude, if I was being snobby and unkind to someone who was just trying to be my friend.

But when I returned to school after the new year, everything took a turn.

NINETEEN
NOW

"NO," my dad says. "*No*. Abso-fucking-lutely not."

But tell me how you really feel, Dad. We're on the phone the morning after the improv class that turned me upside down. I called him to float the possibility of moving back in with him for a bit again, maybe trying to become a flight attendant. The desperate idea came when I woke up, my mind scrambling like a manic hamster on a wheel for a way I could leave this place and not ever see Elizabeth again, and it hits me the moment I say it aloud to him how ludicrous it sounds. Like a five-year-old making life plans for themselves. *I wanna be a flight attendant when I grow up!*

"You just got to Berkeley!" he barks. "Are you kidding me with this? Already? Jesus."

I can tell I've called him when he's in a mood. With my dad, everything's about work. Good day at work, he's sage advice and charming jokes. Bad day at work, his fuse is short and his patience gone.

"I just think maybe the universe—"

"The universe, give me a …" He sighs. I can hear him checking himself and attempting to control his tone. "Can you stop it with the universe shit? You know how I feel about it. The universe doesn't care about you. The universe isn't a grand puppet master pulling the strings, all right?"

"How do you know?"

"Look, I'm not going to get into a theological discussion on my way to the office. But this woo-woo malarkey? Just an excuse to take zero responsibility for yourself. Okay? The universe is vast, exploding chaos. There's no reason to it. You think the universe had some agenda behind giving a thirty-five-year-old woman who was the love of my goddamn life breast cancer and killing her before her kid could even string a sentence together? What kind of fucking universe does that, huh? What kind of lesson is that teaching?"

All right, okay. Dad doesn't pull out the dead mom card often, but when he does, there's no way to argue. "I hear you."

"The universe," he says. "Come on. This is you, kid. This is you and your life. And you're almost thirty years old. You know I love the hell out of you. You're my everything, you know that. I love your free spirit. I think you could do anything you want. But I don't think you can do *everything* you want. Feel me?"

"I guess."

"You have to settle in sometime and see things through. What did I ask of you when you told me you were dead set on Berkeley? I told you I would help you find a place and set you up as long as you, what?"

I roll my eyes. "See it through."

"Which means what?"

"Which means I stay here through my lease."

"And?"

"And ..."

"And don't quit anything for six months. That's all I asked. Six months. It's a fucking blink, six months."

I drum my fingers on the tabletop, thinking of how it will be springtime by then. Cherry blossoms on the trees and buds in gardens. I'll have to suffer through two seasons of knowing Elizabeth Smith is around the corner. Literally! Around the corner, one block away from me. Teaching a class I'm in. Texting me *night night* messages.

I could tell my dad, but when I mentioned Elizabeth and the accident during one of my many rock bottoms—cryptically, testing the waters—he said he had no fuckin' idea what I was talking about and he wasn't interested in high school drama bullshit. I don't know if his memory is that poor or his will to forget is that strong, but either way, I envy him. And I know talking frankly about the reason I want to leave is a lost cause.

"You take that improv class you were talking about?" he asks. "Started yesterday, right?"

"Yes." I clear my throat. "I don't know about it."

"Okay, well, sounds like you're in some kind of funk. I don't know. You taking those antidepressants?"

"No."

"Well, gee, wonder why you're depressed. Please don't tell me I need to keep on you about your doctor appointments, too."

"I think whatever's wrong with me, pills aren't going to cure, Daddy."

"Oh, bunny," he says, his voice softening. "Nothing's wrong with you. You're okay. Right? You're okay."

My chest is filled with fire. I don't know how to answer him, how to tell him that there's just something inside me that never feels like it will be right. That this whole thing with seeing Elizabeth seems to have blown the roof off the part of me that was barely keeping it all together. I don't know where to run, where to hide, when the thing I hate most lives inside me. I'm not depressed. I'm just a shit person. What's the cure for that?

"How's working for, uh, what's-her-face? Suzanne?"

Above my head, someone clomps up the stairs so loudly I flinch. Probably the first of ten thousand deliveries Google Man will get today. Add it to my growing list of disenchantments with this place.

"Suzanne?" I ask, staring at the ceiling and tracking the clobber of footsteps. "Um ... she's really weird."

"A character, right? What's she have you doing?"

"Nothing of importance." I check my tone, knowing my dad doesn't like it when I'm mopey and I don't want any more pep talks. "She says she's going to start writing a memoir."

He pauses. "A *memoir*. Huh. Well, *that*'ll be interesting."

That cryptic tone—there's definitely something there he's not telling me. "What's her deal? What was her case?"

"You know I can't discuss cases with you. Attorney-client privilege."

"Yeah, yeah, fine."

"Google her if you want to know."

"I've tried, but—"

"Hey, just pulled into the office. Hang in there, all right? Text me later and let me know you're okay."

"Have a good one," I say.

We hang up. I cross to peek out the blinds at my living room window. Outside, a car with a siren on top and a weed leaf on the side says CANNABIS EMERGENCY DELIVERY SERVICE. A guy in a green uniform stomps downstairs and gets into the car to drive away. There's a weed club at the end of our block. I can see it from here if I squint hard enough. Google Man is perhaps the laziest person I've ever met in my life.

I get dressed for the day, carefully painting my eyeliner on and taking the time to straighten my hair—you know, trying to pretty myself up as much as possible to cover up the way I really feel. When I powder my cheeks, the voice whispers, *You don't deserve this beautiful face* and I flinch, imagining myself with scars, with tight, raised, pink marks forever marking me. But I ignore it. Look away. Keep moving.

Stepping out into the sunshine to head to work, I turn to lock my door and freeze with my key in midair.

On my white front door, there's what looks like a smeared, bloody footprint. It's stamped in the middle, just a few inches from the knob.

The spirit drains out of me. Goosebumps, all over.

I look around, checking the doorstep—but there's nothing here. I stoop to get a closer look, but what am I, a forensics expert in footprints? I don't know what I can learn from scrutinizing. The foot looks bigger than mine, but not much bigger.

"Why?" I ask it, as if the footprint will answer.

You know why, the voice whispers.

I stand up uneasily. To ground myself, I imagine what my dad would say. I can hear his voice in stereo, saying this is a coincidence, stop reading into everything. I remind myself that Berkeley's full of weirdos. That it's probably paint. Ketchup. That it has nothing to do with seeing Elizabeth again. That Elizabeth only has one real leg anyway, could she even kick the door like that? And why would she? And wouldn't I have heard it if she did?

Blowing a deep breath in and out, I walk away from it and start making my way to work. A man's rapping along with his headphones. A woman is speaking French to a baby in a stroller. I calm down, admiring the interesting houses with so many hidden lives inside. I step in and out of the speckled shade in the shady streets.

At an intersection, while waiting for the light to change, I take my phone out to text Google Man and let him know about the footprint—I don't know, he's a landlord, wouldn't he care? I don't want him to think I did that.

That's when I notice the dark red smear on the palm of my hand—the hand that closed my front door.

I could retch. Someone not only left a bloody-looking smear on my door, they left it on my doorknob, too.

TWENTY

"I WAS BORN in the blustery, moody gloaming on the coast of Maine," Suzanne says.

She's pacing her room, a shawl wrapped around her delicate frame. Her hair is in an enormous silver topknot and she hugs her arms like she's cold. But I've learned, in my few weeks working for her, that this is what she does when she's "thinking," when she's in "creative mode." She hugs her arms and paces. I sit on her rocking chair with a notebook and pen, jotting down notes.

"You got the adjectives, yes?" she asks me. "The adjectives are important. Perhaps even more important than the facts."

"Blustery. Moody. Yes, I got the adjectives."

"Born in an old farmhouse that whistled with salty air," she continues.

I write quickly, my hand cramping, and wonder if I should gently mention the invention of dictation software. But I'm pretty sure Suzanne is looking for more of an audience than a secretary. It's fine. This beats hawking her secondhand books or skipping over to the health food store for probiotics.

"My mother, a former ballerina, was struck by lightning when I was three and turned to ash," she says. "And my father—"

"Wait wait wait," I say. "Your mother was *what*?"

Suzanne stops in the middle of the room and puts her hands in a namaste position. She seems to be gathering something within herself. "I need you to simply write it down. Please don't interrupt the flow of my unconscious."

"Sorry," I say.

She's giving me a stare that could wither a flower. I clear my throat and write down *Mother, ballerina, lightning, turned to ash.* As she breathes deeply, I would say *yogically* if that were a word, I examine the palm of my hand and wonder about the blood on my door. My pocket buzzes and I peek at the text from Google Man. It's just a thumbs up emoji.

What? That's it? I tell him there's blood all over my door and I get a yellow thumbs up?

"Is there something that requires your attention?" Suzanne asks.

"Sorry." I pocket my phone again. "It was my landlord. There was blood on my doorstep this morning."

"*Blood* on your *doorstep*?"

"On my door," I say. "I should have said on my door. A footprint. And on my knob. That's why I asked to wash my hands first thing."

"*Blood*?"

"Honestly, I don't know what it was. I didn't want to know. I just scrubbed it off my hands."

"Good goddess," she says in horror. "Whatever does it mean?"

"That's what I want to know."

"Maybe it's a sign of some kind," she says, pacing again. "An omen. Once a bird flew into my window, just *bam*—" Suzanne claps her hands so loud I startle. "Blood on the pane, shaped like a snowflake. Revulsion! And then ... well." She shakes her head. "That was the week my husband died." Pausing, adjusting her shawl, she inhales sharply. "For your sake, I hope I'm wrong."

"Uh, yeah. Me too."

Another clue in the mysterious puzzle of Suzanne, a woman who has piqued infinite questions with few answers. Her husband is dead. "Expired" means dead. I figured that's what she meant, but now it's official.

"Back to the memoir," she says. "My mother was, indeed, struck by lightning. A freak accident when meandering the bluffs. After her cremation, we sprinkled her into the snarling sea ..."

I chase her words down on paper and tingle with a strange sense of déjà vu.

We sprinkled my mother into the sea, too.

TWENTY-ONE

ALICE COMES for a visit over the weekend because I'm a mess and she's an angel. She brings Sadie with her, who's dressed in a posh coat with leopard print trim. It's weird when a dog is better dressed than you are. I'm still in my pajamas because I barely slept last night—or any night since the improv class on Wednesday. Then there was the fact my landlord was (surprise!) *in my apartment* when I came home from work on Thursday, supposedly checking on whether he needed to "repaint" the door. Add to that three texts Elizabeth sent me wondering if I wanted to meet up to go to a slam poetry thing on Sunday and I'm a hair away from hunting down a shady doctor to dole me some benzos. But I'm not supposed to take those anymore, not after that summer I got strung out on Ativan. So I called Alice. And here she is, her fancy dog under one arm, holding a tray with two coffee cups with the other.

Thank my lucky stars for Alice. She's the only person

besides my dad I'd let see me like this. I might be a disaster on the inside, but I usually put on a nice face. I haven't brushed my hair, gotten dressed, and yesterday's mascara is under my eyes like a scream queen in a horror movie.

"I'm so glad you're here," I say. "Hi Sadie! You look amazing."

Sadie barks at me like I'm Satan himself and I flinch. We have a tenuous relationship.

"We discussed this, Sade," Alice says, setting her down. "Don't bark at Aunt Jo."

Sadie growls lowly.

"You look ..." Alice bites her lip in concern as she assesses my appearance. In contrast, she's in a cute puffer vest over a turtleneck, tight jeans, and clean white sneakers.

"I know how I look."

She pulls the door back and glances at it. "The door looks fine."

"He scrubbed it or painted it. That footprint's gone."

"And he came inside your house?"

"Shhh!" I whisper, beckoning her inside. "Google hears everything."

She steps inside and Sadie's toenails click on the floor, her tail wagging. Sadie might not love me, but I sure love her. She's tiny. She's got chocolate fur and floppy ears. One day, I'll win that pup over. For now, she ignores me, running to explore the apartment.

I close the door and raise my voice to a normal volume. "Yes, he was here in the entrance when I came home Thursday."

"Like, door open? Door closed?"

"Open."

"Well, didn't you text him and tell him about the footprint on the door?"

"I did."

"So ..."

I sigh, shaking my head. Alice. Dear, sweet Alice, always giving the benefit of the doubt. "It was dark, Allie, and a *strange barefooted man* was in my apartment without permission."

"I think that's a bit of an interpretation, he is your *landlord*, but okay, I hear you. Creeped out." She glances around. "It's cute in here! So sunny. You should open your blinds."

"I've kept my blinds closed because I'm afraid of seeing Elizabeth walking by."

"Jo," Alice says, eyes widening. "We're spiraling here."

I called Alice the day after the improv class and told her all about running into Elizabeth again, but Alice interpreted this whole thing as it being serendipitous, a blessing. She called it an "opportunity to heal." She doesn't understand how awful a coincidence this is.

"Can't you just drop out of the class if you don't want to see her?" Alice asks. "I mean, if it's bothering you this much?"

"I begged my dad for the money for the class and he would kill me if I dropped it now."

"Well, talk to him about it. Tell him why."

"You don't understand my dad. He'll just tell me to buck up."

Alice purses her lips and I can read her mind. She's thinking my dad's right.

"How's Elizabeth doing?" Alice asks. "I've still never met her. I'm so curious about her."

"Fine. Fabulous, actually. She's pursuing a master's or something so she can be a therapist. She was a life coach in LA."

"So she's got a great life now," Alice says, like this should comfort me.

And it's true. Elizabeth seems a lot more joyful and together than I am, that's for sure. But that doesn't make me feel any better.

"I don't want to live here anymore," I say, tears pricking my eyes. I breathe deeply to keep them from spilling. "This isn't working."

"Deep breaths, my friend," she says with a little laugh, putting her hand on my arm. "Let's just—let's sit down together and drink some coffee and we'll—we'll talk it out. You're okay."

We sit down on my inflatable couch, which makes farting noises that I'm not feeling humorous enough to joke about. The whole thing kind of tips us into the middle, so we're practically sitting on top of each other. I apologize.

"You need some real furniture," she says.

"I know. This is temporary. But I'm not in a place where I'm about to go looking for furniture when all I'm thinking about all day long is how I can't wait to get the hell out of here."

"You just moved here!"

"You sound like my dad."

"Well, he's got a point." Alice sips her coffee and taps mine, encouraging me to sip, too. I do, but it's black and the only way I enjoy coffee is with enough cream and sugar to put me in a diabetic coma. Tastes like bile to me. "Why did you move here in the first place? What were you hoping to find this time?"

This time. I hear it. The judgment about the litany of times I've up and moved and changed careers. Used to be cute. I was a globetrotter. I lived in Amsterdam and worked at a hostel, taught English in Seoul, picked apples in Washington, chased a girl to Alabama and then, when everything quickly fizzled, made it to New Orleans just in time for Mardi Gras. But now I'm almost thirty and no one thinks it's cute anymore. All the fascinating people I've met in all the cities I've landed in had no sticking power, there was no time for it—Alice is the only true friend I have. A life full of anecdotes with no real plot.

"I was hoping to find a *home*, you know?" I take a beat to ponder the question. "I just wanted to spread my wings in a city not too big and not too small, a weird place I could be myself that wasn't too far away from my dad or you. Somewhere the weather didn't piss me off. I didn't have a plan. I don't *like* having plans."

"Yes, I've noticed."

"I felt like there was something drawing me here—I know, you'll roll your eyes. But my gut just said there was something here for me."

"The 'universe.'" Finger quotes.

"Right."

"Look ..." Sadie comes and jumps up on the inflatable sofa and slides right off like a doofus. Alice slaps her thighs. "Come here, Sade." Her sweet dog jumps up on her lap. I reach my hand out to try to sneak a pet, but she barks at me.

I wonder if she can sense that I'm a shit person.

"You're not using any recreational drugs or unprescribed pharmaceuticals, right?" Alice asks.

"No."

"What about alcohol?"

"I mean, I had a cosmo at a horrible date I went on. Did I tell you about that? Girl was a basket case. And coming from me, that's saying a *lot*."

Alice doesn't look amused as she rubs behind Sadie's ears.

"But no," I clarify. "This isn't me partying my ass off and losing my mind again."

"Are you currently prescribed any medication?"

I kind of love it when Alice goes into doctor mode. I can almost picture how adorable she looks in her white coat with a stethoscope hanging around her neck.

"I was on antidepressants but it just wigged me out even more." I say the words that have been banging around in my head now for weeks. "I don't think what's wrong with me is anything pills can fix."

"I actually agree with you."

"You do?"

Alice nods. There's a hissing noise that I realize is probably coming from the inflatable couch. It's lending a sense of urgency to the conversation—we've got to get somewhere before we both end up in a pile of plastic on the floor.

"Well, so ... what's wrong with me, then?" I ask.

Alice smiles at me like I'm a child. "I can't diagnose you. You need to talk to a professional, this isn't my field."

"Tell me as a *friend*, not as a doctor."

I can see myself in the pupil in her clear green eyes. As usual, I don't like what I see. I find somewhere else to focus

—Alice's arched eyebrows. The wisps on her forehead that have escaped her ponytail.

"I think that what happened with Elizabeth, the accident you caused ... I think that you've been running away from the guilt of it your entire life," Alice says.

Her words are a slap to my soul. I cringe.

"All this moving, this inability to settle down. In some ways, it's you, it's who you are. You're a wanderer. Love that about you. But it all started after the accident, you know? After that, you just seemed itchy. Like you couldn't settle down. So many cities and plans in so many years."

"My *entire life* started after the accident," I remind her. "It's not really fair to act like that defined my character when I literally graduated high school at that time, too—went out on my own, started my life."

"Of course it doesn't define your character, that's not what I mean."

There's a long silence. I'm grateful when Sadie fills it up with her snores.

"Or maybe it does," Alice says, thinking aloud. "Maybe that *is* what I mean."

I shake my head, hating what she's saying. Even just talking about the accident aloud makes me writhe with guilt. I want to run and hide under a blanket. I want to catch the nearest bus and get as far away from here as possible.

"You're spiraling now and it's because you ran into her, that's why all this is happening," Alice says. "That's why you're freaking out and calling me and wanting to run away."

"She wants to be *friends* with me," I say, unable to hold the tears in. I don't snivel with them or anything. I ignore them as much as possible, wipe them away as soon as they begin the slow crawl down my cheeks. "She teaches the improv class I'm in. How can I go back there? Even if I don't return her texts and quit the class—I mean, she lives around the fucking corner! I'm going to see her around."

"Right," Alice says. "And maybe that's a good thing."

My tears have stopped. Just a quick spell of mental rain. I stare at Alice in disbelief. "How could it be 'good' to see someone whose life I secretly ruined?"

"Because you finally have to face it." Alice puts a hand on my knee. "You have to deal with it. You can't keep running from it. Maybe this is what the ... 'the universe' ... what it wanted for you."

I appreciate the fact she's entertaining my relationship with the universe. I sniff, looking at my blank apartment with nothing but that Picasso painting I've kept since high school. Maybe Alice is right, maybe this *is* why I'm here. Maybe if I finally faced this ugliness that has been festering inside me, I could stop living with a head full of bees. I could focus and figure out what I really want out of life. I could be free.

"How do I face it, though?" I ask. "I don't know how. Like, tell her what I did?" Even saying it aloud—I could vomit. I shake my head quickly, wishing I could put the words back in. Jesus, could you imagine? Never, never, *never*. "No. I can't."

"I wasn't necessarily suggesting that. I was more thinking you go to therapy and talk to someone about it who knows how to work through something like this."

"But what about Elizabeth?" I ask. "She wants to hang out with me. I mean, how do I deal with this screwy-ass situation I've landed in? I don't want to be mean to her and not respond."

"So respond to her," Alice says, shrugging. "Be nice to her. You went to high school together. Didn't she look up to you?"

"Yeah, but remember? She was stalker-y."

"Was she *really*? You've always had a flair for hyperbole."

"Believe me, she's a lot."

"Well, you're almost thirty now. People change. Maybe she has some guilt about how she was in high school too and wants to make it up to you."

"Hmm."

"Go to therapy. Call Elizabeth back, be kind to her. What if this is exactly what you need? What if you finally get closure and everything clicks for you?" She smacks my arm, lovingly. "I'm excited for you. This could be a breakthrough moment."

Breakthrough ... or breakdown? I bite my tongue and don't say it. I'll tell you what surprises me: that vicious voice hasn't spoken up once since this conversation started. Whenever I think about Elizabeth, it's there. I wonder what life would be like without that nasty voice whispering in my ear.

As sick as the idea of spilling the truth in therapy and/or texting Elizabeth makes me, Alice might be onto something.

"What if it was her footprint on the door?" I ask. "What if she knows somehow and she hates me?"

Alice rubs her temples, closes her eyes. "Jo, your neighborhood is full of weirdos. A man with no pants on passed me when I was parking my car and told me he was Jesus. Elizabeth is not kicking your door, I mean ..."

I nod. She's right. I reach over and give Alice a long, hard hug. Sadie barks between us. The couch has deflated so much our asses are touching the ground and the situation is so silly and chaotic that suddenly we're both rocking with laughter, holding onto each other tight. For just a flash I feel young again and happy again and like I love being myself and nothing hurts.

Then the moment it's over and I let go, I ache.

TWENTY-TWO

"I FREAKING LOVE SLAM POETRY! Don't you?" Elizabeth asks.

I do not. It's cringey. But ...

"Yeah," I say. "Slam poetry, it's—it's great."

We're hurrying a few blocks to a pub to make it to slam poetry night, "Slam Bam Thank You Ma'am." We look like we walked out of the same time machine: me in my flower-power bell bottoms, she in her go-go boots.

"I love your outfit," I tell her.

"Samesies!"

I can't believe I'm doing this. I'm so nervous with her I feel like I'm holding a pinless grenade. Every time she speaks, I hold my breath waiting for some accusation. Every time she smiles at me, I die a little bit inside because I don't deserve it. But Elizabeth invited me to join her because it's only a few blocks away from our houses. Alice said this would be good for me and Alice is the smartest person I know. So I'm facing my fear and hanging out with Elizabeth, despite the fact I will have to suffer through open mic slam poetry night and I secretly almost burned her to death and made her lose an eye and a leg.

If only she knew, the voice says. *Or maybe she already does?*

Not possible. Shut up. I clear my throat. "So how are you? Like, how's life? What have you been up to?"

"Let's see ... I've been helping Jerry with his classes, painted a set, I'm working part-time as a caregiver to a woman with dementia in the mornings and looking into school applications. Not much."

Her *not much* is my *very much,* apparently.

"Besides that," she goes on, "I went on a disastrous date last night, then cried myself to sleep." She laughs at this, as if it's a joke. "People are so shallow. I can see right through them. They think they're fooling me, finding some excuse to break the date off, to leave early, but I know it's about my scars."

"What?" I ask, horrified. "No."

"Oh yes indeedy! Scars or the fake leg, I don't know which scares them more. I guess I should take a picture that shows my ugly side." She shows off her scarred cheek with a flourish.

Man, people are terrible.

"You're not ugly, you're beautiful." My chest is cramping up. Fighting a heart attack from the guilt I'm feeling. "What assholes. Their loss."

"You know what's worse, though?" she asks. "The people who like it. I met a guy who—I'm not kidding you—asked me if he could 'fondle' my 'stump.' And we were still on the first drink! Like, really? *Really, ma dude?* That date, *I* was the one scrambling for an excuse to leave."

We pass by a house so overgrown with climbing morning glories the windows are barely visible. Swallowed alive by flowers—not a bad way to go. I wouldn't mind getting swallowed by flowers right about now.

"Well," I say. "I'm sure you'll find someone eventually."

"What about you?" she asks, her voice softer. "You seeing anyone?"

Oh God. As we stop at a crosswalk waiting for the parade of cars to let us walk, a horrible thought rings: what if Elizabeth has a crush on me? Remember how she glommed onto me in high school like a barnacle? And then—how dare I be apprehensive about such things after what I did to her? My vision grows spotty and I wonder for a second if this is a legitimate panic attack. I don't know if I can go through with this. But *especially* after what she just told me, I can't bail on this outing with her. I shouldn't have listened to Alice. Even Alice can be wrong.

"Are you okay?" Elizabeth reaches out and touches my shoulder. "You look kind of pale."

"I might be having a panic attack," I say.

Not kidding, I might pass out. I lean over to put my head between my legs. That's a thing, right? That's a real-life thing and not just something people do in movies?

"Oh no!" Elizabeth rubs my back. "What do you need from me right now?"

I shake my head, closing my eyes. A couple stops and asks if I'm okay.

"She's having a panic attack," Elizabeth says loudly. "Y'all, give her space."

Someone walking their dog stops to stare at me. A woman hops off her bicycle and asks if we need to call an ambulance. A small crowd is forming and I can see them, upside-down. I have never wished for a meteor to hit the earth until now. Please. Go ahead, wipe us all out. Anything to stop this. Finally, I stand back up and manage to announce, "I'm okay. I'm fine. Let's go."

Elizabeth hooks her arm in mine (sob) and helps me slowly across the crosswalk. Her concerned expression and the agonizing pace we're walking—it's as if I'm her hundred-year-old grandmother.

"I'm okay," I say.

We get to the other side and linger for a minute in front of an anarchist bookstore. She's still holding tightly to my arm. I wish she wouldn't touch me but I don't want to hurt her feelings.

"I have issues," I finally manage as a feeble explanation.

"It's fine! We all have issues, Jolene. Believe me. Take it from a girl who has the suicide hotline programmed into her phone! LOL." Despite the acronym spoken aloud, I don't know if she's kidding. Her face slackens. "Anywaysies, just saying I understand. I've been through so much therapy I should have an honorary degree in counseling by now."

"Yeah?"

"Are you in therapy?"

"No. Been thinking about it."

"Highly, *highly* recommend the place called Healing Oak Therapy Center up on College. They're spectacular. Sliding scale. Great therapists. They even do psychedelic therapy, ketamine, stuff like that."

"You've tried it?"

"I haven't actually been to Healing Oak myself but psychedelic therapy? Oh yes. Tried it all. CBT. EMDR. Role-playing." We walk up the sidewalk, passing a Mexican restaurant blaring mariachi music. "I've had debilitating PTSD since the accident. It's like this ... shadow following me around the past ten years."

Ugh. Dagger in the gut, those words. And yet—I understand. I too have had a shadow following me around the past ten years. It's shaped differently than hers, but it's still a shadow. We slow down in front of a row of apartments because ahead of us, outside the pub, there are groups of people. And this conversation deserves privacy.

"Every time I think I'm through it, I get some moment of panic, a nightmare, a memory that brings it all back," she says.

"I'm so sorry," I blurt.

And I mean it from my core. I would do anything in the world to take it back. I would trade places with her—put me in the car, let her jump scare me off the road. Before I can think twice, I reach out and hug her.

"I'm so sorry that happened to you," I say.

"It's okay," she says with a little laugh. She squeezes me and then pulls back to look at me. "It's not like it's your fault."

If only you knew.

I inhale sharply. "Yeah."

"It's just—it's something that happened."

"Do you ..." My throat tightens and I can't believe I'm going to ask it, but I have to. "... know what caused it?"

She shakes her head. "I don't remember."

I let out a long breath, trying to not let my relief show. She has no memory of the gorilla suit. But also—how horrible must that be for her to have no idea what happened? Is it a blank space that haunts her the way my drug-fueled blackouts haunt me?

"That must be so hard," I say.

Elizabeth smiles brightly. I look at her good side, focus on her real eye. "For a long time, I was so angry. I was filled with rage, I wished I could lash out at someone, break something. Because why me? Why would something like that happen to me? But sometimes there's no one to blame except the universe."

"The universe," I echo. "Right."

And for the first time in my life, I wonder if my dad's right. If "the universe" is just bullshit.

Inside, it smells like feet and old beer and this is what the man with the wizard beard onstage is rapping:

"We should care about the dolphins/ with their small fins/ the blue whales/ who knew they were so frail? Don't put your garbage in the sea/ see it to believe it/ the bees are dying, mother nature is crying ..."

We are not an audience. We are hostages.

I order us beer. When I hand Elizabeth her pint, she winks at me with her real eye. I gulp beer fast enough that it becomes a painkiller and we stand in the back. Maybe the painkiller is working because for just a moment, I feel lighter. Like maybe Alice was right. Like healing is within reach. But then I look at the floor while someone's onstage yelling about how "patriarchy equals hate-riarchy" and I notice something.

There's a faint hint of what looks like red paint or blood rimmed around the toe of one of Elizabeth's white go-go boots.

TWENTY-THREE
THEN

AFTER WINTER BREAK was over senior year, I returned to school and the first thing I saw when I turned the corner to eat my lunch with the theater geeks just about made me drop my Caesar salad on the pavement: there, perched on a bench, Elizabeth squawked about chemtrails being some mind control method for the population. It wasn't the stupidity of what she was talking about, though why everyone hung onto every word of this nonsense was beyond me. It was the way she flipped her hair over her shoulder.

Her previously blond, now copper-red hair.

She'd gotten a trim, too. Sideswept, feathered bangs. She straightened it. And now it was parted in the middle instead of on the side.

Exactly like mine.

I forced a smile and sat down and caught up with the crew about the holidays, but the whole time all I could do was side-eye Elizabeth. The weirdest part? She didn't even look at me, not once. I was a ghost.

In class that afternoon, she didn't sit next to me, either. Which was fine, I had my own friends, but I was used to her following me around. She found a new spot near the front and seemed a lot more talkative with everyone, as if over the break she'd grown some newfound confidence. I stared at the back of her skull, remembering how her face had fallen when she'd left my house over break. Was she pissed at me? Playing games? What the hell was this all about?

I got my answer when, after the bell rang, I ran into her as we were filing out of the theater. The two of us ended up exiting right at the same time, walking up the concrete steps together. *Click, click, click, click,* harmonized our high-heeled Mary Janes.

Curling my lips up into a smile, I said, "Hi Elizabeth. How was your break?"

"Oh," she said, casting me a glance as if she just noticed I existed. "Spectacular. You?"

"You know, loafed around. Binged bad Hallmark movies." I laughed. "The usual. By the way—thanks for those cookies."

I was trying to be kind, to make up for any coldness I might have exuded when I was blindsided by her visit.

"Did you actually eat them?" she asked, in a sweet-and-sour voice. "Or did you just throw them away like you did to my painting?"

I was being charitable. As soon as she left my house, the thought of her cookies exited my mind and by the time the thought came back around again, the cookies were stale. But still, I was taken aback. We paused at the top of the stairs, where the hall bustled with students rushing to the next period. Skateboards and backpacks, letterman jackets and energy drink energy.

"I didn't throw your painting away," I said.

Just tucked it into my closet where I didn't have to look at it, I didn't add.

"Then can I have it back?" she asked.

"You ... want it back," I said, in disbelief.

"Is there an echo in here?" she asked. "Yes. I want my painting back. Which shouldn't be hard. Unless you *did* throw it away."

Her tone chilled me. It was like she was a completely different person. As she spoke to me, she didn't look me in the eyes. She was focused on another spot, above it—at my bangs, or an invisible hat on top of my head. Like I wasn't even worth eye contact anymore. Then her deadpan expression brightened and she met my eyes for just a moment, as if she cranked the sunshine back on.

"See you later, alligator!" she chirped cheerfully.

And spun on her heel and walked away.

The next day I did give her the painting back. When I handed it over at lunch, she said, "Oh, thanks," and zipped it up in her bag, as if it meant nothing to her. I couldn't help but notice that her bookbag was new and that it looked a bit like mine. And her platform heels were awfully familiar—like the pair I'd found at the thrift store the previous summer, the ones she had complimented the first day she met me. In the coming weeks, there would be more items that she rotated into her wardrobe that resembled mine—

bell-bottomed jeans. Fake eyelashes, thick eyeliner, white lipstick. A jumpsuit. What really got on my nerves wasn't just the fact she was copying my style.

It was that she looked so damn good in my clothes.

TWENTY-FOUR
NOW

> Hi! Thanks so much for helping clean up the footprint on the door situation the other day. Can I please ask that in the future you give me a heads up if you're going to enter my apartment? Thanks again!

CLEAR. Polite. Concise. Creating a paper trail in case there are any future violations (I'm a lawyer's daughter, and don't you forget it). What do I get in return? An apology? An explanation? No.

I get one single yellow thumbs up.

"Seriously?" I shake my head and slip my phone back into my bag. Right now, I'm seated in a beanbag chair in the waiting room of the Healing Oak Therapy Center and trying to hold down the tacos I ate for lunch.

I can't believe I'm doing this.

I can't believe I'm going to therapy.

Yes, I've been through a parade of psychiatrists and a merry-go-round of diagnoses and pharmaceuticals. But actual therapy, digging in deep and talking about my past, is something I have long avoided. It's why I couldn't weather rehab. All those gushy group therapy sessions filled my soul with fire ants and made me sprint the hell out of there. I was afraid the catharsis was contagious and I might start spewing the truth.

I'm terrified of the truth.

A crime confessed to a therapist is protected by confidentiality, I repeat in my head, like a mantra. Google assured me of this last night. I did my research.

I'm jiggling my leg, jonesing for fresh air and casting a longing glance toward the door. I'm the only person in here. Just me and a giant poster of a woman with flowers instead of a brain, watering her head with a watering can. But the longer I stare at it, I can imagine the flowers turning to flames and I have to stop looking at it, instead picking up a pamphlet that says, "When Your Emotional Support Animal Unexpectedly Crosses the Rainbow Bridge" from the table beside me. They really have a pamphlet for everything these days, don't they?

"Jolene?" a voice says.

A woman with deep brown hair streaked with silver smiles at me from her doorway. She's got at least a generation on me and exudes a classiness that makes me feel rumpled and underdressed—her layered bob is glossy, her glasses are posh and probably designer, and she wears silk pants, strappy heels, and a blazer. I could imagine her narrating the news on MSNBC. The website for this place boasts that it caters to "low-income and underprivileged populations" and utilizes "alternative and experimental therapeutic practices" so I wasn't expecting someone this fancy. I was expecting someone a little crunchier, a little weirder, more of a Suzanne and less a Kamala Harris.

"What a cute outfit," she says to me as I stand up, as if she can sense my insecurity.

"Oh thanks," I say, looking down at my jeans and peasant blouse and vowing to use an iron next time.

She beckons me into her office. "Come in, come in."

The room is giant, sunny, walled with leather-bound books. The carpets are cream and the couch is beige and it's got about as much personality as a staged home. The woman, whose name is Maria Markland, gestures for me to take a seat as she settles into an ergonomic swivel chair. There are two options: the beige couch, or a wooden chair farther away from her. I hesitate, uncertain if this is my first test. Do I lay down on the couch like people do in movies, get comfortable? But that would be a mere couple of feet away from her. I'm already feeling like a bug under a microscope. I take the wooden seat and she pulls a yellow legal pad from her leather briefcase bag and writes something down with her fountain pen.

"So, Jolene, I'm Maria. Nice to meet you. What brings you in here today?"

A crime confessed to a therapist is protected by confidentiality. A crime confessed to a therapist is protected by confidentiality. I haven't even opened my mouth yet and I've already got pit stains.

"I've never been to therapy voluntarily," I say. "I really don't want to be here."

She doesn't respond, blinking her gray eyes and waiting for me to elaborate.

"I mean, I hope that doesn't sound rude," I say. "I'm sorry. Did that sound rude?"

"It's quite common to not want to go to therapy," she says, writing something down on her paper. CHICKENSHIT PERSON, I imagine it saying. "Takes a lot of courage for some, but you're better for it. What was it that provoked this visit, what made you willing to push through despite the discomfort?"

"My friend suggested I do it. I'm struggling."

"Define 'struggling.'"

She sits back and studies me with a placid, unreadable look.

"Having ... a hard time?" I try.

"Can you be more specific?"

"I just ..." I swallow, the squeamishness making it impossible to sit still. I wring my fingers, bite the side of my tongue, just to have something to do. "I don't feel good about myself." My eyes burn and my brain fires a warning—no crying, not this early on!

Pathetic, the voice whispers.

"Mmm," Maria says sympathetically.

"I can't stand living with myself sometimes," I tell her. "I can't—I can't even sit still or else I feel like I'm on fire. I've lived in twenty-three different cities in ten years."

"What is it you do?" she asks, as if I have some good reason for it. As if she expects me to tell her something respectable like I'm in the military or I'm a documentary filmmaker or something.

"I don't do anything."

"Anything?" She scrawls something on her paper. I imagine the word USELESS. "Are you sure about that?"

"Okay, well, I've done lots of things. Just not for very long."

I walk Maria through my mile-long resumé of odd jobs and false starts, framing it with a nervous smile and trying to flavor it with a sprinkling of self-deprecating humor to seem more fun and less lost. Maria's Mona Lisa smile is facial cement. It's the most serious and stubborn smile I've ever seen, to the point where, as I'm speaking, I wonder if it's less friendliness and more something Botox-related. Her skin is immaculate.

"Tell me a bit about your upbringing," she says.

Surprisingly, she jots nothing down about the life history I just barfed into the air, as if it's nothing of importance. As if she knows that there's something deeper I'm not articulating.

She knows, the voice says. *Everyone does. It's as obvious as blood on your face.*

"My upbringing?" I ask. "Oh." I force a laugh. "Not very interesting. Grew up pretty privileged. Dad's a lawyer, Mom passed when I was so young I can't remember her. Cancer."

This she scrawls down on her page, eyebrows raised in interest. *DEAD MOM!* Now we're onto something. But I don't know how much space we're going to fill today with a woman who's been absent all my life.

"What are some of your earliest memories?" she asks.

My brain shuffles through a random series of movie clips, none of which I like enough to repeat. There's my dad crying on Mother's Day when I was five or six—throw that one in the bin. Never cared for that one, so out of character for him. When I told him about it once, he was offended.

"I never fuckin' did that, I didn't walk around crying in front of you. Jesus."

Maybe he's right, I don't know. I also have a memory of seeing the glow of the tooth fairy in my room in the middle of the night at that age, too, and I'm pretty sure that's not real, either.

"Hmm," I say to Maria. "I don't remember a lot. Probably just, like ... sitting passenger in my dad's car." I shrug. "Vague stuff like that."

If I dwell on it—which I don't—one of my first memories is, indeed, sitting passenger in dad's car, but there's more to that story I keep to myself. Namely, that a highway patrol officer pulled my dad over and my dad coaxed me into pretending my stomach hurt and faking tears as the cop approached the car.

"Just pretend your tummy's aching, baby, we got this," he said. When the cop knocked on the window, my dad rolled it down and said, "Officer, I'm so sorry for speeding. Pretty sure this poor kid here has appendicitis and I'm rushing her to the ER before it bursts."

I wailed and clutched my gut. I was so nervous my stomach actually *had* started to hurt, like some kind of backwards method acting.

The CHP officer let us go right away and as my dad pulled back onto the highway, he cackled and high-fived me.

"That was good, bunny. Proud of you."

After that memory plays, I cross it out with my mind's red pen. Nope, not telling that one.

"My dad's really pretty great," I say. It comes out kind of

defensive sounding. "I guess you'd call me a bit of a daddy's girl."

Why oh why did I say that? I despise that term. It conjures up images of girls in hot-pink convertibles, a phrase on a glittery bumper sticker. I know therapy's good for people, I know it's a blessing and a lifesaver for many, but I hate this. It's as if my mind has splintered in two since I walked in here. There's the me I'm presenting and the me I truly am and the two don't get along very well.

The next forty minutes, I shift into bubbly babbling mode. I talk about benign things, like my wacky boss Suzanne, my failed dates, Google Man upstairs, how I've considered being a flight attendant. Glancing at my watch, the nausea builds. I only have five minutes left. I don't ever have to come back here again. And I think it's that knowledge—that I never have to see this woman again—that makes me blurt out the horrible thing I've been holding in for my entire adult life.

"I ran into this girl Elizabeth I knew in high school recently." I look at the floor instead of her eyes. "It sent me into a spiral. I'm paranoid, thinking she's ... after me or something. It's crazy. I know she's not."

"Why would she be after you?" Maria asks, genuinely curious now, as if I'm a creature that just became interesting to her.

"There was this bloody-looking footprint on my door and then I saw red on her boots ... it sounds nuts. She explained it when I asked her, said it was from a set she had helped paint."

"But why would you assume that she'd kick your door?"

"She's—she's the assistant in this improv class I'm in—

doesn't matter. She's someone I went to high school with back in Santa Barbara and I never expected to see her again. But I ... there are things I never told anyone. I did something horrible to her." My eyes fill up and I put my head in my hands. "I caused a car accident she was in. A bad one. She's been disabled for the rest of her life and scarred from it. Lost an eye, a leg, she was burned all over and—and I dressed up in this Bigfoot costume and ran out into the road. I saw the car roll off the road and I'll never forget her eyes, how big and scared her eyes were." I let out a sob. "I told a woman walking her dog to call for help and then I ran. I drove away, I didn't even check to see if she was okay. Her car caught fire and she was trapped under the car and had to have her leg amputated and I ... just went home and packed for summer camp."

I sob for a good minute or two and when it subsides, when I open my bleary eyes and have the nerve to meet her gaze again, for the first time, her expression has subtly changed. The Mona Lisa smile has become a Mona Lisa frown. Disgust? Sadness? Disbelief?

She sees what a monster you are, the voice says.

Maria clears her throat. "That is ... quite a story," she says, and I can't read her tone. "I imagine it must feel like a weight has been lifted, to say it aloud."

"Mostly it just feels like shit," I tell her.

She hasn't written anything on the legal pad. I imagine she'll be filling it up the moment I leave.

"Well, our work has only begun, but I'm afraid our time is up." Maria stands, gives me a pat on the back, and accompanies me to the door. "Stay well. Nice meeting you. Be safe and we'll talk more next week."

"Thank you," I say, waving at her as she closes the door.

She hates you. She doesn't ever want to see you again. Did you see that look on her face? She was shocked and revolted by you because you're a horrible human being.

"Oh, shut the fuck up," I say.

And it feels good to say it, to be louder than the voice. Really good. Better than anything has felt in a while. Then I spot a woman sitting in the corner of the room holding her phone and gazing at me as if I've lost my mind. And when people are looking at you that way in the waiting room of this place, that's saying something.

"I was talking to myself," I say, as if that helps.

It doesn't. It doesn't help.

I step out into the night and I'm pretty sure I'll never go back there again—how could I face Maria after that confession? But I've cried myself into a lovely shade of numb. I'm walking one foot above the ground the whole way home. The truth has given me an almost benzo-like buzz and the buzz doesn't wear off until I approach my house and see, up the stairs, Google Man staring out his front window at me and shutting his blinds like he's been waiting for me the whole time.

TWENTY-FIVE

THE TRUTH'S aftermath hits me not unlike the aftermath of a drug binge. The act of it was cathartic, followed the next few hours by euphoria, giddiness, lightness. But by the time midnight rolls around, I'm lying in bed with a comedown that sucks my dopamine levels dry and leaves me shaking and sick with shame. Cold sweats. Images of Maria calling the police to report me, the wind rattling my windowpanes and making me imagine a SWAT team assembling outside. The bang of them kicking my door down, rushing inside and screaming as they pull me from my bed. Flashbacks to blackout weekends spent with liquor bottles and someone else's prescription pills, I'm filled now with an unspeakable dread as I throb with regret. What is wrong with me, telling a stranger my darkest secret that I spent years protecting?

When I text Alice in a frenzy, she reminds me she's on her anniversary trip and asks if it's an emergency. It is, but not the kind that warrants me interrupting her romantic vacation in Kauai. I wish I were in Kauai. Maybe I should move there. I try to calm down by listening to affirmations for people with low self-esteem against watery new-age music and attempting to drown in the comforting ocean of sleep.

I am confident, the YouTube woman's velvety voice soothes as I close my eyes and wait for my racing heart to calm down. *I am valuable. I am in control of my own life. I am special. I am worth loving …*

Finally I drift off into the divine escape of my unconscious. When I jolt awake again, I'm in bed unable to open my eyes, sleep paralysis, but I can hear that ghastly voice in my ear, the volume turned up so loud it's vibrating my brain, hissing like an evil witch. *I am a piece of garbage. I am a rotten human being. I am a wriggling worm. I don't deserve this life.*

A shiver rockets through my frozen body. What kind of fresh hellish YouTube channel is this? These are condemnations, not affirmations. Finally, I kick my legs, able to move my body again, shooting up into a seated position. I catch my breath, wipe the cool sweat from my face. Of course it isn't the evil witch in my brain. It's just a silvery-voiced woman declaring affirmations, same way she was when I fell asleep. *I am grateful. I am healthy. I am successful. I am trying my best …*

I take out the earbuds and send them flying across the room, and right when I do, there's a huge glassy *smack* that seems to vibrate my apartment.

Climbing out of bed, I hang in my doorway and wait for a follow-up, but nothing comes.

My oven clock says it's not even eight a.m. Beyond my dim kitchen that opens into the living room, the gold light of morning slants through my blinds. I have to work today. I blurted the disgusting truth and exposed the ugliest parts of myself to a woman I have no reason to trust and now I have to eat cereal and get dressed and walk to work like it's a normal day.

When I go to open the front blinds, I gasp.

There's a long red smear on my window and a spider-web-like crack in the glass. That must have been what I heard—that sickening slap.

"No," I whisper.

She's coming to get you, the voice says in an eerie singsongy tone. *She knows what you did.*

Behind the bloody mess painted on my window, the day is obliviously cheerful and sunny outside. Leaves shimmy with the breeze. Someone glides by on a bicycle, whistling. A cat licks itself on the sidewalk.

I slip on my shoes and step out my front door to investigate, shivering in the morning sunshine. My breath comes out in a cloud of fog. There, on the ground outside my front window, a tiny dead bird lays in the dirt. My ears ring as I remember Suzanne's story about the bird flying into her window. That must have been what happened, right? An accident. A bird mistaking the reflection for the sky or greenery.

But tell me something. Why is its head severed from its body?

TWENTY-SIX

"A SINISTER OMEN," Suzanne tells me as we sit in her yard. She shakes her head. "A deceased bird, a bloody footprint on your door—you don't need it spelled out for you. Something wicked lurks." She points a long fingernail at me. "And I could tell before you even parted your lips this morning. Want to know why?"

"Why?"

She leans in. "Your aura is red-tinged."

I swallow. "Is it?"

"Indeed," she says grimly, as if she's a doctor who just delivered a cancer diagnosis.

Suzanne's yard is overgrown and unkempt, but somehow that only makes it more stunning. Unlike my sparse yard that looks like it was just delivered off the Home Depot truck, Suzanne's is wild. Passionflower vines crawl over her fences, hand-painted birdhouses hang crookedly from a redwood tree, a hot tub hides in a cobwebbed gazebo. Someday, if I ever actually grow up and have a home of my own, I imagine my house would look something like this. I chew my lip and wonder what Suzanne sees when she looks at me —a woman surrounded by a bloody shadow.

"How do you change your aura?" I ask.

"You've got to get rid of that negative energy that's following you. It's tainting you."

"How do I do that?"

"Only you can answer that question."

I tap my pen on the paper where I've been taking notes for Suzanne's memoir. We're trying to "assemble the skeleton" today by listing off chapters. Right now all it says is *Chapter two: Boarding school, sharp-tongued nuns, brain full of wildflowers. Chapter three: Teenage runaway, my year as a trapeze artist.*

I appreciate that, despite the silly shopping trips and errands Suzanne sends me on, despite this odd memoir I don't ever see getting published, she treats me like a human. She actually seems to care about my wellbeing and she doesn't mind when our conversations veer to me and my life. That's something I can't say about a lot of bosses I've had, who treated me like an exchangeable piece of machinery.

"This might have something to do with me going to therapy," I tell her.

"Oh, so you opened Pandora's box." She shakes her head. "Now the demons are out."

I wrinkle my brow. Not exactly the reaction I expect from most people when I tell them I'm going to therapy.

"Demons?"

"I went after Daveed died," she says, talking over my question.

"Yeah, can be helpful for grief."

"*Grief*?" She puts a hand to her chest, where her crystal necklace catches the sun and nearly blinds me. She begins laughing, rocking with it, a laughter so long and hard I start to wonder if it will ever stop. When she finally recovers, she wipes the tears from her face and looks at me with her cerulean laser focus. "Good goddess. You really don't know a thing about me, do you?"

My cheeks burn and I feel stupid, but I'm not sure why. I'm missing context and I'm too intimidated by Suzanne to dig for it. We turn our attention back to the skeleton of Suzanne's life on paper and all I can think is, if I were to try to assemble the bones of my life in words, what would it look like? It's as if there are no bones. No structure. A series of monologues but no real overarching story.

My last task of the day is to clean out Suzanne's medicine cabinet. We stand in her bathroom together as she talks me through this task. Above my head, there's a framed picture with the word LIVE painted on it, but in the mirror it looks like a backward version of the word EVIL and the sight of it makes my stomach turn like I swallowed something rotten.

"I want you to see if there are any less fortunate individuals to whom you can donate my expired pharmaceuticals," she tells me, opening a dusty mirrored door to display enough orange bottles to fill a modest pharmacy.

"Wow," I say, beholding.

"I used to believe in medicine."

Believe? By the looks of it, I'd go so far as to say she worshipped. The sight of this is like taunting a drunk with an open bar. We've got everything from painkillers to muscle relaxants to sweet, sweet benzos.

"Okay," I say. "I'll see who I can donate them to."

She brings me a reusable grocery bag and, as I pile the rattling containers in, I consider whether the universe is testing me.

"May I suggest you lie naked in the sun?" Suzanne asks me as I sling the bag over my shoulder.

Sometimes I'm able to withstand Suzanne's weirdness, roll along with it, nod and smile. But right now is not one of those times. "Excuse me?"

"Sun exposure can cleanse your aura," she says. "Much better than therapy. You ever notice you can't spell therapist without 'rapist?'"

There's a lot to unpack here. An image comes to mind of me lying naked in my backyard with its brand-new, fresh-from-the-bag dirt and the single skinny tree with four leaves on it that still has the tag stabbed into the earth the way it did at the nursery. Google Man gaping at me from his back window.

"I didn't notice that," I say.

"Have a blessed day, my love," she says, squeezing my shoulder.

When I get home, it probably comes as no surprise that I do not, in fact, strip naked and lie in my yard to cleanse my aura. I also don't research where one might donate old pills.

Instead, I fill my empty medicine cabinet. Stack them side by side, bottles gleaming neon orange with exotic princess names like Diazepam and Amrix and Klonopin and Opana. Beholding this glorious sight of narcotic abundance, a calm spreads through me, one I haven't experienced in a long time.

It's like someone installed a self-destruct button inside me, and what a comfort it is to know the option is there.

TWENTY-SEVEN

> Hey, sorry, but a bird flew into the window yesterday and cracked the glass. I wanted to give you a heads up so you didn't think it was my fault, apologies for having to deal with this. Should I tape the window up or do something to prevent the crack from spreading? Do you want to replace it or take a look? Sorry to bother you!

THE MOMENT my index finger hits the *send* button, I regret my apologetic tone. How many times did I say I was sorry when I didn't even need to say it once? *Sorry I exist!* is the undertone of the text. Not that it matters, because all I get back is—you guessed it—a single yellow thumbs up from Google Man. These responses are microaggressions at this point.

When someone thumps on my door five minutes later, I assume it's Google Man coming to investigate the damage done, which is why I open the door without thinking. It's night outside, getting late, almost ten, so I'm shocked to see Elizabeth blinking back at me. Regret pours over me like a hot flash. I want to shut the door. I want to run away. I want to disappear. *Don't look at her scars, don't look at her scars, don't look at her scars.*

The guilt is suffocating, as if someone vacuumed the oxygen out of the air.

"Oh," is all I manage to say. "Hi?"

"I'm sorry to barge in on you!" Elizabeth says. "I wanted to make sure you're okay."

She's dolled up with smoky eyeliner and a floral print dress and those go-go boots again. Cute, but at the same time, there's a Party City quality to it. *1960s Girl!* costume-in-a-bag. But who am I to judge? I'm in joggers and a *STAFF* T-shirt from a record store I worked at for a week.

"I'm fine," I say, not unlike a robot. "How are you?"

She knows, the voice whispers.

"Spectacular! We missed you at improv class tonight though and you haven't been returning my texts since the poetry slam last weekend." She peers at me, like someone inspecting something broken. "You sure you're okay?"

"Of course, yeah, just busy."

Yes, I actually say this as I stand here looking like someone in the "before" half of a commercial for antidepressants.

Elizabeth holds up a paper bag in her hand. "I brought cookies. I know how you love cookies."

My neck tingles. It's like that visit over Christmas break so many years ago.

"Can I come in?" she asks, crinkling the bag.

I would rather jump into a pit of snakes, but I say, "Absolutely, come on in."

"What an adorable place!" she exclaims, stepping inside. "Omigod, I know that painting well." She points to *Girl before a Mirror*. "In your room in high school, right?"

"Yeah. Good memory."

Elizabeth casts a hesitant glance at the inflatable couch and then instead chooses a stool at the kitchen counter. Understandable. I sit next to her.

"I thought I'd see you at improv?" she asks, setting her crocheted bag on the counter along with the cookies. "Are you not going to keep up with the class? Last weekend you said you'd be there."

"I know, I'm just—" I gesture toward the naked room, as if that means anything. "Busy. The job and everything."

"Right! Okay. Sure. Is that ... is that why you're not calling me back, too? Why you haven't responded to my texts?"

She knows, she knows.

I don't know which eye of hers to focus on—the wide blue one that zeros in on me, or the fake one, the one that's just a hint duller than the other and lacks the same luster and shine.

"Not at all," I say. "No. I've been—I started therapy."

She gasps and squeezes my arm so hard it hurts. "That's so great, girl! Good for you! Working through your issues?"

"Trying to."

"You're having a really hard time, huh?"

Elizabeth has always had this quality to her where she's so eager, it edges on sarcastic. There's a sharpness hiding in her friendly tone and I remember how she was in high school—how she turned on me so quickly.

"Kind of," I say.

"I had such a hard time for so long," she says, opening the brown bag and pushing a cookie wrapped in paper my way. "I was miserable after the accident. The pain was like a ghost that haunted me. And then *this*."

In a shocking twist of her fingertips, she pulls her blue eye out of its socket and it takes everything in me to not look away. The hole where her eye was is dark and fleshy and disgusting.

"Can you imagine, looking in the mirror every day and seeing this?"

"Gosh," I manage, writhing inside, forcing myself to focus on it.

"Anyway, sorry, don't mean to make you lose your appetite," she laughs, pushing her eyeball back into its socket. It makes the faintest little slurp of a sound, the fart of a fairy.

I would dry heave, but that seems impolite. Reluctantly, I open the bag and pull the cookie out.

"It's so good," she says, smiling. "Brown butter chocolate chip. Try it."

This entire scene makes me want to implode. Elizabeth showing up to my house and inviting herself inside; the gross déjà vu that leaves a bitter taste in my mouth; the sight of her without her eyeball; how she brought me a cookie she expects me to eat when I really don't want to; the fact I wonder bizarre things like whether she decapitated a bird and threw it at my window; and then of course, the layer of self-hatred underneath it all.

But I force myself to taste the cookie. One bite. One bite can't hurt me, right? And I rave about how delicious it is, even though it isn't, and say I can't wait to finish it later, though I won't. Politeness is its own special brand of lies.

Thankfully, Elizabeth doesn't stay long. She has to get up early tomorrow because she's got a packed schedule with the caregiving and the class-teaching and she's driving out to see the director of a counseling program at CSU East Bay.

"You drive?" I ask in surprise as I see her to the door.

"Of course!" she says, stopping with her hand on the knob. "Why wouldn't I?"

My mouth drops open. I'm not sure how to say what I'm thinking, but I don't need to. She seems to read my mind.

"Oh!" she laughs. "Because of the accident? Oh, no, no, no." She flashes me a toothpaste-ad smile. "Haven't you learned by now? I'm relentless."

The smile disappears for just a second. The vacancy in her expression is so chilling that my stomach cramps. I'm certain, in this blink in time, that she's going to ruin me. That the voice is right and she does know.

But then she smiles again and says, "Toodle-oo!"

As soon as I lock the door behind her, I run to the bathroom and throw up.

Toodle-oo, cookie.

TWENTY-EIGHT
THEN

MY LAST SEMESTER of high school, the spring production was *Romeo and Juliet*. I'd been trying out for every play in our school since freshman year but only scored ensemble or supporting roles. Juliet was a coveted part. Every girl in our department wanted it—including, of course, Elizabeth.

The day the roles were posted, students swarmed the bulletin boards outside the theater building to scan the cast lists. I squeezed my way through the mob and found myself elbow to elbow with Elizabeth. Although we were dressed almost identically in jumpsuits and platformed heels, we ignored each other as we read the list. When I saw my name under *Juliet,* I squealed with excitement. All around me, students clapped my back and congratulated me. And I won't lie, some of my joy wasn't just joy, it was schaden-freude. Because beside me I could feel Elizabeth's disap-pointment like a cold gust of air. Her name was printed under the name *Juliet* too—only hers said *Understudy.* It was as if the universe was verifying that yes, Elizabeth was nothing but a cheap imitation of me.

"Congratulations," I said to her, turning and offering a bright smile.

Elizabeth smiled back, so wide it almost looked like it hurt, and said, "You too!" When I started to walk away, she pulled my sleeve and said, "By the way, gorgeous, you have lipstick *all* over your teeth."

My smile faltered and I thanked her for letting me know. I checked in my phone on the way to my next class. No, I didn't have lipstick on my teeth. She was just trying to make me doubt myself. And it worked.

There was something about Elizabeth that shook me up, threw me off my game. I had been so confident in my skin. But with her around, now I had a direct competitor. She was a wallflower who blossomed into a copper-red rose. I didn't mind that I seemed to have inspired a change in her. What I minded was that I got no credit for it, that no one else seemed to see it but me.

At rehearsals for *Romeo and Juliet* I did my best to tune Elizabeth out, even though I could see her mouthing my every line from the side of the stage, ready to run in and scoop up the role at a moment's notice. Though our interactions were limited to fake smiles and mutual feigned ignorance, I was ever aware of her, tracking what she was wearing, listening to her tell stupid stories about how she believed in aliens and Bigfoot, noticing that she put the same silver shimmer on her eyelids two days after I did. Was I obsessed with her or she with me? It was hard to tell.

All I know is, I was first.

Dress rehearsal nights are magical, full of buzz and

nerves and tension. It's that last-minute push where the show becomes real and plain clothes are traded for costumes, where you're not playing anymore but embodying the actual character. I braided my hair and wore a velvet medieval gown with bell sleeves, powdered my face while whispering my lines in the mirror. I could see Elizabeth behind me, without a costume, watching me with an unreadable look. I was so sick of her. She was a demon I could never exorcise. For the first time, I wanted to hurt her.

The dress rehearsal went smoothly. I remembered all my lines, *O Romeo o Romeo*-ed, and didn't stumble on any of the blocking. When we got to the fourth act, I could see the finish line. All I had to do was drink a potion, sleep through the remainder of the play, briefly wake up and stab myself again—smooth suicidal sailin'. I downed the potion and had to stop myself from making a face. It burned my mouth and throat. Smelled like cleaner. What the hell did the props crew put in the bottle? I thought it was supposed to be blue Gatorade.

As I lay onstage with my eyes closed, my stomach gurgled. Juliet's sleep potion wasn't sitting well with me. I could still taste the alcoholic burn in my mouth. By the time I woke up and stabbed myself with the retractable prop knife, my gut was on fire. By the time the curtains closed, I had to run to the bathroom to try to throw up whatever it was I had swallowed—but it was too late. Nothing came out.

"Are you okay?" Elizabeth asked when I came out of the bathroom, a wide-eyed look of alarm on her face. She was waiting outside the stall with her arms crossed. "I heard you in there."

I didn't want to give my understudy the satisfaction of thinking I was sick, so I smiled.

"I'm spectacular!" I said, just like she'd say it.

But I wasn't spectacular, of course. At home I broke into a sweat and I had such nonstop diarrhea I basically spent the night on the toilet. And then I cried a river because I knew that I'd probably miss opening night, so I leaked out of two orifices at once.

And yes, Elizabeth played Juliet opening weekend. I'm sure she was over the moon. I never found out what the hell was in that potion bottle, but I suspected it was Windex, because when I took the stage again the following weekend, it was nothing but sweet Gatorade. It seemed too out-there to accuse Elizabeth of it, even if my spidey sense said it was her. I had no proof. Elizabeth had nothing to do with props and the person in charge of the potion was a guy who was so stoned all the time it's quite possible he made some kind of mistake. It wasn't like it did any irreparable damage. Still.

That's when I vowed to get Elizabeth back.

TWENTY-NINE
NOW

THE MORNING after Elizabeth's unexpected visit, I wake up before my alarm because I hear footsteps.

In my apartment.

A disgusting gush of panic washes over me and I scan the room, wondering what the hell I could pummel an intruder with. A boot? My purse? I'm still living like I'm about to flee town at any moment—a box spring and a mattress, a crooked standing lamp I found on a neighborhood curb, my clothes in a cardboard box.

"Hello?" I ask with a shaky voice.

I get up and peek out the doorway. Google Man is standing in my living room in his bare feet, surveying my front window with a guy in a work shirt. They're discussing it in low voices like they haven't heard me, like I'm not even here. I'm stunned at the sight of them. How is this okay? How is this legal? I told Google Man to give me a heads up if he was going to come in and he yellow-thumbs-upped me. Does a yellow thumbs up mean *nothing*?

"Excuse me," I say, louder.

The men turn around, appearing to be shocked to see me here in my own house before eight o'clock in the morning. I'm in a wrinkled nightgown with unshaven legs and my hair is a tangled nest but I'm too livid to be embarrassed about it.

"What are you doing here?" I ask.

"I'm sorry, miss," the window repair guy says, stroking his beard. "I'm here to replace your window."

"You just ... came inside my apartment while I was sleeping?" I say.

Window guy looks at Google Man, who holds his phone up for me to see.

"I texted you, but you didn't answer," he says, with about as much emotion as a text-to-speech app on a computer. "I thought you weren't here."

"I was *sleeping*."

"I texted," Google Man says again. "Last night and this morning. Do you want your window fixed or not?"

Oh. Right. My phone's in *do not disturb* mode. Maybe this is my fault.

"Yes," I mutter. "Go ahead, do what you need to do."

In my room, I sit on my bed and hang my head in my hands, willing the emotion to stay put. I still feel nauseated, remembering the chunk of cookie I threw up after Elizabeth left. Is it possible she put something in it that made me so sick from a single bite? The same way I wondered if she put Windex in Juliet's potion in high school? I am so unhinged. The worst kind of unhinged—sane enough to be aware of how insane I'm acting.

Speaking of which, I'm supposed to meet with Maria

today. I'm terrified to face her after my confession last week. Because we're meeting over Zoom, maybe it will be less excruciating this time. Being judged virtually rather than in person somehow seems easier. I want to skip it—I want to never see Maria again. But I know Alice would get on me about it. There are rows of gleaming, expired prescription medications that are calling my name from the bathroom. I'm aware I need help.

While Window Man makes a bunch of noise in my living room replacing the window, I stay in my bed and waste time scrolling my phone. I try, not for the first time, to look up Suzanne to learn more about her, but only incorrect Suzanne Hills come up in Berkeley. I have so many questions about her that don't seem appropriate to ask. Like how did she get her money? The woman doesn't work and I doubt she's making a single penny off her writing. She told me she's retired, but when I asked from what, she just started reciting a poem called "Working for the Man" she published in some obscure literary magazine a decade ago. I nodded and smiled. A lot of my work with Suzanne involves nodding and smiling—a real-life minimum-wage bobblehead.

The window replacement is done within an hour and I'm relieved when silence floods my apartment again. The new pane is still taped up in the corners and so transparent and brand-new it almost doesn't look there. The memory of the bird with its head hanging on by a thread—shivers. I don't want to think about it again.

It wasn't a coincidence, the voice says. *Don't act stupid.*

I hurry to the bathroom to take a shower, keep moving, don't listen to the voice. Don't think. I imagine a calendar in my head—March. Five months now. I just have to stick this out five months to prove to my dad I'm not a colossal failure and then I can go away from here, I can start over again, I can be someone new.

But you can never run away from me, taunts the voice.

Ignore it. Don't listen to it. I stare at the medicine cabinet, which is a mirror, so really I guess I'm staring at myself.

You're a liar, the voice says. *You lied to your dad that you wouldn't quit improv.*

"I didn't quit," I whisper. "I just didn't go for one night."

You lied to Suzanne that you would throw away her pills and then you kept them like a little junkie.

"I'm storing them here," I say aloud. "Just until I can find a better place for them. I'm not keeping them."

You're the worst kind of liar, the voice says, so loud it buzzes my eardrum. *Because you lie to yourself.*

This is why I can't engage with the voice. When I do, it becomes louder, more powerful, it tricks me into talking to it. The less I pay attention to it, the quieter it becomes.

"You aren't real," I say to the mirror.

I turn to the shower. I make the water scalding and stand in it so long my skin turns pink and pruny. When I get out, I feel temporarily reborn. I wring my hair out and make a towel turban on my head. But when I see the mirror, the floor drops out from under me.

Written in the steam, the smeary words *I KNOW WHAT YOU DID* stare back at me.

THIRTY

"SO YOU THINK Elizabeth is 'after you,'" Maria says.

The use of finger quotes makes it abundantly clear what my new therapist thinks of my theory. She sits there in her cream-colored pussy bow blouse with her taupe lipstick that matches her taupe nails, looking like an aging Banana Republic model. Behind her, a classy, modern fireplace dances with flames. An antique clock is centered on the mantel above it, flanked by framed photographs that have been turned backward—a gentle reminder that this relationship goes one way only. While I may be baring the ugliest and most personal parts of myself to this woman, she gets to keep her private life all to herself.

"I realize how it sounds," I say, folding my hands on my kitchen countertop and sitting up straighter. In contrast to her classy background, mine is a blank room, white walled as a padded cell. "But I looked it up online and someone can write something on a mirror with their fingertip that's invisible until you fill the room with steam. She could have written it when she used my bathroom the night before. And the cookie made me feel sick."

"Do you think, perhaps, the more logical explanation for feeling sick to your stomach is the guilt you've been carrying?"

"That does sound more logical," I agree. "But—there was what I saw in the mirror."

"Written in the steam."

"Yes."

She takes off her glasses and cleans them with a little cloth. "Is it possible ... someone else wrote those words?"

"Like who?" I laugh. "The window guy in my apartment?"

"Did *you* write those words?" she asks, putting her glasses back on her face.

She asks it gently, suggestively. The temperature rises in my cheeks.

"I don't think so," I say. "I don't think I would do something like that and forget about it."

"Okay," she says.

She writes something down on the paper. *LIAR*, I imagine it saying.

"Can we shift tracks for a bit and talk about your psychiatric history?" she asks. "You asked to 'start fresh' last time, which I understand, but I'd like to hear about any medications, treatments, or diagnoses you might have received in the past."

Oh brother, here we go. I didn't want to delve into this—I knew it would color the lens she views me through. "But it doesn't matter. They never officially diagnosed me with anything besides situational depression. I was screened for other things I had symptoms for, but I didn't check enough boxes to be diagnosed."

"And what were you screened for?"

I hate this. The rectangular ruby button that says LEAVE twinkles and begs to be pushed. I could just zap this meeting right now, shoot it dead, never speak to this woman again. I sense her judgment, the same way I can sense judgment from any psychiatrist or psychologist or therapist or counselor—from any human who's made it their life purpose to squeeze other people into boxes. But I've already started down the snarled, frightening path of being honest with this woman, and it would seem a sunk cost to stop now.

I clear my throat. "Well, the situational depression—that was the most recent thing. I saw someone when I moved back in with my dad this last time. I hit a funk, it was hard to get through. Dropped out of cosmetology school and felt like a failure. It's one thing to not be able to hack it through college. It's another level of failure to not be able to hack it through cosmetology school."

Her head is bent down as she takes notes. I don't even want to think about what she's saying about *that*. "And in the past, what disorders were you screened for?"

I take a deep breath and focus on myself, on the tiny me in the top of the screen. "It's a list. A long one. Bipolar disorder. Borderline personality disorder. Schizoid disorder or something. Schizophrenia."

"Schizophrenia?" she asks with surprise, glancing up at me.

"Because sometimes I hear voices. A voice." I shake my head. "And yes, I know how that sounds. Promise—I'm well aware the voice isn't real. It's me. It's my voice in my own head."

"So the voice sounds like you?"

"Well, sort of. It's a mean voice. Low, like a ... a cruel witch." I shake my head. Oh, how I wish there was an unsend button for confessions like this. I haven't spoken about the voice aloud for a long time, and to talk about it with someone else—it terrifies me that it might give it even more power, make it more real. "Please don't start thinking I'm schizophrenic, I've already been down this path and it was ruled out."

"I believe you, Jolene, there's no need to get defensive."

I let out a long breath through my mouth. "Okay. Thank you."

"Tell me more about the voice. When's the last time you heard it?"

"Yesterday."

"And it said?"

Flatly, I tell her, "'You're the worst kind of liar because you lie to yourself.'"

"Let me hear what the voice sounds like."

"Like—imitate it?" I ask, in horror. "I don't know if that's a good idea."

Maria peers in closer. This must be how a specimen on a slide feels under the glare of a microscope. "Why wouldn't it be a good idea?"

"Because—because, I don't know. I try not to think about it, not answer it, not engage with it as much as possible. The less attention I give it, the more it seems to disappear."

"But is that really true?" she asks. "Has it disappeared?"

I chew my cheek. "You want to hear the voice."

She nods.

I clear my throat and close my eyes. "It sounds like this." My throat burns from the low growl of it. I open my eyes again. I can't keep going. I shake my head. "Like that."

She writes something down and I wonder what she would say if I asked her to turn around and burn her notes in the fireplace. I imagine her just shaking her head and writing *that* down.

"So it's a mean voice. Criticizing you."

"Yes."

"And it feels separate from you."

"I know it's me," I tell her. "I know it's in my head. I'm not thinking there's some entity I'm engaging with. I'm not psychotic."

"Jolene," Maria says, with a half-smile, as if I'm a silly child. "I'm not implying you're psychotic. *Everyone* has voices in their head."

These words she uttered—they undo something in me, like the woman just loosened a vise grip on my skull. She doesn't think I'm crazy. She's not trying to put me in a box. For a fleeting second, fresh relief rushes through me. "Right."

"Can you walk me briefly though medications you've tried?"

"None of them worked."

"I understand. I'm more curious about the treatments that psychiatrists thought might help your condition."

Condition. I don't like that word. It's a little too close to the words *disorder, disease.* I swallow. "I've been on a lot of things, but for short periods of time. I was addicted to Ativan. So when I went to rehab for a few days, they prescribed me Paxil while I tapered off. That started me down the rabbit hole. Paxil gave me the cold sweats, so a few months later, they put me on Prozac, which made me horribly anxious. So I went off that. A year or so later I gave Zoloft a shot, but the headaches were awful. I didn't try anything again for a while after that, until just a few months ago, when the doctor gave me Wellbutrin and it made me have blackouts every time I drank so I stopped taking those."

I'm breathless. I'm sure I'm giving Maria's hand a workout as she furiously takes notes.

"All antidepressants," Maria says, finally sitting back and giving her pen a rest.

"Yes."

She taps one of her elegant fingers on her cheek. "Have you ever tried psychedelic therapies—MDMA, psilocybin, ketamine?"

"No, never."

"Have you used any of those drugs recreationally?"

"Since high school, I've quite honestly been so terrified of the contents of my own brain I steered very clear of anything like that." I shake my head. "I'm scared of what could happen."

"What if healing happened?" she asks. "Have you considered that confronting your issues might be exactly what you need?"

"That's what Alice said," I murmur. "My best friend. She thought that by becoming friends with Elizabeth, by going to therapy, maybe I could work through my issues."

"Alice sounds like a smart woman."

"She is. But ... I don't know how deep I can go here."

"What do you mean?"

"Like ... I don't know. She thinks this all stems from Elizabeth. She even suggested I tell her what I did, try to free myself of the guilt."

"What if you did?"

"I will *never* do that." I shake my head. "What good would that do? She would hate me. I destroyed her life."

Maria doesn't disagree with me. Instead, she sighs and turns to look at the clock behind her. Subtext: *how much longer do I have to listen to this basket case?*

"Psychedelic therapy can be very beneficial," she says, "especially for patients who don't respond to other treatments. The doses we administer are low and they're given in a very relaxed environment. You lie down in a darkened room, wear an eye mask, listen to relaxing music. I've seen it do wonders for dozens of patients. In a few cases, it's entirely reversed symptoms of anxiety and depression."

In the pause, I let myself imagine that possibility—the possibility of an *actual* new beginning. Of being freed from the shadow that's been following me for years. Not another false start, but the real thing. Wouldn't that be wild, if drugs were the answer this whole time, but I just chased all the wrong ones?

"I would be with you the whole time, ensuring you're safe," Maria assures me.

Don't do it, the voice hisses in my ear, from nowhere. It has an edge of desperation I've never heard before. *Don't go there. You think it hurts now, just wait until you see what lies beneath.*

And that's when I know that this is what I need to do.

Because I've never heard the voice sound like that before—like it's genuinely scared. Like our roles have reversed for a flicker in time and *I'm* the one in control.

"Okay, I'm convinced. How soon can we do it?" I ask Maria.

THIRTY-ONE

"FOR THE FIRST time in longer than I can remember, I'm recharged by this decision to do something new," I say into my phone as I walk breathlessly up tree-lined Ashby Avenue. "For years, I've been stuck in this cycle of same but different, same but different, same but different. I keep thinking I'm changing, but I'm not."

"Jo, this is so amazing to hear you talking like this," Alice says in my ear. "Do you hear yourself? This is progress!" I can hear Sadie barking in the background. "Sade. Chill."

"She can probably smell me from a hundred miles away. Your dog hates me."

"She does not. You're so paranoid."

I stop at a red light and push the walk button with my elbow. Next to me, a jogger runs in place, having his own corporate-speak Bluetooth phone call.

"That's why we need to shift our KPIs, so we can figure out our ROIs and nail the MVP," he says.

Meanwhile, traffic sails by, each car filled with a person

on their own mission. Sometimes it seems the whole world is bubbles of mutual ignorance, each of us a little world of our own.

"Hello?" Alice says. "Still there?"

"Still here," I say, obeying the light signal and crossing the crosswalk. "I'm on my way to get my hair cut."

"Nice. Self-care. Here for it. Big change or just a trim?"

"Big change. Pixie cut."

"Really? What inspired this?"

"I don't know, symbolism. I'm ready for something new."

"Send me a picture when you're done. Immediately."

"Of course."

"I have to go though. I have back-to-back appointments all day."

"Keep the masses healthy."

"You know it. Don't forget to send me a pic."

"Promise."

I hang up, a bounce in my step as I take the next block to the salon. Inside, it smells like sugar and rain, endless mirrors on the walls, bottles and sprays and blow dryers, the calming snipping sounds of scissors. It's been a while since I treated myself to a haircut—usually I trim my ends and bangs myself. And I've never gone this short. The most extreme thing I ever did to my hair was dyeing it red in high school.

"So how short are we going?" the hairstylist asks me.

"We're going Mia Farrow in *Rosemary's Baby*," I tell her.

She wears a bandanna, hiding her own hair. Is that suspect? Should I not trust a hairstylist who doesn't flaunt her hair? Too late now, she's draping a cloth around me and leading me to the sink. With my hair back in the warm water, my eyes closed as this stranger soaps up my hair and runs her fingers all over my scalp, my skin prickles gorgeously. It's been so long since I've been touched. It's only when I get too close to somebody that I realize how lonely I am.

Back in the chair, bandanna hairstylist starts snipping and a blizzard of brown hair surrounds me on the floor. I scroll my phone to keep myself distracted from the possibility of regret—it's just hair. It'll grow back. A text comes in, my phone glowing with the name *Elizabeth*. It's a whole block of text with a LOT of all-caps.

Suddenly I feel like I've swallowed a brick.

> Hi Jolene, I'm going to be STRAIGHT UP with you. I'm feeling UPSET with how you've been treating me. I'm not sure what I did to deserve the COLDNESS and the GHOSTING 🪦 IS THERE SOMETHING YOU'RE NOT TELLING ME?? I've texted you EIGHT times with no response. You skipped improv ..... is there a reason you're AVOIDING me??? I've been WORRIED about you, that's why I stopped by the other night, I thought we were FRIENDS. But you made it ABUNDANTLY CLEAR with your VIBES that night that you don't want me around. I'm not MAD, just SAD and CONFUSED. What did I do??? You'll be glad to know I'm in LA for the week so you won't have to see me around!! Feel free to go to improv this week, I WON'T BE THERE!! I do hope you're OK........

Yikes. What a text.

I turn my phone over in my hands like a tiny wheel, a cold unease flooding through me. This is the Elizabeth I remember from high school—unpredictable. A hurricane of bizarre emotions. Oscillating between loving me and hating me, often for no detectable reason. But is there more to this? I read the text again, scouring it for subtext.

Does she know?

I blink and see it in the mirror of my mind: *I KNOW WHAT YOU DID.*

How would she know?

Elizabeth's deranged text has ruined the joy of my haircut. Now I'm sick in the pit of my stomach and all I can focus on is what the hell to say back, how to extinguish the ridiculousness.

> Elizabeth, I'm so sorry if I've seemed cold to you or anything! I'm just going through a lot right now. It has nothing to do with you. I really appreciate you swinging by the other night to check up on me and value your friendship. Hope you have a good time in LA!

I send it and see her three dots light up right away. I imagine her there, hungrily staring at her phone for my reply. The wait on my end now is mildly sickening. With her, the incoming response could be anything.

> Oh I'm so RELIEVED to hear that!! THANK YOU BABE!! Wanna do DINNER Tuesday?? I get back that afternoon.

Complete turnaround. Do I want to do dinner Tuesday? No. No I don't. But how can I say that now?

> Sounds great!

Exclamation point and everything. She hearts my text.

SEE YA NEXT TUESDAY!

God, I hate this friendship I've struck up with her. It's like trying to dance on hot coals and not get burned. Thankfully my phone doesn't light up again and I tell myself I don't have to think about her until next week.

"Ready?" the bandanna hairstylist asks me, swiveling my chair to face the mirror.

At first, I don't know what to say. I've never seen my hair this short—inches long, moussed and a little fluffy. My ears stick out. I touch my naked neck and wonder if this is a mistake. Do I resemble an elf?

"Shocking, right?" the bandanna girl asks.

"Very." I turn my head from side to side. It starts to sink in and I like it. I do, I like it a lot. I smile at myself. This is a new start.

Your beauty is nothing but a lie, the voice whispers.

I stand up, break eye contact with the mirror, pay for my haircut. I ignore the voice and step back outside, feeling the cool breeze on my neck for the first time in a long time and I tell myself: I'm new again. I'm starting over again. I'm okay.

THIRTY-TWO

SUZANNE GASPS and shields her eyes when she opens her door to behold the new me, as if I've morphed into a being made of blinding sunlight.

"What have you done?" she asks. "Good goddess, what have you done?"

"I ... cut my hair?"

"No, my love. You *slaughtered* it."

After a beat, I go with, "I take it you're not a fan."

She beckons me inside with a curl of her fingers, then lays a hand on my back as I come in. The way she looks at me, it's as if I just hobbled into her living room with a broken leg. "What made you *do* such a thing?"

Lord. This woman has no filter. Doubtfully, I rub my bare neck. "Because I wanted shorter hair?"

"Don't be daft." She holds my hand and squeezes. "You're trying to hide from yourself. Sever a part of yourself, murder it to oblivion."

This is quite the dramatic reaction to a simple haircut.

Even though I recognize Suzanne has got some out-there beliefs, she also has this way of being so convinced of everything she says that she starts convincing me, too.

"Hair is a cosmic transmitter, the connector and receiver to the universe. When you *mutilate* it, when you *disrespect* it, it's like severing a spiritual phone line."

"I see," I say.

I don't see. Hair, I always thought, is nothing but a collection of bizarre protein strands growing from our skulls. Shows what I know. The pity glittering in Suzanne's river-blue stare shrinks me. I'm a disappointment.

"Is my aura different now?" I ask.

"Thankfully, no," she says, giving me a hug. "You're going to be okay."

She takes me by the hand and pulls me through the chaos of her cluttered living room and into the breath of fresh air that is her tidy kitchen. Thinking it's teatime, I take a seat at the table, but she opens a cupboard instead and pulls out a box. The cupboard is stocked—and I mean *stocked*, like a store. There must be at least two dozen identical boxes in there.

She plops a box of salt in front of me.

"Sprinkle it in the corners of your rooms. You're in an *extremely* vulnerable place right now spiritually after what you've done to yourself. This will keep the negative energy at bay."

I tap the box with a finger. She's kooky, but I do appreciate someone's looking out for me. "Thank you."

She lets out a puff of a sigh, as if this interaction has been taxing. "Did you donate my expired pharmaceuticals to someone in need?"

"I did."

No lies there technically. It's me. I'm the one in need. Still, I'm terrified my aura is telling her something my words aren't, the way she narrows her eyes—like a lioness about to tear my guts out. I stand up and tuck the salt in my purse, which I'm still holding onto as if I'm ready to spring out of here at any moment.

"All right then. Let's get to work," she says, leading the way up the stairs, her rainbow crocs clip-clopping on the wood. "I've decided to compose my memoir in verse ..."

THIRTY-THREE

TONIGHT, I put on my big girl pants and go to improv. It's a lot more fun this time without the torturous presence of Elizabeth. I'm able to completely let go. I'm able to be the best version of myself, me on my brightest setting. Compliments rain in for my daring, fashionable haircut. Handsome man either winks at me or has an eye twitch; I choose to believe the former. I make the group laugh when I pretend to be Santa Claus hitchhiking and the only thing that brings me down is the fact that Jerry calls me "Liz" not once, not twice, not even thrice, but *four* times. As I'm packing up after class is over, he does it a fifth time.

"Jolene," I say through my teeth.

"I'm so sorry," he says, pantomiming smacking himself upside the head. "Why do I keep doing that?"

"People used to tell us we looked alike," I tell him, trying to lessen the sting of his mistake for him. "You're not the first person to get us mixed up."

"Yeah, yeah, yeah, that's right, you went to high school

together." He zips up a hoodie and slings a courier bag over his shoulder. It's an outfit you'd expect a twenty-year-old hipster to wear, not a silver-goateed dude old enough to have an AARP card, but it gives him a rumpled kind of charm. He points to the door, where the rest of the class has already left. "Walk you out?"

"Sure," I say.

I don't really want to walk out with him, I'm ready for pajamas and silence, but he's my teacher. What choice do I have?

"So you knew Lizzie back in the day, huh?" he asks me as we creak through the swinging metal doors and step outside into the smack of fresh night air. "What was she like back then?"

He has this playful smirk on his thin lips and his dark eyes dance. That look—it's like when we walked outside, he went from respectful teacher to flirtatious zaddy. I can't tell if he's horny for me or horny for Elizabeth, but either way, I'm really wishing I hadn't strayed behind and gotten stuck in this conversation.

"Was she as much a handful then as she is now?" he asks.

"I mean, she was … spirited," I say.

Spirited: a kind euphemism. I'm rather pleased with my word choice.

He cackles and puts some fingerless gloves on. "Bet she was the best damn actress in your school. Lead in every play. Am I right?"

"Actually, I was the lead," I tell him. "Juliet. She was my understudy."

"Funny," he says, leaning in, his smile dropping. "'Cause she said you were *her* understudy."

My eyebrows wrinkle. "No."

He studies me, like he thinks I'm lying. And there's this energy that shifts between us, as if the earth tilted imperceptibly on its axis. Something isn't right. It's askew.

He knows what you did, the voice whispers, and hearing it so loud here, now, out on a quiet street talking to my teacher —it's so unexpected it practically stops my heart in my chest. But then his face melts into a goofy smile and he shakes his head.

"My pot-addled brain can't remember shit, what do I know?" He slips a beanie over his bald head, folds up one pant leg, and walks over to a bike rack. He bends down to undo a lock and then gives me a serious look, pointing at me. "Stay safe out there."

"Sure, thanks," I say.

As I walk away from him, relieved to be done with the conversation, I can't help but hear his words ringing in my ear. And with every echo, they seem to grow more menacing.

Stay safe out there, stay safe out there, stay safe out there.

THIRTY-FOUR

"OKAY, so ... your teacher's out to get you," Alice says, holding one finger up. Another finger joins the first. "Your landlord's out to get you." A third. "Elizabeth's out to get you, of course. Are we sensing a pattern, Jo?"

It's Saturday. Alice surprised me with a visit, no warning, just knocked on my door this morning with Sadie in her arms. We're at a dog park in a neighborhood on the north side, where the houses are immaculate and unfunky and you can't blink without seeing a Tesla. No graffiti on the street signs or beat-up furniture abandoned on the curb like the south side where I live. Sycamore trees, trimmed grass, designer dogs smelling each other's butts. When I complimented a Pomeranian's rainbow dress, the woman told us, "Oh, this isn't my dog. I'm just her au pair."

Dog. Au pair. That's the kind of neighborhood this is.

I'm worried that my dad sent Alice to drive from Sacramento to Berkeley because he knows how miserable I've been since I moved here or, worse, that she's so worried about my mental health she's doing weekly wellness checks now.

"Do you think I'm out to get you?" Alice asks me. She crosses her arms and watches maternally as Sadie runs in a circle chasing her own tail. A dizzying idiocy. Yet somehow, I relate.

"Of course not."

"At a certain point when you think everyone's out to get you, you've got to realize it might be *you* who's the problem."

I fight the urge to roll my eyes. But she's right. Alice is always right.

"I can't get over how adorable that haircut is."

"I'm into it," I say, rubbing a hand over my head.

"How's therapy?" Alice asks, scooping Sadie into her arms and holding her like a baby.

"I'm starting this 'psychedelic therapy' thing on Monday."

Alice's expression changes, as if a rain cloud just floated above our heads.

"It's legit," I tell her. "It helps with PTSD, anxiety, depression."

"No, I'm aware. I just feel like since you've been to rehab and everything ..."

"I went to rehab for three days. And I'm not about to get strung out on psilocybin—psychedelics aren't addictive at all."

She scratches Sadie's tummy. Sadie eyes me with her beady brown eyes and when I smile at her, she growls. She might be an eight-pound chiweenie in a sweater, but she scares me.

"I looked in your medicine cabinet," Alice says.

Oh hell. Not this. Alice has switched modes from warm friend to worried medical professional. I gaze across the street at a bus pulling up to a stop and wonder if I should go throw myself under its wheels.

"Why do you have an arsenal of medicines prescribed to other people?" she asks.

"Why are you looking in my medicine cabinet?" I snap back.

"Jo."

She says my name like she says Sadie's when she's doing something bad. Bad Jo! Bad girl!

"They belong to my boss," I say, enunciating every word. "I haven't taken them. She asked me to get rid of them."

"Then why haven't you?"

This time, I give in to the urge to roll my eyes. "Can you not? I will. I'll get rid of them. Swear on my dad's life, I haven't taken a single pill."

"I don't understand why you'd even want the temptation." Alice puts Sadie down and lets her run across the stretch of green to have an awkward interaction with a yippy terrier. "And why would that woman *do* that to you?"

"Because she thinks I'm a normal human being. It's not like I told her, 'hey, I'm a loser who got strung out on Ativan once and dropped out of rehab.' Not exactly information I advertise to my boss."

"I need you to get rid of them," she says. "Promise me."

"I promise!" I can't help the anger rising, but the way Alice is looking at me right now, like I'm a very bad dog— our friendship is tipping off-kilter. It suddenly doesn't feel like we're on even ground anymore. I want a friend, not a mother. "Why are you even here, Alice? Tell me the truth.

Why are you giving me surprise visits on your day off and checking up on me? Don't you have better things to do?"

Alice doesn't answer, just shaking her head at me. "Please check your tone. I'm here because I love you."

"Did my dad put you up to this?"

"No."

"Are you talking to my dad behind my back?"

"Geez, do you hear how you sound?"

My mouth is open to continue defending myself, but the wind is sucked out of me. I look up at the trees with their fiery leaves. I wish I were a tree. Wouldn't life be grand? But no, I'm stuck with Jolene. And then there's Alice, who is correct and right and wonderful, of course, as Alice always is. I let my anger and shame recoil into a dense little ball and I swallow it for now.

"I'm sorry," I finally say.

We hug and Sadie comes over and ruins it by barking at me as if I'm her enemy.

She knows how evil you are, the voice whispers. *Animals can sense it.*

Silently, I say back to it, *I can't wait to kill you with psychedelic therapy.*

And to my shock and my delight, the voice doesn't say a word.

THIRTY-FIVE

I am aware that my experience with psilocybin administration may be challenging and cause discomfort. I accept that there may be one or more of the following side effects: headache, palpitations, drowsiness, confusion, auditory or visual hallucinations, the unearthing of past traumas, and more. I also accept that there are rare serious side effects such as cardiac disturbances or psychotic episodes.

I TAP my pen against the clipboard, rereading this.

"Questions?" Maria asks as she watches me from across her desk.

"Psychotic episodes," I say, pointing to the clipboard.

"Extremely rare. Please don't let that faze you. I've been administering psychedelics in therapeutic settings now for years and I've never had anything but positive results." Maria re-ties the scarf around her neck, merlot like her lipstick. I wonder if she was born with that kind of class or if she bought it somewhere. I've never been able to figure out where to get any of my own. "Now, I won't lie, it might be uncomfortable. But there's no way to heal without discomfort. If healing was easy, no one in this world would hurt."

I sign my name, a scribble I can barely read. Maria takes the clipboard and smiles at me, as if I've made her proud.

"You know what haircuts represent?" She points to my head. "Letting go of the past. I have the feeling you might be ready for that."

No, no, no, hisses the voice, as if it just woke up within me. *You can't. Don't listen to her!*

It's the sweet, uncharacteristic sound of a demon in despair. I relish it and smile, feeling like I just got into the driver's seat of my own car for the first time in years.

"Yes," I tell Maria. "I sure am."

Maria folds her hands on her desk and studies me. She has this wise, steady gaze that reminds me of something—an owl perched atop a tree, maybe, or the self-satisfied knowing of a cat. I can't help but wonder what her life is like, who she goes home to at night. Even this office gives me no clues. She probably jogs every morning on a treadmill. Donates generously to Planned Parenthood. Shops at Williams Sonoma, a place I wandered into once in a mall while searching for a teapot only to be told their cheapest one was five hundred dollars, made of copper. Like that teapot, Maria seems out of my league.

"Now, we need to discuss payment options," Maria says. "The sliding scale we agreed on for sessions goes up a bit when we move to psychedelic therapy."

This news arrives with a sting. Nothing like the reminder that this is a transactional relationship. My bank account is currently in the two-digit range. I imagine my dad's exasperation when I need to call him for another loan. *Do I look like an ATM machine to you? You think I shit hundred-dollar bills?*

"Oh, I didn't realize," I say.

"My approach is conducted via multiple sessions," she says. "Beginning with this first session today, which is considered our consultation. We're going to go over expectations, goals, preparatory information. If all goes well, next week we'll move onto ingestion with a smaller dosage, then another ingestion session with increased dosage, and then the final integration session where we explore your takeaways from the experience and how you might synthesize it into your life as you move forward."

"How much does the whole thing cost?"

"The total cost is one thousand five hundred dollars," she says.

Oof. I tell my face not to betray how much that hurts. I could buy three unaffordable copper teapots with that amount of money.

"I do accept payment plans, though," she goes on, "and I can work with you on spacing out payments in whatever way works for you."

You don't need this, the voice pipes up. *What a stupid waste of money. You can find a dealer and enjoy a drug trip for twenty bucks. You're being conned.*

If the voice is telling me not to do this, then I definitely have to do this. It's a new brand of reverse psychology for me —whatever the evil witch in my brain says, do the opposite.

"Can I get back to you on the payments later today?" I ask.

"Of course. For now, let's delve into expectations, shall we?"

I nod.

"The sessions will take place at my home office, which is in the Montclair neighborhood in Oakland," she says. "This is because psilocybin is decriminalized in Oakland, but not in Berkeley yet. To stay within legal limits, ingestion takes place in my home office. It's very comfy. A warm room with a sofa and daybed. We dim the lights, put on headphones with soothing music, and you wear an eye mask. This will be mostly an internal experience, but I'll be there with you the whole time."

"What am I supposed to do?"

She leans forward and says, "I would suggest you take time to really listen to that voice, to talk back to it, to explore and confront your guilt."

No! the voice screams within me.

"No!" I can't help myself from echoing. A ghostly, cold hand of panic grips my throat. "I'm sorry, but that sounds terrifying."

"It won't be terrifying, I assure you. Disturbing? Perhaps. Uncomfortable? Undoubtedly. But the only way to work through your depression and self-esteem issues that stem from the wrongdoing you committed is to confront them."

I sit back, stunned, the words *wrongdoing you committed* as jarring as yellow police tape flapping in the wind around your home. My God, the way she says it, like it's a crime. Like I'm a criminal.

Criminal, the voice whispers.

"I don't know," I say in a squeak, because I feel like an internal pipe's about to burst.

"Jolene, do you want to heal or do you want to continue to suffer? I'm asking this in seriousness. Because you need to be a hundred percent ready for work, for committing to this method." She leans forward and points to me. "The same way you did with your hair—you didn't turn back. You didn't doubt yourself."

"True."

"I want you to close your eyes."

I do as I'm told and the whole world goes dark.

"Breathe in, slowly," she says in a velvety voice. Tingles all over my scalp. "One, two, three, four, five, six, seven."

My lungs expand, my body fills, I could float away, I could burst.

"And let it out. One, two, three, four, five, six, seven, eight, nine, ten."

My chest caves in, my stomach extends, I'm drained of air, I'm hungry to breathe.

"You're calm and relaxed and safe here," she says. "Feel your body. Feel where your feet meet the floor. Feel the weight of your limbs. The tickle of your breath leaving your nose …"

She continues guiding me through a mindfulness exercise and though I can feel my mind squirming, the voice thrashing and resisting, as she names each body part and assures me I'm relaxed, I succumb. And it works—I do relax. She tells me I'm in control and I *am* in control. And when I open my bleary eyes again, I'm lighter.

And it truly is like Maria is an exorcist because after that, the voice doesn't speak to me again all day.

THIRTY-SIX

"LEMME GET THIS STRAIGHT. You're asking me for fifteen hundred bucks so you can trip your balls off?"

I can hear the 60-mph wind through the phone pressed to my ear. My dad's driving home with his sunroof open. I can picture him, one hand on the wheel, brights on the whole time because he's *gotta see the damn road*, taking the hairpin curves like they're straight lines.

"That's not what I said—"

"But it's what you're asking me. You're telling me this lady charges you almost two thousand bucks so you can eat some shrooms and lie on a couch and, what, cry about how your old man treated you?"

I let out a sigh. It's Monday evening. Should have known this was what I was in for when I called my dad to ask for money. I'm standing in front of the microwave watching my frozen burrito turn, turn, turn in the puny yellow spotlight.

"That's not what I talk about."

"How rough you had it, you know, growing up in a

fuckin' paradise beach town with everything you could have asked for?"

"Having money isn't everything!" I say loudly, wanting to throw my phone against a wall, but knowing then I'd probably have to have yet another conversation like this because he'd have to be the one who would buy me a new phone. Get me off this carousel.

"You say that, but you sure as shit ask for a lot of it."

"I'm sorry," I say, softer. "I have issues."

"You won't take your antidepressants because, I don't know why, but you'll do this," he says. "I mean, Jesus. Listen to yourself."

"You know what? Never mind. I'm sorry I asked."

I hang up the phone. A second later, it rings again.

"What?" I say.

"I'm sorry, bunny. I just don't get it. Issues. What issues? Someone abuse you? 'Cause if so, I'll find them and I'll cut them into bite-sized pieces and feed 'em to raccoons."

It's a very specific and very strange threat. I can't help but laugh, which I know is what he wants.

"No one abused me," I say. "It's not that. It's—it's something I did to someone else." I lower my voice. "Remember right after I graduated? The thing that happened?"

"I don't know what you're talking about. You know what? I don't care." He lets out an exasperated puff of a sigh. "Whatever. It's three billable hours for me. I'll wire you the money if you promise you've been going to work, paying your rent, going to that improv class I paid for."

"I have been, I swear."

"I'm pulling up to the house right now. I'll do it in a couple minutes, I gotta take a whiz."

"Thanks so much. I appreciate it, Daddy, it's really going to help me."

"Yeah, yeah, fine. Talk to you soon."

"Wait, one quick question."

"What? My bladder's about to explode."

"Did you send Alice here to check up on me?"

"Did I send who to what? Huh? Why would I do that? Alice your friend Alice? The doctor lady? No, of course not. I gotta go."

He hangs up and I honestly can't detect if he was being defensive or not there. Thou doth protest too much and all that. I can picture him there in the dark, climbing out of his car and muttering to himself as he goes inside. My childhood home is a gorgeous stone-covered cottage on the hill hidden by oak trees where he now eats frozen meals with plastic forks and leaves the toilet seat up and has a custom-built hot tub with algae growing all through it because he never uses it. Last time I went home, he had a new dining set and three out of four of the chairs were still covered in shrink wrap because he never has anyone over.

When I was a kid, he didn't date. The one time he did bring a woman home—Lacey I remember her name was, Lacey like a piece of negligee, and that's how she was, wispy and useless and sexy—I was probably seven or eight and even I had the good sense to know that this woman was closer to my generation than his. I sat at the kitchen table pushing my mac and cheese around in my bowl with my spoon and when Lacey went to use the loo (yes she called it the loo, strike two), my dad whispered, "Psssst. What's up?"

"I don't like her," I said.

"You don't like her," he repeated.

The moment hung in the air and he studied me. I couldn't tell if he was about to break into a laugh or start yelling at me. It's always been hard to tell with him. Then Lacey came out of the bathroom and my dad stood up.

"Lacey, this isn't gonna work out. My kid doesn't like you," he said.

She looked so stunned there, hands on hips, eyeing me like he'd just told her I was a vampire.

"Are you serious?" she asked with a nervous giggle.

"As a heart attack," he said. "Sorry."

My dad's apologies are often fired out of his mouth like bullets and don't feel apologetic, and this was one of those times. We both watched as Lacey slowly and disbelievingly walked to the doorway where she'd just hung her coat and purse. She grabbed her things and left, her high heels clicking down the stone steps.

"And that's the end of that," Dad said, sitting at the table and rolling up his sleeves. "How's your mac and cheese?"

I never saw him with a woman again.

THIRTY-SEVEN

ELIZABETH'S HOUSE is around the block from mine, a Victorian triplex that must be what my house looked like before Google Man bought it and renovated the soul right out of it. Hers is a sea-foam green. Weather-bleached and shaded by redwoods. Christmas lights strung around the roof—a couple months early or many months too late, who knows. Someone upstairs is playing a classical song on the piano with impeccable flourish.

Like me, Elizabeth lives in a downstairs unit, though hers is through the back. As I stand on her doorstep and eye her flowering hanging plants and the adorable concrete fountain with a spitting cherub, I can't help the stab of envy, because this is what I imagined when I moved here. This is what I wanted. I knock on her door. Already, I can't wait for this night to be over. Quick dinner, light conversation, get the hell out of here. That's the plan.

"Hey!" Elizabeth says as she opens the door.

Then her jaw drops.

Mine drops too.

An eerie feeling drips over me. Have we gone backward in time? Are we onstage again, conducting a mirror exercise?

Because we both have the *exact same fucking haircut.*

Same cute little pixie. Same light brown color.

Both of us touch our fingertips to our hair.

"How?" I manage.

Elizabeth bursts into laughter and grabs my arm. "Are we twinsies?"

She's delighted, but I'm horrified. *Horrified.* How could this possibly happen? "When did you ...?"

"When I was in LA! Omigod, this is so *crazy.* You and I are two peas in a pod, aren't we? Remember how this happened in high school? How we randomly ended up with the same haircut?"

'Twasn't *random.* She straight-up copied me then and she must have somehow done it again. But I offer a tight smile. I ruined her life, I'll let her keep her illusion. "Right."

She beckons me inside. "Come in, come in!"

Elizabeth's apartment is a studio. The intimacy of being near her bed, the pillow she rests her head on at night, makes me squirmy. I've barely stepped a foot inside and I'm already sneaking a peek at my phone to check the time. Shivers. That identical haircut. *Did* she copy me again? She was out of town when it happened, how could she have known? But what are the chances it was accidental?

She knows. You know she knows. She knows you know she knows.

Hush up, voice.

Elizabeth's space is smaller than mine, high ceilings and philodendrons slithering around the perimeter of the ceiling. Though the place is funky and hung with colorful paint-ings, I can't explain why, but it screams expensive. It's so well laid out I can imagine an interior designer did this all for her. An espresso machine gleaming on her kitchen coun-tertop probably cost three thousand dollars. No inflatable couches here—she has a legitimate antique Victorian tufted velvet sofa. Her bed is not a mattress on the floor, it's canopied and flanked by curtains like she's a medieval queen.

"I love your apartment," I say, and I'm not lying.

"Oh, thanks." She bats a hand like it's nothing and heads behind the counter into her tiny but adorable kitchen. "Still haven't quite settled in yet."

Doesn't look that way. Not an unpacked box in sight. I scan the walls, all the paintings in matching gold frames, and my eyes stop on the picture that I instantly recognize with a striking and intimate familiarity, as if I've caught my own reflection—a reprint of Picasso's *Girl before a Mirror*. The sight of it tightens a sickening screw in my stomach.

"I didn't know you had the same painting?" I say, pointing at it.

"Yep!" Elizabeth says. "Had it for a long time."

"Interesting," I say through my teeth.

She's doing it again. She's copying me. The haircut, the painting, these aren't coincidences.

"Have a seat!" Elizabeth says. She points to a wine rack, bottles aplenty, another clue that the girl's still rich. "You like vino?"

"I'll just have water," I say, sitting. I don't trust my tongue if I begin drinking with her. The kitchen's set up a little like mine, long marble counter, stools. "Smells good."

"Pot pies are in the oven. Hope you're a carnivore."

"I am."

She gets a glass of water and slides into a seat beside me, pulling up close, too close, close enough that I can smell her minty breath. She smacks my arm. "How've you been, girl?"

I sip my water, mostly to hide my face behind the glass as long as I can. "I'm okay."

"Sorry about my cray-cray texts. Sometimes I get a little weird when Aunt Flo comes to town," she says.

Sure. Blame it on your uterus. It's all your uterus's fault.

"Oh, I get it. Totally fine."

It's not fine, of course. I'm scared of her. I don't know why I came here, but I'm in too deep with her to back out now. And I'm sorry to say that I'm seated next to her burned side. I try not to notice it, just focus on the unscarred half of her face, but it's so hard to pretend it's not there. To not want to shudder at the sight of it.

That's your fault, the voice whispers. *And she hates you for it. She wants to hurt you like you hurt her.*

As the horrendous voice whispers in my ear, I offer a plastic smile to Elizabeth and focus on her good eye. I ask her about LA and let her rattle off a monologue about all her friends who live there and how unsure she is about whether she's making the right decision by going to grad school but she wants to help people. Do I know what she means? And coaching is helping the *privileged* and really she wants to help *underserved* people and also she just loves the Bay Area because it's so *real* and *authentic* and in LA everything is *performative,* do I know what she means? That's why she admires me, she says in a random segue, because I'm so *authentic,* I've always been so *myself,* do I know what she means?

Do I know what she means?

She's staring at me and I swear there's a maniacal twinkle behind her grin.

You know what she means, the voice says.

"That's why I guess I've been so thrown by how closed off you seem with me, how *worried* it made me," Elizabeth says, pinching my arm. "I felt like we really bonded that night at the poetry slam and then it was like a light switch went off and even now, I'm looking at you and I'm wondering, is there something she's keeping from me?"

A cold sweat breaks over my skin. She is examining me like I'm a painting on the wall of a museum, like I have many meanings she's here to uncover. She has to know. Right? She's testing me, that has to be what this is. She's slowly torturing me. There's no other explanation for the grilling she's doing. But then, for just a second, I imagine what I must seem like to her—closed off and stuck in my own head all the time, nervous and paranoid. Maybe she doesn't know.

What a tiring teeter-totter of guilt.

I force myself to laugh. "Of course not." Swiftly, I turn the conversation back to her. That's the easy part of hanging out with Elizabeth—she loves to talk about herself so much that pivoting the spotlight of conversation her way is a piece of cake. "Hey, what's up with Jerry?" I ask in a gossipy tone. "What exactly is your relationship with him?"

"Oh, he was kind of my mentor," Elizabeth says.

"Does he have a thing for you?"

"We're keeping it professional."

She hops off her stool and her unscarred cheek flushes

pink. She clears her throat and busies herself with checking the oven. Looks like I'm not the only one who's got a lie in their pocket.

"Ding ding ding! Pot pies are ready!" she sings.

Ding ding ding! I shouldn't eat anything this woman gives me, how am I going to sit here pretending to eat her food? My brain hits the gas and all the thoughts come at once as she removes the tray from the oven. Did she poison me in high school or did I imagine it? Did she poison that cookie she brought me, or was it nerves that made me throw it up? I only took a bite. It must have been nerves. Elizabeth shows me the pot pies with a little grimace.

"I burned them, I'm so sorry. They look awful."

"They look fine!" I say.

Lies. All lies.

"Which one do you want?" she asks. "Take your pick."

I look at her smile, bright as the moon. Okay. I breathe a little easier. They can't be poisoned because she's letting me take my pick. I point to one and thank her. It doesn't look appetizing, but I start eating it anyway.

Dinner is agonizing. Besides the writhing swamp of my own mind, Elizabeth's pot pie has a burned crust that makes the whole thing taste bitter. She's all apologies and tells a convoluted story about the time she almost set her house on fire heating up frozen pizza rolls. She gets up and investigates her oven, which is smoking, and has to stand on a chair to remove her beeping smoke alarm from the ceiling. Good old schadenfreude again—I don't know why it brings me satisfaction to note she's a poor cook. Something I can't do too well myself, but at least I know how to not burn a frozen pot pie.

"Isn't this wild, that we're practically neighbors?" Elizabeth asks as she gets down from her chair. "I could peep over my back fence and wave to your back window!"

She's watching you all the time, the voice says.

"So fun!" I say.

She sits back down and tells me how spectacular it is to have me here. Isn't it spectacular? Everything's so spectacular. How's therapy going? Am I feeling better? What's bothering me, do I want to talk about anything? Elizabeth's here for me! Elizabeth's my friend! She squeezes my hand so hard that I wonder if she truly loves me or if she's trying to crush my bones.

She knows, she knows, she knows, she knows, she knows.

I'm the puppet and the puppeteer. The smiling girl and the shadow person inside her. I'm the supportive friend nodding and listening and I'm her despicable enemy who nearly destroyed her.

I chew, I swallow, she talks, the lump in my stomach grows, grosser and grosser.

There's this pressure mounting with every tick of the clock. I don't know how I can keep pretending. I don't know how much longer I can stand to be around her. There's nowhere to comfortably rest my eyes on the sight of Elizabeth. Her haircut creeps me out so much I want to run home and shave my own head. Her scars make me gag with self-hatred, her good eye sees too much into me, her glass eye spooks me.

"Isn't this the best, getting to reconnect?" she asks. "There aren't a lot of people in my life who know ... the old me. You know, the *before* me. The me who didn't look like this."

Elizabeth gestures to her leg, her face, and there's a flicker of darkness, of sadness that makes me want to bury myself alive.

"I never had the luxury of choosing what defined me," she says, her voice dropping to a lower register. It's jarring. I'm so used to her high-pitched optimism. "Once the accident happened, this was it. This was who I was. This was what the world would see every time they looked at me. But you—you remember the girl before. Do you still see her when you look at me?"

"Yes," I say, barely above a whisper.

And for the first time, I do.

My mind has a magic eraser that can remove the pink, ropy, tree-like scars from her face, that can replace her glass eye with a real one, grow her leg back, that can age her backwards. She was once whole and unhurt. I took that away from her. The past is nothing but an ache. As we maintain eye contact, I wither like a salted snail.

"I hate not knowing what happened," she says. "The accident. Not remembering anything. It's this blank space I've had to carry around with me my whole life."

"That must be so hard," I say, an invisible hand squeezing my heart.

She shakes her head. "I was getting in my car one evening and then when I woke up, I was in a burn ward screaming from the pain. And then my dad took my hand, sobbing, telling me the doctors had to amputate my leg."

"I'm so sorry—"

"They put me under general anesthesia," she says, her voice rising. "When I woke up, I was still sedated. I thought I was dreaming. When I finally realized this was real life, when it sank in, the sobbing started. A freaking *ocean* poured out of me. I thought I was going to die of dehydration. A month or two later, the phantom pains started—like my leg was on fire, like my ankle was twisted the wrong direction."

My stomach gurgles and I push my plate away. All at once, a wave of nausea hits and I really do wonder if this has become too much, if I'm going to throw up.

"I'm so sorry," I say.

She laughs a chirpy little laugh, her face suddenly softening, her pitch rising again. Like an actress—but I can't tell which is the character and which is the real person. "Why would you be sorry? Was it your fault?"

Swallowing, I meet her gaze. Her nostrils flare and I detect a deep, controlled rage beneath her smile. But maybe I'm imagining it.

You're not.

I have a pathological imagination.

No you don't.

Is she joking, the way her tone implies? Is she really asking me this nightmarish question? What if I answered her truthfully right now? What if I told her what I did?

Never. Never, never, never, never, *never.*

Coward.

Go to hell, voice.

You should know by now that monsters are best kept under the bed.

Or better yet, locked inside my brain.

THIRTY-EIGHT

"I'M ACTUALLY NOT FEELING WELL SUDDENLY," I say, eyeing the goopy pie pan in front of me.

"Oh no! Did me talking about my amputation gross you out? Omigod, so sorry."

She rubs my arm as if trying to wake up a limb that fell asleep. She's either far too kind and understanding or she's cruelly sarcastic, I cannot tell. Either way, her cheerful tone is an invisible knife to the gut. My bowels seethe and I don't know what's happening, what is the mind, what is the body, it's all tangled up and I know suddenly I'm going to be very sick.

"I have to go," I say, standing up.

"Already?" she asks with a crestfallen expression. "You just got here!"

"I'm sorry," I say.

I'm an apologetic parrot. *Sorry! Sorry! Sorry!* Queasy, crampy, sweaty, I stand up. I can't tell what's going on right now inside me. Is this avoidance? Am I just looking for an excuse to sprint out of here? Or am I actually feeling sick? No, this is real. I'm sick to my stomach and I'm either going to spew tepid pot pie on her floor or I'm going to shit my pants if I don't get out of here.

Elizabeth poisoned you. She poisoned your pot pie.

No, she didn't. Maria would say my guilt is making me sick to my stomach again.

Maria hates you and lies to you.

"Are you having another panic attack?" Elizabeth asks, her eyes wide with concern. "Can I do something for you?"

"I'm just—I just need to go," I say. "Thanks for having me."

Elizabeth follows me as I hurry toward the door, waddling stiffly because I am so ill.

"Hope you're okay!" Her eyes shine with worry. "Please text when you get home!"

"I will," I say, rushing out the door.

The route to my house is one block long. I walk it like a stiff-legged cowboy and I have never, in my thirty years on this earth, had to concentrate so hard on controlling my sphincter. It's dark outside. The streetlamps click on and the crickets sing and I am going to explode. I fantasize about making a beeline into a neighbor's yard to duck behind a rainbow PRACTICE RANDOM ACTS OF KINDNESS yard sign, pulling my tights down and crouching to take a shit like a dog. But no. No, I have to make it to my door. And I do, thank the universe, I make it, and I haven't exploded into a mess of bodily fluids yet ... but when I put my hands in my pocket, my keys aren't there.

They're not in my other pocket, either.

Dancing on my doorstep, my stomach drops again and I tighten every muscle in my abdomen and beg the universe to protect my intestines right now. I emit a sad whiny noise, trying my doorknob but knowing it won't open. This is an emergency. A bodily *emergency*. I slowly make my way up the stairs, breathing deeply as I can, and when I get to Google Man's door, I ring the doorbell over and over again, *dingdong-dingdong-dingdong*, sweating profusely and clutching my belly as if I can keep it from spilling open.

Google Man comes to the door and opens it, not speaking a word, regarding me with the emotionlessness of a man retrieving his Amazon package from his front porch.

"I need to get in my house, right now," I say. "It's an emergency. I'm not feeling well. I don't have my keys. Please."

"Okay," he says, adjusting his glasses.

He turns around, disappears for a moment and I can see into his place as I stand here breathing like a woman in labor. It's blank and white but there's a hat rack in the foyer with wigs hanging on it, very odd, very unexpected, and I would ask about it but I'm a ticking time bomb and I'm clenched like one giant muscle right now with only one objective in mind—bathroom.

Bathroom.

I need the bathroom.

Should I just run inside and use his bathroom? Before I can decide, Google Man comes back with a key in hand and a mask on so he doesn't catch my plague and I whisper a thank you and head down the stairs, one by one, clutching the railing like I'm a hundred years old and the steps are slathered in butter.

Finally, *finally*, Google Man opens my front door for me and I rush inside yelling "thank you!"

"You can keep the key," he yells after me. "I have a few."

"Great, thanks!"

Never have I wanted to be home in this apartment more than right now. I run to the bathroom and pull my tights down and my dress up and moan as I sit on the toilet and an absolute hell blasts out of me. I dry heave as I sit here, wondering if it's about to come out of both ends and thinking, rock bottom moment, this is a rock bottom moment, but what did I do to deserve this? My other rock bottoms were my own damn fault—drinking myself into a blackout state, nauseated and twitching from Ativan withdrawal. Why is this happening?

Don't be stupid. She poisoned you.

Did she? Was Elizabeth's pot pie laced with something? How would I get sick this fast? And she offered me my pick of the two, so it makes no sense unless ... unless ...

Wait.

The oven was smoking. The smoke alarm went off and she had to remove it from the ceiling. Then she sat down and she talked and talked and talked and—did she even eat a bite? She might have. She might have not. I wasn't paying attention.

I close my eyes, in pain, every muscle in my middle constricting. And I think of Juliet's potion in high school, the cookie, now this. What did she give me? Will I die? Should I call an ambulance? Go to the hospital? Call Maria, declare this a psychiatric emergency? I am unraveling here, so sick, so sick I feel shaky and weak, sick to my bones, I don't know what to do.

After an unspeakable eternity on the toilet, I finally get up again. In the mirror, my face is pale and moonish and hollow-eyed as a ghost. I'm shaking and sweating and feel like I weigh half of what I did when I woke up this morning. My ass is on fire. My stomach is spasming. All I want is to crawl into bed and pull the covers over me and disappear into the welcoming oblivion of sleep.

I wash my hands in the cool water and shiver. The water in my sink has been draining slower than usual lately. Right now, it's barely draining at all. Timing, universe. You need to work on your timing. The last thing I want when I feel like I may or may not be dying of either poisoning or guilt-induced hypochondria, take your pick, is Google Man having to come into my apartment right now. That's a thumbs down from me. As I rinse my hands, the sink water sits, placid as a pond, going nowhere. I turn the faucet off and push the sink stopper a few times, pumping it. Exasperated, I pull the stopper out completely and when I see what's at the bottom of it, I gasp.

Every follicle of hair on my head stands on end.

Every inch of my skin hardens with goosebumps.

There's an eyeball staring at me from the bottom of the drain.

THIRTY-NINE

DON'T PEER into a mirror in a dream.

Promise, it's not pretty. First, it's hard to even find a mirror when wandering the labyrinth of unconsciousness. Dreams are like casinos—no clocks, no mirrors, no sense of time or self. But if you do happen to find a mirror and gaze into one, you won't like what you see. You don't look right. You don't look like yourself. It's like Picasso got hold of your face or someone tried to generate you with AI. Asymmetrical, features misplaced, your skin all wrong, your shape not quite right. I've always wondered what this means—if it betrays a deep lack of a sense of self innate to us. Not sure what it is about the human mind, but it's almost like mirrors in dreams make us glitch. We're not meant to do such a thing.

Tonight I dream I look into a mirror. I'm hunched and my teeth are too sharp. I'm deformed and shriveled and monstrous. One eye is crooked and duller than the other. I'm devastated, not just because my beauty has rotted before my eyes, but because I don't recognize me. It's a special kind of emptiness, the ultimate loss, a death while alive, as if someone just snatched my whole world away. And then I hear a scratching noise. *Scritch-scritch-scritch.* Footsteps echoing in my ears and a low, witchy hissing voice saying, *Ugly on the inside.*

I awaken in my bed drenched in sweat, jolting upright. I swear I just heard the thud of a door shutting.

It's the middle of the night. My hand is pressed to my chest, panting as I catch my breath. Then it all comes back to me, a garbage tsunami of memories. I'm blinking and trying to pick apart the waking nightmares from the sleeping nightmares. Elizabeth's uncanny haircut, me almost shitting my pants—those were real. The eyeball in the sink, the footsteps, the sound of a door thudding ... those, I don't know.

"Hello?" I ask weakly.

My belly flip-flops, empty and making noises. I imagine it's screaming, *what have you done to me?* My poor, war-torn bowels. I slip out of bed and tiptoe into the darkness of my living room, nothing but blue moonlight spilling into a quiet room with a deflated couch and a single picture on the wall. Above my head, there are the creaks of Google Man's footsteps. It occurs to me how easy it was for him to grab my key and help me inside last night, how he said he has more keys. My belly flip-flops again now, for different reasons. Encore.

In the bathroom, I switch the light on. I still look like someone who crawled out of a bunker during the apocalypse. Ravaged. Chapped lips. Zombie complexion. My hair's standing on end like a sick bedheaded child's. Holding my breath, I peer down into the dark hole of my drain and am electrocuted by the sight of the eyeball still there, still right there, it's *real*. A pale blue eye gazing back at me from the depths. I gag and duck out of the room.

Hands to my mouth, I pace the darkness of my kitchen. I don't know what this means. What does it mean? What would Maria say about this? Would she try to tell me it's a figment, a hallucination? Because it's not. It's in there, and there's no logical explanation for it except Elizabeth put it there. Right? I take a picture with my phone, to have proof. To solidify this in reality. I'm dizzy. My apartment seems angled and bobbing, a boat on a stormy sea.

Maybe I should be asking myself instead what Suzanne would say about this. Suzanne would think it has a deeper meaning. She would tell me to meditate on it or go lie naked in the sun.

Salt! That salt she gave me. Where did I put it?

I open my nearly empty cupboards until I find it. Then I go back to the bathroom and I pour piles of salt in the corners, covering vile slime of grout from strangers who lived here before.

I try to go back to sleep, but I can't. My heart is pounding so loud it could be someone pounding on my door. It could be footsteps in my house. All I can think of is that eyeball down there, imagining Elizabeth dropping it in, but when? She's only been to my house once—do I really think she brought an extra glass eyeball for the sole purpose of dropping it down my drain when she went to the bathroom? That she wrote a message on my mirror at the same time? I'm crushed under the weight of these questions and this night is eternal and my stomach is still rotted and I am wrung like an old rag from how sick I was last night.

After a little while, I creep back into the bathroom, not to peer down the drain. Don't look at the drain.

I see you, I imagine Elizabeth's singsongy voice echoing from the sink.

"Nope," I say, opening the medicine cabinet.

I scan the poetic names on the bottles, dreamy made-up words, Soma and Lozol and Ambien. I can imagine stuffing them all in my mouth and swallowing and shutting the lights off for good. It's just a thought. It doesn't mean I'll do it. Just like the voice is just a voice, I know it isn't real.

My fingers hover over the temptress Klonopin, but no, it's a cousin of Ativan. Not that. I pull out the Ambien instead. Shaking it, I get tingles from the sweet maraca noise of the pills. The name on it is Daveed D'Angelo. It's the medication of a dead man. The bottle says it expired three years ago. Better take two.

I knew you were going to break, the voice says as I eat the pills and swallow them dry.

It's funny, that word. *Break.* That's what I need, a break.

A break from my own brain, before it breaks me.

FORTY

"VERY WEIRD," Google Man says as he stares down my drain.

Some men stroke beards. Others twiddle mustaches. Not Google Man—he squeezes his man-bun instead. He's still masked and clearly trying to keep a few feet's distance from me.

It's ten a.m. I skipped work, texted Suzanne: *sorry! got food poisoning.* Every time I think of Elizabeth and that fucking pot pie I want to walk into the ocean with pockets full of stones. The Ambien helped me sleep, but now I'm groggy. And my landlord is barefoot in my bathroom. He's wearing a faded shirt that has Google's old slogan *Don't be evil* on it and right now it reads a little accusative.

"I don't know how to get it out," I say again. "And the sink is draining so slowly now I can hardly use it."

"How did it get there?" he asks, pointing to the eyeball.

"I'd like to know the same thing."

Our eyes meet. Google Man has dark ones with long

lashes and the steady, unfazeable gaze that reminds me of either a guru or a serial killer, haven't decided yet. He turns and sticks a finger down the drain, but it's too deep for him to fish it out that way.

"The guy who used to live here before was an odd duck," he says.

"Oh?"

"A sculptor," he says, as if that means something.

"You think ... he left the eyeball in there?"

"Wouldn't put it past him. Whole place was full of mannequins. Do you have a wire hanger or something?"

I'm still digesting the image of my apartment crowded with plastic people. "Let me look."

After rifling through my closet, I return with the hanger. Google Man straightens it, plunges it down the drain, wiggles it around and grunts as if he's moving a mountain. Finally he's able to pop the eyeball out of the drain. A glass eye, hideous and covered in hair and slime. If I had anything left in my stomach, I would throw up again.

"Want it?" he asks, holding it out.

"No." I shudder. But wait—evidence. Maybe I need evidence that this is real, that this really happened. "Yes actually. Okay."

I take the eyeball in my hand and wash it gingerly in the sink. Shudder. I can see Google Man behind me in the mirror. At first, I think he's checking out my ass but then I realize he's looking at the piles of salt in the corners of the room. I'm too tired to be embarrassed right now. Plus, who's this guy to judge? He's got a hat rack full of wigs in his foyer. I dry the eyeball with the care of someone shining a crystal and take it into my room, put it in my box of underwear that sits on my bedroom floor. The sight of it there among my G-strings is so creepy I get a shiver.

Back in the bathroom, Google Man is beholding the contents of my wide-open medicine cabinet. Just helped himself to my shame, no permission asked.

I spoke too soon a minute ago. I do still have it in me to be embarrassed.

"Wow," he says.

"Hey, excuse me. Those are, um—my boss, she wants me to donate them."

"Donate them," he repeats, shutting the cabinet.

"Right."

"Mmm-hmm."

The moment hangs long and ripens with awkwardness. At last, he gives me a thumbs up and says, "Well, sink is unclogged now."

"Thank you so much," I say, maybe too loudly.

He gives me a nod, casts one more sorry glance at my medicine cabinet and my sickly self, and leaves.

This isn't a good look for me. Bloody footprint on my door, broken window, locked myself out of my house, eyeball down the drain, and now the cherry on top—my landlord thinks I'm a drug addict.

He thinks you're a mess because you are a mess.

"Shut up!" I burst, so loud it scratches my throat.

In my semi-empty apartment, the sound reverberates. Fighting tears, I hesitate in front of the medicine cabinet, craving another dose of oblivion—but then I catch a glimpse of myself there in the mirror, almost as shrunken and ugly as a dream-mirror version of myself. Instead, I turn into my bedroom and dive back into bed.

FORTY-ONE

MY LIFE MUST BE A REVOLVING door because I dream that I'm right back in my bathroom again.

This time, the lights are flickering a sallow blue. The sink is splattered with something dark, muddy or bloody, I don't want to know. A woman's fingers are reaching out of the drain, wriggling like worms. Sludgy, dirty, with red painted fingernails. I can smell ash and burnt meat in the air.

I know what you did, Jolene, Elizabeth whispers in a singsong voice. *Jolene. Jolene. Jolene ...*

"Jolene," a voice is saying to me. "Jolene."

I open my eyes, confused. No idea which world I'm in. But as I blink the blur of sleep from my eyes, it dawns that I'm awake now and Elizabeth is hovering over me. Her jasmine perfume hits me like a slap in the nostrils. That déjà vu haircut. That halved beauty of her face.

"Jolene," she says again, sharper.

I sit up, freaked out, wiping the sweat from my brow. "What the hell are you doing in my apartment?"

Elizabeth's mouth drops. "Geez! Sorry I care about my friend. I've been worried *sick* about you. I was afraid, I don't know, you had appendicitis or something. That you needed to go to the hospital. You haven't answered any of my texts."

I pick up my phone from the floor. Fifteen missed texts.

"But how did you get in here?" I ask.

Widening her eyes as if I'm a fool, she jangles my keys in the air. "You ran off in such a hurry last night that you left these at my place." Gently, she places them next to my phone. "Are you sick? What's wrong with you?"

This state I'm in—wizened from last night's diarrhea extravaganza, balloon-brained from sleeping pills, dirty in my bed and vulnerable as a snail without its shell—is not a state I would ever want anyone to see me in. Not even my dad. Not even Alice. But *especially* not Elizabeth. It's like someone walking in on me naked or something, I am so speechless and uncomfortable.

"What's wrong with you?" she asks again.

"I'm sick," I say.

She reaches over and touches my forehead with her fingers. Red painted fingernails. I flinch at the sight of them.

"You feel warm," she says, biting her lip with concern. Real? Fake? I don't know. "Let me get you some water. Do you have tea? I can make you tea."

Her go-go boots click out of the room and I sit in my bed, trying to breathe normally. I can't tell right now if this is sweet of her to come check on me or if she's deranged. I definitely know that no matter how thirsty I may be, even though my mouth is the Sahara desert right now, I'm not drinking *anything* that woman gives me. I can hear her singing "Jolene" in the other room and it's so sugary sweet it could be the soundtrack to a horror movie.

Standing up, I check and yes, there it is—the glass eye staring back from my underpants box. Not a sight you see every day. I hold out my hand to assess myself. It's shaking. I blow out a breath, considering my options. I need a moment to process.

"I'm getting dressed," I call to the other room, then shut my door.

What fresh hell is this? I'm still trying to get my bearings after taking two of a dead man's Ambiens. There's a very good chance the woman currently making me tea in my kitchen tried to poison me last night. That she stuck an eyeball down my drain. No matter what's true, I do know she let herself into my apartment and watched me sleep for who knows how long. That's creepy, right? That's crossing a boundary. I can't even think right now. I don't know what to say to her because, quite honestly—and after last night, quite literally—she scares the living shit out of me.

I pull a dress over my head and when it comes back down, there's Elizabeth, smiling with a cup of tea in hand.

"Excuse me," I say, unable to believe the audacity of her walking in on me getting dressed.

"Excuse *me*," she says. "Sorry! I didn't realize you weren't decent."

"I said I was getting dressed."

"Well, I didn't hear you."

The way her tone drops sends chills down my spine. Like a petulant sister.

"Besides," she says, her tone climbing again, a chipper

little birdy tweeting. "It's not anything I haven't seen a hundred times in the green room back in high school."

"Yeah, well, we're not in high school anymore."

I can't help it. I'm done playing nice. I want her out of here.

"Why are you talking to me this way?" Elizabeth asks, tilting her head. She holds the cup out. "Drink some tea. You're not well."

She's right. I'm not well. But I don't take the tea.

"Did you put a fucking eyeball down my drain?" I demand.

Once those nine words fly out of my mouth and sail through the air, the weather seems to change. Both of us stand totally still. Elizabeth's expression crumples in confusion. My hands come to my hips. I study every movement of her face, every deliberate contortion of her expression— because it has to be deliberate, right? She's an actress, a better one than I gave her credit for. She inhales sharply and finally says, "What on earth are you talking about?"

It does cross my mind that this sounds insane. It *is* insane. But that doesn't mean it isn't true. "You put an eyeball down my drain." I point to my underwear box. "Wrote a message on my mirror. You tried to poison me twice."

"Jolene, are you ... are you all right?" she asks, something new quivering in her eyes. Fear? Is that fear? If it is, it has to be fake. She's the scary one, not me. "Do I need to call someone? I'm a little freaked out by what you're saying."

"Don't. I know what you're doing," I say. "It's not going to work on me."

She lets out a breath, as if she's too stunned to speak.

Finally, she crouches and puts the tea on the floor. "Look, I have been nothing but nice to you. Making you dinner last night. Bringing you your keys. Making sure you didn't die in your apartment—I mean, seriously, you really scared me last night!" Her eyes fill with tears. "You're welcome for being a friend."

She spins and clomps away from me, her footsteps getting lighter and lighter, until finally I hear the sound of my front door thudding shut. I blow a steady, long sigh out, savoring the relief of having her gone. In the gorgeous quiet, I tiptoe to my front door and lock it. There's a worm of doubt in my mind that I was in the wrong, but the voice pops up and it says, *You were right about her. Everything you said was true.*

It's alarming that, for once, the voice and I agree.

FORTY-TWO
THEN

AFTER *ROMEO and Juliet* ran its course and the cast was left with hoarse voices and sour sweat stains on our costumes, the only assignment left to focus on in theater senior year was our final scene.

Of course, because the universe holds special plans for me, our teacher paired Elizabeth and me as partners. We were performing a melodramatic number from an old movie called *Terms of Endearment* and we had to spend class together practicing.

Elizabeth and I sat outside in the grass that first day, bare legs and copper hair catching the sun, twisting clovers between our fingertips as we tried out our lines. When we first sat down, I couldn't help the way I still felt—bitter, like the taste of Windex in my mouth. But after a bit, us one-on-one, nobody else around, Elizabeth softened and so did I. Then I questioned whether that potion had ever made me sick at all or whether it was just that wild imagination of mine.

"You're such a spectacular actress," she gushed when we ended our first read-through. "Seriously!" She turned to the empty quad and yelled, "Give this woman the Oscar!"

"Heh," I said. "Thanks. You're good too."

My words fell flat, underwhelming and unconvincing. Maybe I wasn't such a spectacular actress after all.

"Are *we* good?" she asked, meeting me with her twinkling blue eyes. Her eyes that matched the sky behind her. Her eyes that matched her shift dress. She had high cheekbones, the creamiest skin with just a light dusting of freckles, and full lips. I wondered which one of us was prettier and was afraid to know the answer. "You and me. I feel like ... somehow things got weird between us?"

"No, they didn't get weird at all." I smiled. "We're good."

"Yay!" she said, like she won a prize. She glanced back down at the script in her lap, which fluttered with the lazy breeze. "Ugh, so depressing. Why couldn't we have gotten a comedy? This scene! Bummer city."

"I know. Maybe I should have said I was too triggered to do it, I probably could have gotten out of it."

Elizabeth tilted her head at me quizzically.

"My mom died of cancer," I explained.

She gasped, hand flying to her mouth.

"Long time ago," I made sure to add. "When I was a toddler. I hardly remember her." The way people reacted when I told them—the pitying shock—was one of my least favorite things in the world. I always felt the need to excuse her death somehow, to make other people comfortable with my loss, to assure them it didn't scar me.

Her eyes widened and shined. "Omi*god*."

"It's okay, really," I said, adding a laugh to let her know how not a big deal this was.

Elizabeth reached out and clutched my arm. She squeezed. "Girl, my mom also died of cancer when I was little. What kind? How old were you?"

Suddenly, as if a cloud passed overhead, it all became sadder. Tragedy's often sadder when someone else is wearing it.

"Breast cancer," I said. "I was two."

Her mouth dropped. "Same, but I was three."

I got a chill. My first thought: liar. But my second thought was, why the hell would anyone lie about something like that? Copying my hair was one thing. Copying my dead mom story was next level.

"Wow," I finally said.

"*Very* wow," she agreed.

Her red-penciled brows furrowed. She fanned herself with the script, deep in thought, and for maybe the first time, I truly became curious about Elizabeth. I wanted to peer inside her skull and know what movies played in there. What her home life was like. Who she was under the me-shaped costume. Since we'd met, I'd been so put off by her too-muchness and annoyed by the way she co-opted my style that I'd never given her a chance. But maybe we did have more in common than I thought.

The bell rang and we got up, slinging our bags over our shoulders.

"Want a ride home?" she asked as people came pouring out of the classroom doors.

This was a truce, a peace offering. Whatever rivalry we had before, now it blew away in the wind. Elizabeth and I smiled and she took my arm and we went to the parking lot as if we were cosplaying sisters.

She drove a silver Jaguar, easily the slickest car in the parking lot. She got whistles and looks from the boys as she jumped into it—whether it was the car or her they drooled over, who knew. I'd never seen Elizabeth in this context before, slipping on her rhinestone-studded sunglasses and cranking up some wailing guitars. I'd never ridden passenger or paid much attention to where she went after school was over, because I was too busy riding the city bus like a loser. My dad offered to pay for half a car, but that still only gave me half a car and I didn't have much saved yet. All this time, I'd thought I was the cool one, I was the enviable one, but as Elizabeth slammed her foot on the gas and burned rubber, it hit me that I'd had it all backwards.

"Are you going to prom?" she shouted over the guitars.

"I was thinking about it," I shouted back, the warm 60-mph-wind in my mouth as she sped down the highway.

"With who?"

"Joey maybe."

Joey was the stoner whose negligence may or may not have led to me drinking window cleaner. My standards were too low to limbo under. He was a red-eyed, stoned himbo, but damn he was good-looking. He was sweet, too. We'd been flirting at lunch the past few weeks.

"I'm not sure if I want to go," Elizabeth said. "Prom. I mean, isn't it just so predictable? So cheesy?"

"It is pretty cheesy," I said. "Maybe I won't go, I don't know."

Why was I agreeing with her? I don't know what it was about her, but her conviction was contagious. She turned onto the pass that snaked up the mountain and then cut through the back road, the narrow one without guardrails that was overgrown with brambles and sprawling oak trees. Only us hill people took this road, especially with the ease she did, one hand on the wheel. As if she could read my mind, she told me, "I live up this way, too, you know."

"Right."

"Yeah," she said. "Watch this."

With a screech of tires, she pulled onto a shoulder. Dirt flew up in the air, dust clouds around us. She unclipped her seat belt and we got out. She beckoned me to come to the edge of the road. When I looked down, chaparral and jagged rocks edged steeply down into a thicket. But the view—it was like nowhere else, one of my favorite spots on earth. You could see the whole city sprawled out below like jewels as you stood higher than the clouds. Then, beyond the violet twinkling city, there was the blur of ocean bleeding into the sky.

"That's my house, over there," Elizabeth said, pointing up the hill a bit, where an impressive white mansion clung like a barnacle to the side of a cliff. I'd seen that house before. It had a pool that winked at you and begged to be noticed.

"Damn," I said.

She turned to me, her hair whipping around. And then she took a step toward me with this sleepy gleam in her eyes, reached her fingers out, and touched my lips. She was going to kiss me. I could feel it in the air, I could tell what was happening, and it threw me off so much I stumbled on my feet, tripped over a rock, and almost tumbled down the hillside. But she grabbed my arm and pulled me back.

"Omigod!" she said, laughing. "What are you doing?"

I was taken aback, rubbing my leg, which had a long scrape on it from a rock. "What are *you* doing?"

"I'm saving you from your death, girl!"

"You were going to kiss me."

At this, she threw her head back and laughed so hard I could see her uvula dancing. "*What?*" she finally managed. "Are you on drugs?"

"You touched my lips."

"A fly had landed there! Ew, I wouldn't kiss you." She smacked my arm. "Geez, get over yourself."

Her smile melted and the moment seemed to land with a thud, killing the lightness we'd felt so far. All at once my doubts came back about her. I touched my lips, questioning reality yet again.

"You might want to wash those lips," she said, heading to her car. "Flies love shit, you know."

Feeling upside down, I rubbed my mouth and got into the car. She turned the music down, way down, but all that filled the air now was our bloated silence.

"Must take you forever to get home on the bus," she said suddenly as she made the turn for my house, easy as if it was her own. I didn't even have to remind her where I lived.

"It does," I said, grateful that she killed the silence with her cheerful tone, happy that it seemed like we could silently agree to move on and abandon that bizarre confusion of the fly or the almost-kiss or whatever it was. As she pulled up to my house, so modest and small, like a hobbit's home compared to hers, I pointed to the Karmann Ghia that was parked on the road with the FOR SALE sign on the windshield. "I've been saving my money to buy that car."

"Oh, cute." She pronounced it *cuh-yoot.* "Love Karmann Ghias, my dad has one. You so should."

"I have a summer job and I'm hoping it's still available then. It's been parked there forever."

"Fingers crossed!" She smiled at me and waved. "Have a spectacular rest of your day. Oh—and I don't know if you ever walk these woods at night, but be careful if you do. Swear on my life, I saw Bigfoot the other night when I was taking out the trash."

I laughed.

"I'm dead serious," she said.

And she was. Not a trace of humor in her tone. In fact, she looked terrified.

"Um, okay," I said as I hopped out. "I'll be careful."

"Toodle-oo!" she cooed.

She drove off, peeling a little rubber in her exit. I stood there in my pebbled driveway, pondering the spread of oak arms above my head, listening to the engine of her car fade quieter and quieter and then vanish completely. Then the worm in my belly turned. I touched my lips again and my heartbeat raced. It was frightening what a dizzying effect she had on me. I truly did not know how I felt about what just happened, about her, whether I was foolish or she was foolish or whether we were friends or enemies.

After the weekend, on Monday, as I hopped off the school bus, an orange Karmann Ghia—*my* orange Karmann Ghia—stopped in the middle of the road. Behind the wheel, Elizabeth honked the horn and yelled, "Hey girl!" and then drove away with a finger-wave.

My breath hitched. I bit my lip in the exact spot she touched it, so hard I tasted blood.

FORTY-THREE
NOW

you'll be happy to know i didn't sleep A
WINK after yesterday. SO CONFUSED

srsly I have shown you NOTHING but
kindness since we reconnected.

Feeding you!! Checking in on you!!! Cuz I've
been WORRIED about you!!!

But you want to spiral & lose your mind in
that SAD little EMPTY apartment?? Pushing
away the only SANE person who is showing
you KINDNESS??

This is IT

I'm DONE

I'll be CIVIL to you of course in improv
because I'm a PROFESSIONAL and (unlike
you) a DECENT PERSON but consider this
friendship OVER

And of course TYPICAL you don't even
have the decency to text back

THANK YOU FOR SHOWING ME WHO
YOU REALLY ARE!!!

THIS DIGITAL mayhem is what I wake up to the next morning when I get up to go to work. I stare at Elizabeth's flurry of insecure texts. So many of them. So much all-caps. Frankly, after the adrenaline rush of reading them all wanes, I'm left with nothing but relief. Fine, let's be done with it. No more pretending we're friends. Good riddance.

I get dressed and eat a bowl of cereal and head to work. It must have rained a spell last night because there's a sweet fresh stink in the air and the pavement is dark and damp. Walking is something I've learned to love, the place where my thoughts seem to make the most sense and where my brain is the kindest. When I'm out among the traffic song and the shivering trees and the endless river of same-but-different houses, that vile voice tends to disappear and the world opens up, bigger than me, so much bigger than me, and it's a blessing to be swallowed by it.

By the time I enter the expansive luxury of Suzanne's neighborhood, a peacefulness has blossomed within. I'm lighter. I forgive myself for the stupidity of eating pills I shouldn't have, I accept that I'm not sure what the hell happened with Elizabeth or who is wrong, and I'm relieved it doesn't matter because she and I are no longer apparently on speaking terms. My obligations with her are done (DONE!! as she would say) and the sun is shining on the dewdrops and the day is wide open. I smile at my reflection in Suzanne's Mercedes Benz as I walk up her driveway. There I am, intact, symmetrical, no dream-mirror Picasso face, not even thirty yet, still have my life ahead of me. Hashtag blessed.

On Suzanne's door, there's a sticky note.

> *Here comes sweet Jo to babysit the junkmen!*
> *Expect their knock-knock at 10AM.*
> *Inspiration struck yesterday …*
> *The memoir is officially underway*
> *When the muses speak, I listen*
> *Thou shalt not disturb*

I read this cryptic message twice. That's it. These are my instructions. I shake my head and open the front door, which she's left unlocked, because she lives in a neighborhood where the rules change and you can do that sort of thing.

Inside Suzanne's house, it's quiet, nothing but the white noise of a refrigerator. Speckled sunlight all over her antique labyrinthine living room and its claustrophobic contents, which the junkmen are apparently picking up at ten. I assume Suzanne's in her "inspiration station" writing cave in the backyard, which is rare. She's never not been here to let me in before, but I've been doing this tango with her long enough to know what needs to get done. The ferns that need watering. Her supplements collection that needs replenishing. The kaftans that need steaming. I can't help a little whiff of disappointment that I'm not part of the memoir writing session today; it's been the task where I've felt the most useful and I've been excited to tack it onto my mile-long resumé.

But soon the junkmen arrive, two sweaty unsmiling men who speak in grunting Russian, and I sit on the fainting couch in the corner and point at what they need to take away. Boxes. Tables. Lamps. Stacks of water-stained paperbacks. I feel luxurious and useless, a breathing piece of furniture while they do all the work to haul away Suzanne's dead husband's "detritus" as she calls it. Meanwhile, I scroll my phone. In a mini epiphany, I Google Suzanne again, hungry for the real story, but this time I use her first name and Daveed's last name—the one printed on the pill bottles. *Suzanne D'Angelo.*

And ... holy shit. The results that come in: images, news articles, a fucking *mugshot.*

A mugshot!

Suzanne with wild silver hair and a stare so sharp it could cut you. Eyes I peer into regularly, eyes that assess my aura.

Jackpot.

BERKELEY POET ACCUSED OF HUSBAND'S MURDER

I prickle to attention like an exclamation point. Down the rabbit hole I fall, clicking, scrolling, devouring headlines with bated breath.

A little over two years ago, Suzanne was arrested for the murder of her husband Daveed, the man whose junk is currently getting hauled by grunting, sweaty men in the very room I'm seated in. Junk that, who knows, could be evidence. Goodbye, evidence. After her arrest and a local media frenzy, Suzanne stood trial but was ultimately acquitted, thanks to my dad. Which—sidebar, your honor—my dad set me up to work for a woman accused of homicide? I have questions.

But putting my own safety and wellbeing aside, the case is gruesome. Daveed's corpse was found in their hot tub. He'd been in there so long, the coroner described what was left of him as "human stew." Flesh slipped off the bones. Internal organs bled into the water. The man was left to boil and simmer in his own Jacuzzi so long that his cause of death was undetermined and that's how Suzanne got let off the hook. My jaw remains unhinged as I scan comment sections of local papers, the know-it-alls, the armchair psychologists and wannabe conspiracy theorists. I don't know what to think. I try to imagine Suzanne killing someone. Slipping poison into his tea, shutting the lid on the hot tub with the click of a lock and walking away from it.

I send a text:

> Dad, why the hell didn't you tell me about Suzanne??

"Well, it appears the junkmen ravaged the room," Suzanne's voice says, making me jump and slip my phone back into my pocket guiltily.

She looms in the doorway to her kitchen. Behind her, the back door is ajar. Birds chirp. A breeze blows her shawl majestically, her hands on her hips. It's probably the new context that she's an accused murderer, but she looks like some kind of white-clad witch to me right now. I shiver.

"Yeah," I say, just noticing I'm sitting in a nearly empty room by myself. "They did their thing."

"The slate has been washed," she says, stepping inside

and assessing the blankness. Her eyes travel around the room and then land on me.

Please don't tell me my aura has changed.

"You look like a frightened rabbit," she says. "What's wrong?"

"I found an eyeball down my drain," I blurt.

The words might have physically come out of my mouth, but mentally? I have no idea where that came from. Just reaching for another scary thing to blame my guilty-scared expression on because I'm not about to admit that I figured out she may or may not have made a stew out of her husband.

Suzanne steps closer, her lips straightening into grim concern. "You found an *eyeball* down your *drain*," she repeats, with the flourish of not just an actor, but the kind of actor who would call themselves a *thespian* with a straight face.

"Yesterday," I say.

"An *eyeball*."

"A glass eye. In my bathroom drain."

She inhales sharply, as if I stuck her with a pin. "I see." The intensity she studies me with is annihilating. "Have you done anything to cleanse your space of negative energy?"

"I put salt in the corners of the room," I say, kind of defensively.

"Some divine and beastly spirit is watching you." She folds her arms. "You need more than salt, my love."

"I know, I need something. I don't know what." My voice cracks as I say it. Somehow, I've accidentally stumbled upon telling Suzanne the truth. "I'm afraid this woman from my past is stalking me. Or not. I don't know." I force a bitter laugh. "I'm a fucking mess."

Suzanne steps closer, her rainbow clogs clicking on the parquet floor. "I think I know what you need."

I wait for the next sentence, expecting something along the lines of a tarot reading, sage smudging, astral planing. Instead, she sits beside me and says, "A hug."

And even though she has a gaze as dangerous and blue as a gas flame, and even though I now know that she might have killed someone, I let her put her arms around me and I put my arms around her, too. Disappear into the scent of her patchouli, close my eyes and stay there, soaking it up like sunshine, and say, "Thank you."

FORTY-FOUR

MARIA IS LOOKING at me like I'm her child and I brought home a report card full of Fs. Even via Zoom, her disappointment is profound. She's tenting her manicured fingers and shaking her head.

"I must admit, Jolene, I feel like we're backtracking a bit." She folds her hands in front of her on the table. Today she's blurred her background, as if I'm not worthy of seeing her living room at all. "I thought you decided on psilocybin therapy and made a commitment."

"I know." I'm cross-legged on my mattress on the floor in my room. If anyone should be blurring their background, it's me—a rainbow hill of shoes behind me, blinds that hang crooked on my window. "Look, weird stuff has been happening and I'm already paranoid. I'm afraid I'll be even more paranoid if I go down the psychedelic path. I'll be the fine print on your waiver, you know what I mean? Psychotic break."

"Let's slow down a moment, shall we?" She takes a sip of

water from a crystal glass. Maria hydrates. Maria does everything right. "Tell me about the paranoia."

I breathe in deeply, as if I'm about to blow up a balloon, then dive into the past week with Elizabeth: the creepy identical haircut. The diarrhea attack after she fed me pot pie. The eyeball down my drain and waking up to her staring at me in my own apartment. When I think about these things, it makes perfect sense to me—it all stacks up, it equals a wicked scheme with me in the crosshairs and Elizabeth the mastermind. But somehow, when I speak it aloud, when I try to explain it, it sounds insane. And even though Maria's facial expressions are subtle, I can see, by the perk of a single eyebrow, by the twitch of her mouth corners, that she doesn't believe me.

"I can understand feeling frightened by those coincidences," she says, leaning in and giving a sympathetic nod. "Imagining that someone is after you is incredibly stressful."

Coincidences. Imagining. I want to scream.

"Look," I say, taking out my phone and scrolling through it so I can find the eyeball picture. I hold it up to the camera. "This was down my drain."

"Okay," Maria says. "I see it, yes. Very odd. Remind me though of what your landlord said ...?"

"Well, that the guy who lived here before was a sculptor and he had mannequins, but does that explain it?"

"It might not explain it, no, but it does lead to other possibilities. Right?"

Nodding, I dig my fingernails into my knees.

"Has the voice been speaking to you?" she asks.

"I mean, the voice is always there somewhere inside of me. I try to not listen to it."

"What does the voice say about Elizabeth?"

"She's after me. She knows what I did and she wants to seek revenge."

"And you believe the voice?"

Hmm. Do I? She's stumped me. I'm not sure how to answer.

"Do you think it's possible that, when it comes to Elizabeth, your guilt is causing you to see patterns where there are none?"

"Maybe."

"It's a lot like conspiracy theories—they're all about cherry-picking, confirmation bias. Are you familiar with confirmation bias? You come into something with a belief and every fact you find will confirm that belief. And when facts disagree with your belief, well, the blinders go on."

I never really thought about it that way. I remember listening to Elizabeth prattle on about idiocy like chemtrails, UFO abductions, and (shudder) Bigfoot. Am I doing that? Is that exactly what I'm doing—a conspiracy theory that's a one-woman show?

"Do you think, Jolene, that a part of you imagines that Elizabeth is doing these things because it would mean you're being punished for what you did to her—and that maybe an unconscious part of you *wishes* you were being punished?"

"Punished," I echo. "Maybe."

"What would justice look like?" she asks curiously, leaning in. "I wonder if you felt there was justice, if you made things right, if that would free you of the voice, of the guilt, of the paranoid delusions."

Delusions. She might as well slap me in the face. I hate

that word. I hate that word the most when it's a psychologist saying it to me. It's so dismissive.

Run away from this woman, whispers the voice. *She hates you. She wants to hurt you.*

"I need a sec." I close my eyes and massage my temples, ignoring the voice and untangling what Maria just said. I open my eyes again and turn around, looking at my shoe pile. Before this call, I was counting shoes. I'm missing three shoes. Where did they go?

You know where they went, the voice says. *Elizabeth took them when she was here the other day.*

And it's so ridiculous, so absurd a suggestion—as if I wouldn't have noticed Elizabeth leaving my apartment with an armful of shoes!—that I start laughing. The voice is so full of shit.

Maria squints her eyes at me. "What's so funny?"

"Oh, nothing. Hard to explain. What was it you asked me?"

"About justice," she says, sounding irritated.

"I don't think justice is possible," I say. "I don't think there's anything I could do at this point that would make what happened right."

Maria contemplates this with a face of stone. She adjusts her cashmere cardigan and I spot the glint of a cross necklace, which kind of surprises me. I don't know why. I guess any detail I can glean about her as a real-life person outside of our expensive fifty-minute hours comes as a surprise. "Are you familiar with restorative justice?"

"Sort of. I've heard of it, yeah. Why?"

"Well, part of its focus is on repairing harm done to an

individual. Have you considered what it would look like if you repaired the harm done?"

This suggestion flips my stomach. "How would I ever be able to do that?"

"I'm not sure. That would be up to you."

"I mean, that's partly why I've been so nice to her. Trying to be her friend again and all that—because I wanted to kind of ... make up for what I did."

"Do you think that's helped repair the harm?"

"Look, I can't repair the harm," I say, frustration a burst pipe inside me. I wish I could just shut the computer and walk away and never return to this subject. "I mean, what am I supposed to do? Give her my leg? Pay for laser removal for her scars? What could I ever do that would make up for it?"

"What about starting with being honest with her?"

"I am not going to do that," I say. "Absolutely not."

Usually, I'm a reed that blows in the wind. I lack conviction on many things. But here's one thing I know for damn sure: I will never be able to look Elizabeth Smith in the one functional eye and admit to what I did. It's not just that I won't—it's that I can't. I am pretty sure if I did, I would have a heart attack and die on the spot.

"Understood," Maria says. "Well, let's focus on what we can accomplish here." I can tell she doesn't think I'm giving her much to work with, but she's trying. "Let's go back to talking about psychedelic therapy. I know that you've voiced concern about psychotic breaks, but I can assure you I've guided many patients through these sessions and have never had anything of the sort happen. It's mainly a concern with schizophrenic patients. Are we still open to exploring this as an option?"

I take a deep breath and nod. "Yeah, I think so."

"I'll work with your timeline. When do you think you might be ready for your first session?"

Never, hisses the voice.

Well, I'm nowhere near ready to explore my already terrifying psyche on shrooms. But at the same time, I don't want to obey the voice, because the voice is wrong about everything. I try to think of sometime between now and never and I come up with next month. Next month might as well be another lifetime. Kick the can down the road to a place that doesn't yet exist—that's the way to do it.

"How about November?" I ask.

FORTY-FIVE

LATER THAT NIGHT, a flurry of knocks on my door. *BAM, BAM, BAM.*

My immediate thought is: Maria called the police to turn me in. There's a SWAT team out there in full gear, ready to bust my door down with a battering ram. There's no peep-hole to peep. Should I answer the door and put my hands in the air, go with them quietly? Or should I hide in my room and let them break in and have to find me? I decide on the former but when I open the door, there are just three sullen prepubescent boys in costumes—a splotchy white-faced vampire, a kid with an ax through his head and fake blood all over him, and another in a monster mask.

Relief is too weak a word for what I feel at the sight of their ugly faces, but then I realize it's Halloween and I have no candy. Totally spaced on the date today. Can't believe the end of October snuck up on me like this.

Man, I suck at being a grown up.

"Shit," I say, then realize I shouldn't have said that, either.

They snicker. "Um, I mean, shoot. Hey, sorry but ... I don't have any candy."

The look these kids give me—it's as if they're trying to set me on fire with the power of their minds alone.

"What?" the vampire finally says.

Behind them, I can hear the laughter of children in the dusk. Jesus, there are more. More candy-hungry children to humiliate me and remind me of another one of my petty failures.

I gulp. "Yeah, sorry about that."

"Are you fucking serious?" the one with the ax through his head says.

"Hey," I say. "Language."

"How about we come back and egg your house later?" he volleys back.

What a little jerk. I think about kicking him, but he's probably twelve years old.

"Try my landlord upstairs," I say, then close the door.

I hear a smack on it, like one of them kicked it. I turn off my porch light and my living room light and go back into my bedroom. Halloween night and here I am, hiding from kids in my bare bedroom—my "sad, empty apartment" as Elizabeth put it.

I'm at that life phase where holidays no longer matter. I'm far too old to get excited about them and I'm childless. They don't exist in my world. Maybe I should get back on dating sites or something—I might be solitary by choice, but I am getting a little weird. Singing loudly in my room to cover up the whisper of a voice that doesn't exist. Sitting here rolling the glass eyeball around in my hand, spending way too much time counting and recounting my shoes. I've looked everywhere. I'm missing a cowgirl boot, a slingback flat, a T-strap platform, a jelly. Just one of each. It's driving me up the wall. I call Alice, my lone voice of sanity.

"Is it crazy to think that Elizabeth broke into my house and stole my shoes?" I ask when she picks up.

"Um ... hi to you too."

"Hey, hi."

"Yes, it's crazy. Who would do that?"

"I told you about how she came into my house."

She groans. "Haven't we gone over this? She thought you were dying. She was performing a wellness check on you. I'd come into your house if I had your keys and you weren't responding to me too."

"Yes, but you've been my best friend since high school. She hasn't."

"She's known you just as long though."

It's weird to think that—that I go that far back with Elizabeth, that deep. "Yeah," I admit.

"Hey, we're getting ready for a Halloween party over here," she says.

Sadie barks as if she can sense her nemesis is on the line. In the background, Liam says, "Hey Jolene, hope you're okay" in this tired way that makes me wonder what Alice tells him about me. Rolling her eyes when she hangs up, saying, *she's calling because she thinks someone's stealing her shoes now.* And Liam saying, *oh honey, you're such a saint for dealing with her.*

"But anyway, I'll be coming into town this weekend. Lunch Saturday?" Alice says.

"Why are you coming into town again?" I ask, suspicious. What am I, a charity case? Is my dad paying her to check in on me like a pet sitter? He acted like he wasn't when I asked him, but it's just so bizarre that the busiest person I know is driving hundreds of miles out of her way during her precious days off to just swing on by to say hi.

"Sadie, no!" she yells. "Sorry, I have to go. Sadie's chewing up her marshmallow costume. We're going as s'mores—Liam's the graham cracker, I'm the chocolate, Sadie's the marshmallow except—" Here her tone gets higher, an admonishing baby voice. "—wittle miss marsh-mallow might have chewed through her outfit, didn't she?"

I love Alice, but I hate Alice's baby voice. If my half-crazy phone calls are her charity work for the week, then mine is listening to her talk like this.

"Okay, yeah, I have no life, I'm around Saturday. Just call when you're on your way."

I hang up the phone and see I got a text. I haven't been getting many texts this week, since Elizabeth ghosted me— the most welcome ghosting in the world. I open it. It's from a number that just says *Unknown*. All it is?

One single clown face emoji.

I text back:

?

No response.

It's her again, the voice says.

A few goosebumps prickle—but no. Not taking the bait tonight, voice. It's a wrong number. Not everything is a conspiracy against me. It's my guilt, my wish to be punished, like Maria said.

I'm brushing my teeth later when the knocking starts. *Knock-knock-knock*, so quiet it's nearly tapping, little butterfly thumps. Who the hell would be knocking right now? It's almost midnight, Halloween is over, when will those tiny sugar junkies stop harassing me?

But the knocking keeps up. My heart rate speeds right along with it. I'm not about to go opening my door at this hour. Whoever it is, I'm sure I don't want to know.

It's her, it whispers.

Tap-tap-tap. Rat-a-tap-tap. Less like a knuckle and more like fingernails drumming. I ignore the sound while I'm brushing my teeth and keep on ignoring it while I get in bed, turning my light off and staring at my ceiling, spiderweb patterns of moonlight through tree branches. Finally the knocking stops and my heart slows back down. Above my head, I can hear the creaks of Google Man walking back and forth in his house. I like to imagine his presence is an odd arms-length comfort. That if I screamed, he would come check on me.

After lying here for some time, I can't sleep. All I can think about is the knocking. Even though the knocking has been gone now for well over an hour, I still hear it in my head.

You're in danger, the voice says. *You're prey, you silly fool.*

"Why can't I get a lobotomy?" I mutter, getting up out of bed.

I blow out a sigh and tiptoe through my dark apartment. It's still and silent as a mausoleum in here, but I can hear the world alive and whirring outside my windows—the ghostly whine of the last subway train pulling from the station, the cry of a distant police siren, the wind gasping through the trees. I'm not going to be a geriatric baby scared in my own place right now, I'm thirty years old. I unlock my door and, what do you know? Nothing. Just the streetlamps flickering and leaves skittering on the sidewalk.

But then I look down.

Here, on my porch, are the shattered pieces of something. I crouch to examine them, my pulse skipping a beat. What am I looking at? An eye. A hand. Red smiling lips. Green and white. Jagged chunks of white porcelain. With a closer look I recognize what I'm looking at.

They're the broken pieces of a clown.

I told you so, the voice murmurs in an eerie singsong.

In a lightning flash, I dodge back into my apartment, locking the door.

FORTY-SIX

> Hey, sorry to bother you, weird question, but do you know of any possible reason someone would leave a creepy broken clown doll on my doorstep? Like you said, the guy who lived here before was weird ... I don't know, just wanted to check. Sorry to pester you, I know I'm probably the most annoying tenant you've ever had lol

I TOOK LONGER CRAFTING this text than a novelist probably spends writing an entire first draft. And what do I get in response from Google Man? A single shrugging guy emoji. Thanks, buddy. He probably thinks I'm nuts. Can't blame him, either.

Click. I take a picture of the horror show on my doorstep, send it to Alice along with a screenshot of the text I got.

> Hmm

is her response.

Odd

No shit, Alice.

To be fair, she's probably busy with patients today and not in the mood. I clean up the broken clown this morning, but I can't shake how it's scared me. Who put it there? Elizabeth? Asshole kids playing a Halloween prank because I answered the door sans candy? And I'm missing another shoe this morning. A sneaker.

When I tell Suzanne about these things as we sit on her back patio this morning drinking tea, she listens with a stony expression and then takes a deep breath, nostrils flaring as she lets it out, as if exercising some deep control over her emotions.

"I knew there was a reason your aura was smoky today," she says gravely.

"Smoky," I repeat.

"Grayish. Cloudy." She gestures wildly toward my head, bracelets clanking like the wind chimes hanging behind her. "The violet hue has been consumed by smog."

"Oh Jesus."

"Jesus can't help you now, love, he's long dead. And has there *ever* been a man more overrated? Let's not speak of him, please, not in my casa."

I open my mouth to explain it's just an expression, but she rolls right ahead with her speech.

"I'm deeply *concerned*," she says, leaning in. "That you might be curséd." (Yes, she says it like that—curse-*ed*.) "Bound by some kind of *hex* that needs undoing. You know I adore you, sweet Jolene. I've often mused we're twin flames —not romantically, of course. But perhaps we were family in some other lifetime. You were my daughter, or my mother, or who knows—chimpanzees bound in the same society or elephant kindreds parading the savanna."

There's a dramatic pause, where I try to process what she's said. It's dizzying. There's a lot there.

"Yet I selfishly worry," she continues, "that I may be contaminated by your hex—a secondhand hex, if you will—if you don't find a way to rid yourself of it."

"How do I do that?" I whisper.

A part of me is aware of how ridiculous this is. Curses, auras, dumping salt in the corners of my rooms to rid myself of negative energies—I was raised by a cutthroat lawyer who worships the god of science and has a picture of Einstein hanging in his bedroom. But another part of me wonders if there could be something to it. It does feel like since I moved to Berkeley, the universe has put a dark spell on me. If Elizabeth isn't doing these things to me and the clown emoji and the broken clown and the eyeball down my drain are all coincidences, then it seems like there must be some funky universal energy. I can't determine what is going on. It's spun way beyond my understanding.

"That I cannot help you with," she says. "The healer I used to work with converted to Islam and the psychic I knew got hit by a bus and perished."

I bite my tongue to stop myself from making a terrible joke about the psychic not seeing that one coming.

"I'm sure there are resources online," she says. "But you must do *something*. And I mean something tangible, not that therapy nonsense."

"Okay." I nod. "I'll dig in later."

She reaches across the table and squeezes my hand. I can

feel her bones, the chill of her skin, and her eyes glimmer. Behind her, the gazebo with the hot tub inside reminds me that she may or may not be a murderer and that her husband might have "expired" in that very spot. I try to not let the jolt of that memory show in my face as she studies me.

"Now," she says, sitting back. "I'm almost done with my memoir. I need your help planning my book launch party. I'm thinking later this month at a local bookshop, advertised heavily via fliers and ads. Do you know anything about ads?"

"Don't you need to edit the book though?" I ask.

"Pish posh," she scoffs. "I don't believe in editing or second drafts. Writing a memoir should be like life, messy and true. You don't get chances to fix your mistakes in life, so why should you when you're writing a book about your life?"

She's let me read excerpts of her memoir. It's laden with typos. But who am I to judge? I've never written a book. I can barely compose a text.

"Okay," I say. "I'll look into it."

Behind her, a tiny bird swoops into a birdfeeder. I get a gross gut-flutter as I recognize that it's the exact kind of bird that I found nearly decapitated outside my window. And even though I'm sitting here in the sunshine, my blood turns cold.

"Something the matter?" Suzanne asks me.

I shake my head. "Nothing."

In my ears, I hear the haunting, weird breath of the voice, not saying anything, but letting me know it's there all the time. It's here with me. It's here and it's never going away, no matter what I do.

FORTY-SEVEN

TONIGHT, I would rather cuddle a tarantula than go to improv, but I go anyway for a few reasons. One, I actually love improv when Elizabeth isn't ruining it. Acting is a respite where I can forget myself a little while. Two, I hate disappointing my dad more than anything and he made me promise I wouldn't drop out. And three, I don't want Elizabeth to win this weird game we're playing. Whether she's doing shit like shattering clowns on my doorstep, I need to keep my head high and show her I'm not caving. I'm guilty of nothing. Go on normally as I would have before. You know, do what I do best—pretend. Which is why I'm in improv in the first place.

I get to class a few minutes late. I'm sweaty and frazzled. Because I can't find half my shoes at this point, I'm wearing a pair of ankle boots that are absolutely killing me after the mile-long walk. My heels are on fire.

"Hey Jolene!" Elizabeth sings, waving at me with a smile. "So happy to see you. Come join the group."

So happy to see me? Okay. So that's how it's going to roll today. I expected the cold shoulder, but this is what we're dealing with instead. I put my purse and jacket in a seat, feeling like I'm the one onstage as everyone waits for me.

"Come over here, I've got a spot open," Elizabeth says, gesturing to an open spot beside her in the circle.

"Great, thanks!" I say with a grin.

Two can play this fakery.

She pats my back as I sit beside her and whispers, "Nice to see you!"

"You too!" I say.

What the ever-loving hell is going on with her? Actually, what am I saying—this is classic Elizabeth. She hates me, she loves me, I'm her favorite person, she wants to shun me forever. I guess our little world has turned and the sun's shining on me again. But despite this performative friendliness, the energy has shifted between us. No matter what she says or how big she smiles at me, we've crossed a line that we can't uncross.

As usual, Jerry claps his hands and springs to his feet in the center of the circle with the energy of a man who had a triple espresso paired with a couple lines of cocaine. While we might all be the actors, it truly sometimes feels like Jerry's show. He likes to sprinkle in random mentions about celebrities too, how he worked for Rob Lowe for a summer, how Will Ferrell once told him he was funny when they were in line at Starbucks. Now that I think about it, Jerry might be just as deluded as Elizabeth—that's probably why they get along so well.

"Get up here, Lizzie, let's show the group our warm-up exercise today!" he says.

Elizabeth gets up a little slowly, a little awkwardly. Usually I can't tell she has a fake leg unless she's moving from a seated position to standing. I cringe but try to not show my cringe. But when she gets up beside Jerry, then I truly cringe, because I see her T-shirt for the first time.

It's Bigfoot. A picture of Bigfoot. It says *I BELIEVE.*

She knows! the voice says suddenly, so loud it seems to echo in my ears. *She knows, she knows, she knows!*

The two of them demo the game. It's called One-Word Story, where we all build a story together around the circle, each person just saying one word. I'm not hearing anything. My skin gets hot and prickly, from my scalp to my pinky toes. And all at once it's like I'm in that gorilla suit again. I'm overheating and heavy and I want to faint, but I have to stand up with the rest of the class and try to concentrate right now.

As we play this game, I split into two people. I'm a body with a mouth moving automatically and I'm a person floating above my body, watching. It's a relief to retreat into this other part of myself, the self outside the self.

She's torturing you, the voice whispers.

I know she is, I imagine I whisper back.

Why else would she wear that shirt? it asks.

There could be other reasons. It could be that she's the same old weirdo she's always been who loves conspiracy theories. But my gut is saying that the voice is right. And it's really off-putting to be standing here in class looking like a normal human being when, internally, I'm having a discussion with a witch-voiced demon in my head. I shouldn't speak to it, it only makes it louder. But it's the only thing that seems to agree with me right now.

After an hour of playing games and not having one

ounce of fun, class is dismissed and I go slip my coat back on. Elizabeth taps my shoulder before I get a chance to run out the door. Her smile is bright, as if I'm her best friend and she hasn't seen me in ages.

"How *are* you?" she asks. "I've been thinking about you."

"I'm fine," I say, with a tight smile.

She has this look in her eye, like she shares a joke with the universe, one I'm not in on.

Thank her for the gift, the voice says.

"Thanks for the gift, by the way," I say, slinging my purse over my shoulder. "Real cute."

Good girl, the voice says.

I've never made the voice happy before. A tiny fire lights up in me, like I did something right for once.

"Gift?" Elizabeth asks, tilting her head.

Go on. Tell her, the voice says.

"You know." I cross my arms. "The broken clown on my doorstep? The one you left me Halloween night, right after you texted me the lil emoji from that blocked number?"

Elizabeth has an expression on her face like she smells a fart. "I'm sorry, *what*?"

"I know," I say, in a hiss that is alarmingly close to the voice in my head.

"You know what?" Elizabeth puts a hand on my arm. "You know *what*, Jolene?"

She's trying to get you to admit what you did, the voice says. *She wants to hear you say it out loud.*

Well, fuck that. I'm not giving her the satisfaction.

"Jolene," she says slowly, as if I'm three years old. "I have literally no idea what you're talking about. I was with Jerry

Halloween night. We went to a party in the city, we were out until the sun came up. Swear on my life."

"Uh-huh," I say, shrugging her hand off my arm.

"Omigod. Jer-Bear!" she shouts. "Can you come here a sec?"

Jer-Bear? They're on cutesy nickname terms and they stay out until dawn together? These two are definitely banging. Jerry breaks from a conversation with another student and walks over to us.

"Sup, Lizzie?" he asks, flipping his hoodie over his shaved-bald head.

"Jer, can you vouch that I was with you Halloween night?" Elizabeth asks. "Jolene is under the impression I left some—what was it?" Elizabeth looks at me and sputters a giggle. "Left a *clown* on your doorstep?"

"What?" Jerry asks, breaking into a laugh.

It's appropriate that the word *mortified* is rooted in the Latin word for death, because I wish I was dead right now. As they laugh at me, my brain remembers all those orange pill bottles in my medicine cabinet and how I could just press the end button on myself like a phone call I don't like any second I choose.

"Nah, nah, Lizzie and I went to a party together Halloween. We were out all night. A clown? That's fuckin' out there, man."

"See?" Elizabeth says. "I promise. It wasn't me."

Ask her about the eyeball down the drain again, the voice says.

Nope. Been there, done that. I'm an idiot for listening to the voice. I shouldn't have engaged with it. I certainly shouldn't have repeated the insane things it says to me.

"Sorry," I tell Elizabeth and Jerry. "Have a good night."

I hurry out of there and rush home like a monster is chasing me, my poor feet in these painful shoes be damned. By the time I get home, by the time my door is shut behind me, I burst into sniveling tears. My raw, broken feet, my raw, broken psyche—it's too much. I can't hold it in anymore. I try and try and try and sometimes I have to blow like a little Vesuvius. When I'm done, when I've expelled my emotions for a while, I get up and wash my face.

In my pocket, I get a text from the blocked number again. It's just one word.

Soon

Never have four letters seemed so ominous. There's something about the bareness of it, the simplicity, that is utterly terrifying. My breath gets shallow. It has to be Elizabeth. It has to! Right? Who would say that? And what does that *mean*? It's so chilling, so foreboding. *Soon.* Soon what? What is going to happen?

She's going to hurt you, the voice sings. *She's going to finally get even.*

I can't take it anymore. The voice, the texts, Elizabeth—but most of all, myself. I can't take myself anymore. I swing open the medicine cabinet. This time I take an Ativan and two Ambien. I could take so many more. This is me showing restraint. This is me being responsible. I take pills and I go to bed and part of me hopes I never wake up again.

FORTY-EIGHT

MY EYELIDS ARE SUPERGLUED.

No flutter to them, no matter how hard I try.

Everything is a pitch-black sea of endless dark. My arms and legs are floating balloons.

I'm aware of where I am: my bed. It's the middle of the night. I'm stuck. Sleep has gravity. Sleep has stone-cold hands that still me, hold me down. *Shhh*, sleep says. *You're mine now. You're not going anywhere.* My heart throbs in my chest, begging to wake me up.

Tap-tap, tap-tap, tap-tap.

A pulse. A clock ticking. A faucet dripping.

Tap-tap, tap-tap, tap-tap.

I'm aware of my body, the chill of the midnight air on my skin, the breath coming and going through my lips, the rise and fall of my chest. But my muscles aren't working. My bones are made of lead. Don't panic. It's okay, this happens sometimes. Just wait. Just give it a moment. It'll pass.

Tap-tap, tap-tap, tap-tap.

Finally, I wiggle a single fingertip, flare my nostrils, and my mind and my body find each other and unite again. My eyelids unstick slowly and through the goo of sleepiness I spy my ceiling with its familiar crisscross silhouettes from the moon's spotlight hitting the tree branches outside my window. Except there's a strange shape in it, a shadow-mountain.

Where did that shadow-mountain come from?

I'm woozy from the pills and as I try to sit up, I get the spins, whirly whirly, five-second carnival ride. I gaze at my dim room and wipe my eyes. I adjust to my seated position. Shouldn't have taken so many pills. That was unwise. Still, I feel pretty goopy and nice.

Tap-tap, tap-tap.

That sound again. Coming from behind me. I turn around to try to locate it. There's a looming figure there, like somebody standing outside my window. My breath gets stuck in my lungs as I glance up at the ceiling, matching the shadow-mountain with the looming figure.

Tap-tap.

Someone's out there.

Tapping my window.

A strange sound comes out of my mouth, a whimper, like a cornered animal. I cover my face and squeeze my eyes shut again—go away, go away, tell me I'm not seeing what I'm seeing.

But when I open my eyes, the figure remains. Pressed up to my window. Waiting.

Heart thumping, tremors mounting, I stand up as slow as if I'm walking through water. The faint slanted light in my room is an eerie, moonish yellow-blue, and I tell myself I'm dreaming. I must be. I'm still dreaming. This is only a dream. Waiting here in front of my window, where the blinds are drawn, I can still see the shadow of the person out there.

I swallow, hand clasping the cord that pulls the blinds up. Tight fist. Held breath.

Tap-tap-tap.

There's a violence to it that makes me flinch. Just inches and one thin glass pane divide me and whatever is on the other side of the blinds.

With a single yank, I pull the blinds all the way up until they snag and catch at the top, open now, and what I see there on the other side pulls a bloodcurdling scream out of me that is so long and so shrill I don't even recognize the sound of my own voice.

Someone is fucking standing there in a fucking gorilla suit.

Black and hairy, wrinkled face, round beady eyes glinting, mouth open to bare its sharp canines. Monstrous and horrible. It puts a giant black hand up in a wave, and then turns and runs away, down the driveway, toward the street.

Suddenly, adrenaline electrocutes me, awakening all my senses.

"No!" I scream, tearing out of my room.

On a panic-fueled rampage, I rush through my living room, almost tripping over my shoes, and pull open the front door. Running out in my bare feet onto the sidewalk, I look both ways up and down the street.

They're not there.

But I know who it is—I'm a hundred percent sure. Would bet my life on it.

In a surreal sprint, I take off running around the block toward Elizabeth's house. The street is silent, house lights off, a few dead leaves drifting up the asphalt in a lazy breeze. I turn a corner, ears ringing, and my sole focus is catching her. I know I've got to be just as fast as her, if not faster, especially if she's wearing a fucking gorilla suit. I have personal experience and can vouch that they're heavy and clunky and impossible to run in. But me? I'm a blaze, a flash.

I'm at Elizabeth's house in under a minute and I rush straight to her back door and pound on it, pound on it until my hands sting, an adrenaline rush spurring an inhuman rage in me.

Fuck her. Fuck this. Fuck these games. See? See??

That bitch isn't home because she's out terrorizing you. She's trying to drive you insane.

"I know," I say, panting. "I know."

But then a light flicks on inside, the windows suddenly bright and alive. As I catch my breath, there's a pitch in my stomach as if I'm in an elevator falling down a shaft. The door cracks open and a groggy, surprised Elizabeth says, "Jolene? Is that you?"

She squints. She's wearing flannel pajamas, her hair is bedheaded, and she has some kind of clear mouthguard in her mouth. Most notably, though, she's using a pair a crutches because her prosthetic leg isn't attached. Which ... my brain scrambles, trying to justify what I'm sure she did. Calculating whether it would be possible for her to run all the way here wearing the gorilla costume, then shed her costume, take her leg off, turn off the light, and be ready to answer the door. There's just no way. But it has to be. It's the only explanation for what I saw.

"Jolene, what's going on?" she asks with alarm.

I'm still catching my breath. I'm also speechless, because

suddenly it's like I've woken up from a dream and I realize that I'm standing on Elizabeth's doorstep in the dead of night in a little nightgown and my bare feet and I need to pee so badly and I don't know how to explain myself.

"You were—you were at my window," I manage to say.

"Jolene?" she says again. "Are you ... okay? Do you need me to call someone?"

Then it hits me like a slap—it wasn't her. It was someone else. Someone she's close to.

"Jerry," I say. "It was Jerry."

"What was Jerry?" she asks. "Do you need me to get Jerry? Hold on." She turns and says, with an edge of emergency in her tone. "Jer-Bear, it's Jolene. I don't know what's going on."

You're kidding me. He's *here*?

I hear a long moan. She opens the door wider as she turns to him and I can see his shape there in her bed.

"Jer-Bear," she says, louder.

Finally, he sits up. He's wearing a CPAP machine and resembles an alien. Unstrapping it from his face and emerging from the bed in a T-shirt and boxers, he says, in a raspy voice, "What the fuck is going on?"

They both stand here looking at me like I'm a complete freak. And I suppose I deserve that. I wish, more than anything, that this wasn't real. That I could take this moment and simply delete it from my life. I pinch myself harder than I've ever pinched myself before and I'm very sorry to say that I'm not dreaming right now.

"I—I don't know," I finally answer. "I think I'm sleep-walking."

"Are you on drugs or something?" Jerry asks me.

"Yeah, are you high?" Elizabeth asks.

"No. I mean, maybe. Yeah. Yeah, it must be that." I put my hands on my face. "Sleeping pills. I took some sleeping pills and a ... anyway, I'm really sorry. I had a nightmare, I guess. I don't know." I start laughing, but there is zero joy, only self-deprecation. They decline to join me in this laughter, instead exchanging an uncomfortable look with one another. "Anywho," I say. *Anywho?* I don't know, okay? I've lost it. "All's well!" I wave. "See ya later."

I turn around.

Elizabeth yells, "Jolene! I'm worried about you!"

I don't respond, instead hurrying back to my house, feeling my half-nakedness in the freezing air as I round the block this time. I tiptoe up my driveway and go looking at my bedroom window from the outside, trying to make sense of what I saw—or thought I saw—out here. The bushes do look trampled on. I don't know. Upstairs, a light is on, and I wonder if Google Man heard my screams.

What if it was him?

No, that makes no sense. I shiver and return to my apartment, where I left the door wide open. As if he's reading my mind, I get a text from Google Man that is just an emoji that says *OK* and a question mark emoji.

> Sorry! I thought I saw a person in a gorilla suit outside my window. Did you see anyone like that? Sorry again

All I get back is a yellow thinking face. I stare at that response, head swimming, and then put my phone down. I don't know what to do with that.

I go to the bathroom, release the world's longest pee,

then get back in bed, shivering. Although my head remains light and airy and there's a strange haze surrounding the night, the pills seem to have worn off and I'm left with the horrors of my bare, sober mind. I lie here for a long time playing horrible reruns of tonight's humiliation. Imagine what I must have looked like to them.

I swear, it was real. It was *real.*

I've always had a wild imagination, but I can tell the knife-sharp line between fact and fiction, between waking life and dreams, between reality and pill-induced reverie, between real people and voices in my head.

At least, that's what I believed.

Am I not who I thought I was?

FORTY-NINE

"OKAY," Alice says, slowly, the way you might talk a jumper off a bridge. "Let's take a breath here."

"I'm taking a breath," I say, inhaling. "See? The problem isn't asthma. The problem is that I don't know *what the hell is real*."

Alice is seated across from me at a sunny lil brunch place in north Oakland. Around us, bougie hipsters are clinking mimosa glasses and eating millionaire bacon and laughing Saturday laughs. Mockery. Meanwhile I'm sitting here with bags under my eyes losing my damn mind. I know Alice is trying to get me out of my apartment, cheer me up, but I don't think she gets that these are not ordinary blues I'm dealing with. I'm straight-up unraveling.

"Excuse me, can I get another bourbon?" I ask the waitress, wiggling my empty glass in the air.

Alice's mouth is open, like she's not sure what to say. Granted, we haven't yet ordered food and I'm about to down my second drink. This is where I'm at, Alice. Deal with it.

Sadie growls at my leg and nips at my ankle.

"Sade," Alice says, bending down and pointing a finger.

I glare at Sadie. Go ahead, dog, hate on me. Guess who's going to outlive who?

"Okay," Alice says, staring at the menu with concentration, as if gathering much more than her thoughts on pancakes. She looks so together, like someone who has a gym membership and knows what's up with her city council members. She smells of her husband's soap and is wearing a Patagonia jacket. Why does she even want to be my friend? "I'm ... I'm wondering if maybe living here hasn't actually been good for you."

"Ya think?" I say, leaning in.

"What's with the hostility?" Alice says. "I'm here to visit you."

The way she says it, it's like she's checking in on me at Rikers.

"Make sure you're okay," she adds.

Charity work, that's what this is.

"Which clearly you're not," she mutters under her breath.

"So you think I'm crazy," I say. "You think Elizabeth couldn't have possibly done that."

"Babes," she says, leaning across the table and squeezing my hand. Her palm is warm. Her wedding ring is icy. "You think a woman who is *missing* a *leg* rented a *gorilla suit* and put it on in the *middle of the night*—"

I put a hand up to stop her. It's too painful to hear it spoken aloud. "I get how it sounds. Look, my therapist said the same thing. She squeezed me in for a last-minute session yesterday and talked me down."

"All right." Alice sits back, relaxes a little. "That's good. How ... concerned is she?"

"Like, does she think I should hop in a wheelbarrow and get rolled on down to the nuthouse?"

"You know what I mean. What does she think about it all?"

"That I should shroom my ass off Monday and have some revelation. Dive deeper into my 'guilt' which is 'manifesting' in 'pill-induced nightmares.'" I'm generous with the finger quotes.

"Pill-induced?" Alice frowns. "What pills?"

My mouth hangs open. I scramble for an excuse, but she's too sharp and I'm too dull and immediately, Alice's green eyes widen in a mix of aggravation and disappointment.

"You didn't get rid of the lady's pills, did you?"

"I—"

"You've been taking someone else's expired prescription medication."

"To sleep," I say.

Sadie barks at me once, as if she too sees through my bullshit. Thank God for the server who comes to deliver me a much-needed second drink and takes our order. Alice, of course, orders a veggie omelet, subbing fruit for potatoes: healthy. Mindful. Me, I order benedict: all carbs, processed meat, sodium, and hollandaise. You could learn everything you need to know about our characters from one simple brunch order.

I down the drink as fast as possible, hoping to numb the pain of this conversation.

She shakes her head. "Sometimes I feel like I'm dealing

with my teenage sister."

"Sometimes I feel like I'm dealing with my mom," I shoot back.

"Maybe that's what you need," she snips. "Maybe you need your dad to come rescue you again."

"Is that what why you're here? You think I'm so pathetic I need 'rescuing?'"

I don't enjoy the hag-like edge to my voice, but the alcohol is loosening my tongue. And I'm convinced that an unadulterated shot of the truth is what's needed right now.

"You take everything for granted," Alice says. "You know that? You're lucky I'm still here."

I shake the glass, sad there's nothing but ice already. Four Roses on the rocks sure went fast. "Why are you here, then? Tell me." I flag the server, who's leaving another table, and point to my drink. "Excuse me, I'm so sorry, can I have another one of these?"

"Can she not, actually?" Alice asks, sweetly, with a dimpled smile.

"Don't listen to her," I say.

"She's had enough," Alice says, covering my glass with her hand.

The server looks, understandably, uncomfortable. "Um —why don't you two figure it out and I'll be back to check in on you soon?"

After they leave, Alice pulls her hand off my glass.

"You're unwell," she says.

"That your official diagnosis, doc?"

"You become kind of a bitch when you drink."

"Well, you don't need to drink to be a bitch."

She rolls her eyes, unhurt and unfazed. Right now, I'm so

charged up I could set it all on fire. At the same time, another me is watching and saying, why are you being like this? What is wrong with you?

She thinks she's better than you, the voice says, speaking up for the first time since brunch started.

"You think you're better than me," I say. "You think you know everything. Well, you don't know what it's like to have someone stalking you and copying you—"

"I was your friend when it all started," Alice says flatly. "I'm aware of every detail. You talked about her constantly— just like you do now."

"And you didn't believe me then," I say, remembering.

"I mean, I don't know. I didn't go to school with you two, I only knew you through the music and arts conservatory. I've never met her. I don't know what to believe."

"When have I *ever* shown myself not to be trustworthy?"

"When you took pills you said you wouldn't," she says, putting a finger up like she's about to start a list.

"Okay, okay," I say, not wanting to hear any more.

Sadie bares her teeth at me and barks. Despite Alice protesting, she won't stop.

You hate that fucking dog, hisses the voice, and before it even finishes its sentence—

"I hate your fucking dog!" I yell.

That sentence seems to have ripped time and space. The entire outdoor patio grows silent, the mirth dying in the air as everyone turns to look at me. There's disbelief bordering on horror in most people's expressions—who on earth would hate a dog wearing an adorable little sweater like that? What kind of *monster*? Protectively, Alice pulls Sadie into her lap, who whimpers like I hit her, or like she knows what the fuck the f-word is. My face is hot, flames behind my cheeks, and I wish I could just teleport out of here.

"Sorry—" I start to say, but I can tell that I've done it. It takes a lot to piss Alice off—Alice is cool. Alice is placid water. But right now, Alice is pissed. Her cheeks are as red as mine feel, but hers are due to pure, justified rage instead of bourbon and embarrassment.

"I think we're done here," she chirps.

She flags the server down to cancel our meal. I stew in my shame, crossing my arms.

"You know what?" Alice asks, twitching her nose. She's trying not to cry. I almost made Alice cry. I'm the worst person in the world. "I've been coming to Berkeley every weekend I can for acupuncture. There's this amazing woman who specializes in fertility and Liam and I have been having so much trouble." She hands the server her credit card, not meeting my eyes. "I had two miscarriages and it's been really hard. But I didn't bring it up with you because you've been having problems of your own and I know you need someone right now."

"Allie—"

"So, anyway, I just—I need a break from this. I'm tired, Jolene." Now she looks at me and the shine in her eyes is the stake to my vampire heart. "I'm tired of trying to fix you and figure out your problems with you. I just need a friend. You know? And you're fun as hell and unpredictable and you make me laugh but sometimes, I don't think you're a very good friend."

"I'm sorry," I say feebly. "I had no idea you were going through that. I'm sorry, I really am."

I might as well have let out a burp, the apology rings so meaningless.

Sadie licks her face and makes Alice smile. That chiweenie might have a shorter lifespan, but let's face it—she's a much better companion than me.

———

At home, alone once more, I'm numb. Not a fun numb. Not a pilly cloud-headed numb or a buzzy whiskey numb—just a blank-hearted walking corpse numb. I think about that text that said *Soon*, how I've been getting them every night at the same time, the same hour. *Soon.*

I don't know what it's supposed to mean, but I know what meaning I can derive from it.

In my bathroom, I stand in front of the mirror. Mirrors are tricks. Shiny lies. I'm not really there at all and neither is my image—a mirror is nothing but light bouncing back at us without scattering. It doesn't mean anything. What I see, what I think I see, is only an illusion.

I open the medicine cabinet and take out each pill container.

Soon.

Make a heap of pills in the middle of the counter—a rainbow heap of circles and ovals and square shapes, as varied as my mountain of lonely shoes.

Soon. Soon. Soon.

Aren't you tired? the voice asks. *Aren't you so tired of reality?*

"I've never been a fan of reality," I say to it.

Neither have I.

"I know. We have that in common."

We have so much in common.

I contemplate the pile and wonder, am I really going to do this? Is this what it comes to? And then my phone buzzes in my pocket. It's my dad. Just the sight of that familiar palindrome undoes something in me, snags me.

Don't answer it, the voice says. *He's only going to be disappointed with you.*

I break the gaze with the mirror and leave the room, answering in a quivering voice that sounds much too young for my age.

"Daddy?"

"Alice called me," he says in a low voice. "I'm coming up there, bunny. I'm in the car already. I'm on my way."

FIFTY

"I WANT to see you do it."

My dad's got his hands on hips. Hair slicked back. Sleeves rolled up. Here we are in the bathroom mirror, apple and tree. Things I inherited: his dark eyebrows, pensive brown eyes, and thin lips. Things I did not: his Roman nose. His intimidating stare. His ambition. He opens the toilet and points to the bowl.

"Flush 'em. Go on."

"Dad." I eye my rainbow pill mountain on the counter longingly. "I don't think you're supposed to flush pills, it can pollute the ocean—"

"I don't give a shit about the ocean, I give a shit about my daughter. Do it. Now."

With a quiet sigh, I take a handful of pills and rain them into the water, pitter-patter. It's heartbreaking to peer at them floating in there, a colorful soup, so much beautiful, mood-altering potential. I show him a few stray Ambien still on the countertop.

"But these are for sleep—"

"Toilet."

"I've been having trouble sleeping—"

"Toilet."

Plink. In they go, my wee gorgeous friends who helped me fight insomnia. Goodbye.

"Flush," my dad demands.

I do. As they swirl, I tear up, I actually tear up. When will I ever get my hands on such a rich array of medication? Never, that's when.

"I can't believe Suzanne gave you all those in the first place," he mutters, leaving the bathroom. "I should have warned her about you."

"Should have warned *her*?" I follow him. "What about warning me I was working for a murderer?"

"*Accused* murderer," he corrects me as he goes into my kitchen. "Let's get that straight. She was acquitted. She'd never even had a parking ticket, her criminal record was nonexistent. She's harmless."

"Still!"

He opens my fridge, the glow of its light yellowing his face. He shakes his head and slams it shut. "You have no food in here. What the hell have you been eating?"

"Takeout."

"And what's this?" He gestures toward the living room where it's clear no living is actually happening. Nothing but a sad deflated plastic couch on the ground. "Is this a fuckin' pool toy? A floatie? Where's your furniture?"

"Furniture's expensive."

"Maybe if you weren't spending all your money on takeout, you'd be able to afford furniture. Where are we supposed to sit? The floor? Christ."

"Here." I slip onto one of the two stools at the counter.

Sighing, he sits beside me. In the long silence, I can hear the back-and-forth rhythm of Google Man's footsteps upstairs. I used to hate that sound but now it makes me feel less alone. A little safer.

My dad puts his face in his hands. "What am I going to do with you?"

I lean my head on his shoulder. "Sorry."

He leans his head on mine and I close my eyes, breathing in the scent of his cologne. I don't know what it is, but whenever I smell it, it's him—spicy, woodsy. It makes me feel small and okay again.

"I don't know what I've done wrong," he says. "What am I doing wrong? I give you everything you need, I help you follow every damn whim that crosses your mind, and then —it's like trying to tame a hummingbird. You just keep flying from one thing to the next, crash and burn and repeat."

"I know it seems that way," I say. "This time, though, it's different."

"Uh-huh."

"I mean it. There's this woman—I swear, she's stalking me. And the other night, in the middle of the night, there was someone at my window. Dressed like a gorilla—"

He pulls back. "Do we need to go back to rehab? Do I need to call a—I don't know—a psych ward or some shit? Because the last time you started doing this and seeing things and the paranoia came in, you were strung out on pills—"

"It's not like that this time, I swear. This woman, I knew her in high school. And back then—"

"Back then, back then. Stop it." He eyes me unrelentingly, a warning. "Stop looking backward, what does it do? Stop obsessing about the past."

"But I did something terrible—"

"Bunny, we all did something terrible!" He smacks the counter. "I used to yell at your mother when we fought, even when she was dying of cancer. I broke a guy's jaw once in a bar fight, I used to steal cars when I was in high school. Jesus. If I sat around dwelling on that shit I would curl up in a ball and lose my mind. Your problem isn't the past, damn it, why can't you see that already? Your problem is now." He points at the floor. "Your problem is the future. Where are you going? Who are you going to be?"

"A flight attendant?" I try.

"Aye yai yai." He runs both hands through his hair. "You're going to give me a stroke."

"Sorry."

In the pause that stretches, I try to imagine a future and it's impossible. It's like imagining death, or what's beyond the universe—endless blankness, blackness, a bottomless void.

"What about the therapy shit?" he asks in a defeated voice. Ugh, that voice. It's the voice of me exhausting him, of my perpetual messiness snuffing out the fire in him. "That helping?"

"I haven't done the psilocybin therapy yet. I'm worried it's a bad idea now."

"I thought you called me because you needed money for that last month. Where the fuck did the money go?"

"I paid the therapist, I just put off the session."

He shakes his head. "Of course you did."

"She wants me to do it Monday—"

"So fuckin' do it! What are you waiting for?" He takes my hand. "You need help. Everyone's trying to help you. Accept it. Figure out what's next for you. Because, bunny, I'm not getting any younger. At some point I'm not going to be around to come rescue you anymore."

"Don't say that."

It's the worst, to imagine a world without him in it. I can't think about it.

"It's true." He squeezes my hand. "It's reality. You know, reality? You've heard of it, right?"

I bite my lip, not saying anything, but hearing a faint whisper in my ear. *Reality's overrated.*

"It's not so bad living in the real world," he says softly. "In the real world, you have a clear head and food in your fridge and furniture. You have friends. Maybe even a boyfriend-girlfriend-nonbinary friend or whatever you're into these days."

"I'm graysexual," I say. "Grayromantic."

His mouth is still open but his eyebrows furrow. "The hell is that? You like old men?"

"No, I only feel romantic feelings or attraction some of the time, in very specific circumstances."

"You mean, like everyone in the fuckin' world?" He scoffs. "'Graysexual.' I try to keep up with you and your generation, but Jesus."

I didn't expect him to understand. I barely understand it myself.

"Look, I drove all the way up here for you." He heaves a

sigh. "And I'm terrified of what would have happened if I hadn't. Were you going to off yourself? Do we need to check you in somewhere?"

"No, I was just ... having a dramatic moment."

His stare might be hard, but his eyes are soft. "You've put me through a lot of bullshit, but I've never had to worry if you're going to bump yourself off. Promise me right now. Promise me."

"I promise."

"No more dramatic moments. Get your shit together. Trip your balls off this week with your therapist and figure out your life."

I nod. "Okay. I will. I promise."

He offers me a smile accompanied by a sigh. "All right. Now what do you say we drum up some groceries and I cook us some spaghetti and meatballs?"

FIFTY-ONE

BACK WHEN I had a therapist who was considering possible mental disorders for me off the abundant menu of the DSM-V, schizophrenia struck me as the scariest outcome. I mean, none of them seemed particularly fun. But the idea of losing your grip on reality, of experiencing hallucinations that you can't separate from the real world, terrified me most. The word itself means "the splitting of the mind." I was relieved when that was ruled out. But I've been experiencing the splitting of the mind anyway, living in two realities at once. Though don't we all to some degree? Actors on a stage. A reader scanning a page and imagining a world that doesn't exist. A writer, a liar, a person who goes to a retail job and smiles at people they despise. Saying "fine" when someone asks how you're doing. Aren't we all splitting, all the time?

FIFTY-TWO

I WAKE up Monday to another text from the blocked number. Every time I see the word *Unknown* lighting up my screen, my heart tightens like a fist. I expect another *Soon*, which I've learned to live with. Better than smashed clowns on my doorstep. But this one is a picture and when I squint at it, when I realize what I'm looking at, I can't breathe for a second.

It's a photo.

Of me.

Sleeping. In my bed.

Someone added exes over my eyes in black marker. It says:

Done with you

I throw my phone with a tiny scream as if it's a spider. The room spins, whirling white walls, and I close my eyes.

Oh my God. Oh my *God*. There's a weight on my chest that makes it hard to breathe.

Someone took my picture. Someone's been in here.

When was it taken?

Had to have been sometime in the last month because my hair's short.

It was Elizabeth.

She had my keys and she was in here while I was sleeping that day and woke me up.

Or Google Man.

Maybe him.

I know nothing about him, he could be a complete creeper who's been coming into my house.

All those extra sets of keys …

I pick up my phone to screenshot the text and debate sending it to someone. Shit, I need to go to work.

LEAVE ME THE FUCK ALONE!!!!!

I text back.

I wait a moment to see if I get a response, but nothing. My phone's screen goes dark.

Okay. I'm okay. I fight frustrated tears, emerge from bed, dress myself pretty, wash my face, moisturize, get ready for work, but every step I take, I'm two people. I'm freaking out internally and I'm going about my day normally. Putting on my makeup in the mirror with trembling hands.

You're in danger, the voice says.

"Please stop. You're scaring me."

You should be scared.

"Just shut the fuck up."

To my surprise, it does. Utter silence follows. And I head to work, sick to my stomach.

The day is cold and gray, no sun, all clouds. I shiver with my hands in my coat pockets, smiling at people I pass even though I want to go hide in a hole. Passing overenthusiastic houses that have already strung up Christmas lights, shops with closed signs, a woman sparing change, a man walking around banging a set of bongos hanging from his neck. My mind's frantic, trying to find a solution to my problems. I'll change my locks. I'll call a locksmith. Cameras! I'll get a security camera. Should I call the police, file some kind of complaint? Create a paper trail? My dad would say, make a paper trail. This could be a lawsuit. Harassment. But then what if Elizabeth tells them what I did to her ten years ago and I get investigated for attempted manslaughter? Good God. I don't know what the statute of limitations is for what I did. I need to do some googling later.

When I get to Suzanne's, I've hurried so fast and I'm so stressed that I'm out of breath. I'm holding in my sobs as I get to her door, which just has a sticky note that says:

Come in, love,
laptop awaits,
book launch research!
Memoir's nearly spun,
a glorious dewy spiderweb
teatime is teamtime

I open her front door, letting myself in. Her living room is as empty as mine now. Maybe we should go furniture shopping together. I think it jokingly, but then it sinks in seriously. I fight tears as I stand here alone and realize—here it is. That future, that blank blackness I'm so scared of? This is it. I'm going to be some eccentric crone living by myself and never thinking about the terrible things I've done. She and I are both criminals. The only difference is my guilt is certain. Hers is unknown.

My mind is jumbled. All I see, every time I blink, is that horrible picture. Me with exes for eyes. It's a threat. What do I do with it? Should I text my dad? No, I've already exhausted him plenty over the past couple of days and he's back home and at work. Alice? Alice hates me. I dissed her dog and I'm a shit friend.

I sit at Suzanne's kitchen table and stare at her laptop in disbelief. How can I continue with anything? How can I work, how can I go to therapy today?

I'm so desperate I back get up and go out Suzanne's back door. Walk through her overgrown yard, knee-high crabgrass obscuring the stone path. I need Suzanne's advice. She'll embrace me with her chilly arms. She'll tell me what color my aura is. She'll know what to do.

Knock knock knock.

No answer. I try again.

Knock knock knock knock.

As I wait out here, the wind tickles the morning glory vines with their curious blue-violet heads. There's a damp bite in the air and gray clouds shift above, near and quick. The rain will be starting soon. I wait and wait and as the wait stretches longer and longer, and my continued knocking goes unanswered, a new, fresh fear opens up like an ugly blossom.

Suzanne is elderly. What if she died?

What if she's dead in there?

What if I'm going to discover her bloated, rotting corpse behind the door?

I try the knob, but it's locked. Crap. Locked, and I don't have a key. Then I start banging on the door with my fist, banging and singing her name in a nervous, shrilly voice that sounds like someone else.

"Suzanne! Suzanne, are you there? Suzanne, are you okay?"

At what point do I call 911? Does she have an emergency contact? I'm so inept. No one should ever trust me to be their assistant. Finally, after I've tied myself into a stressed human knot, the door creaks open and there she is—alive, well, with eyes blazing and a downturned quivering frown on her face I've never seen before.

"Oh, you're all right." I rest my hand on my chest and breathe. "I'm sorry, I started thinking—"

"Did I not warn you," she says, in a draconic, vicious hiss, "never to disturb me when I am locked within my inspiration station? Did I *not*?"

I'm stunned, as if slapped. The loathing that is contorting her face—I'm a spider. I'm gum on the sole of a shoe. Never have I seen this expression or heard this tone from Suzanne. It sounds horribly close to the witch who lives in my head. She's trembling, a human volcano ready to blow.

"You did, yes," I manage. "I'm sorry. I'm so sorry—"

"You're *sorry*," she says, curling her lip. Then mockingly, dripping with saccharine, she repeats, "You're *sorry*."

Not kidding, I'm afraid this woman is about to put her hands around my throat and strangle me. She has this deranged fire in her eyes and suddenly I imagine my dead body floating in her hot tub, the jets gently massaging the meat from my bones.

"I—I am. I am." I put my hands up. "I'm sorry. I'll go."

"The inspiration station is my *sacred chamber*," she says louder. "And, along with *shattering* my concentration, *interrupting* the river of my creative flow like a goddamn dam, you've shattered my trust."

"So sorry," I repeat, the word a tic I can't quit. Backing up on the brick path, I trip a little bit. I'm wearing two different shoes that I'm hoping the world won't notice aren't a matching pair. The fact I can't find a pair of shoes is an issue I have no capacity for today. I steady myself. "Really, Suzanne. Sorry."

"You bungling fopdoodle," she hisses. "Get out of my sight."

Despite wanting to giggle at the word *fopdoodle,* I'm still stabbed by the insult.

"Okay," I say. "Sure."

She gestures wildly, her bell sleeves in the air, a sorceress casting a spell. "I release you!"

"From ... like—"

"Fired!" she shouts.

My mouth drops and I stop at her porch, a pinch in my chest. "Wait, you're *firing* me?"

"You're lucky I don't do more than that!" She laughs sharp enough to make me flinch. "I've done far worse when someone wouldn't follow my simple directions to *stay the fuck out of my inspiration station!*"

Oh. It clicks in my mind like a trigger.

I think I just figured out what happened to Daveed.

This woman has lost her ever-loving mind. Her face is purpling with anger. I expect smoke to come out of her ears at any second. And still, I'm stunned with hurt—that she would let me go for something this trivial. That apparently she didn't love me, I meant nothing to her.

"I thought we were twin flames," I say in a small voice. "Chimpanzees on the savanna."

"And I thought you were capable of *hearkening directions*. Apparently I misjudged you."

"It was *one* mistake—"

"Once is enough." She swallows and for just a blink I see something other than maniacal rage. In the shine of her eyes, I glimpse the ghost of a hurt person. In a lower voice, she says, "Thank you for your service and best of luck to you."

"All right." I nod and wipe my eyes before I can give her the pleasure of seeing my pain. "Okay. Sorry again."

"Begone!" She points toward the side gate. "Begone, disobedient wretch!"

With a surge of adrenaline, I stumble out of her yard as if she's chasing me, leaving the gate open to tear down her driveway and into the street. I don't stop running until I turn and her house is out of sight.

On the corner here, in front of a regal colonial mansion where a gardener is trimming a hedge, I stop to look at the sky. The endless gloom, a silver sea I could imagine jumping into and disappearing forever.

"Why are you like this?" I ask the universe. "Why do you hate me? What did I do?"

You know what you did.

I stop, catching my breath, a cold sweat breaking over my

body. "So that's why," I say, voice cracking. "You're punishing me."

You get what you deserve.

A creepy-crawly sensation spiders through me, from the inside out. And I wonder something for the first time.

"Are you the universe?" I ask.

I can hear it breathing, gasping and raspy. As if someone is pressing their lips to my ear. *If I said I was, would you finally listen?*

"No," I say. "It's a trick. You're not real."

Snapping out of my temporary insanity, I glance over my shoulder. The gardener is standing upright with his eyes pointed at me, shears in midair, a pitying expression on his face. I've stepped through the looking glass. I'm now the person talking to themselves on the street. Swallowing, humiliated, I turn and walk toward home.

The maple trees have rained fiery star-shaped leaves over the sidewalks and they crawl in the breeze. I can smell the rain coming. At four p.m., I have my appointment with Maria. I was scared before. But I'm not anymore. In fact, I cannot wait to get there.

"I'm going to kill you with poisonous mushrooms today," I whisper to the voice.

You'll be sorry.

But I've already been sorry. I've been sorry my whole fucking adult life. Sorry is the cage I live in. Sorry is the shadow that chills my every waking moment. Sorry is the boulder to my Sisyphus.

I'm done being sorry.

FIFTY-THREE
THEN

AFTER ELIZABETH SHOWED up to high school *beep-beep*ing at me in her cute orange Karmann Ghia, something shifted.

Rage simmered when I saw her pulling in and out of the student parking lot. There was no way to ignore the car. It was bright. It was loud. It stank of exhaust. Now every time I came home and saw the identical Karmann Ghia parked on my road, I glared at it. I knew I could never afford it, that my dad wouldn't buy it for me. And even if he did, I would just look like the copycat now.

It was like Elizabeth and I were playing a game invisible to everyone else. She was a vampire slowly sucking all the Jolene-ness away from me—my fashion, my hairstyle, my dream car. Invading theater, my sacred space. A bubbly presence making everyone laugh, pulling everyone's gaze to her. A loud voice telling the stupidest conspiracy-laden stories. She spun into my life like a soul-sucking hurricane and copied everything I did and made me feel crazy and no one else cared because they all liked her version better. She was a new and improved Jolene.

"I really think you're, like, reading into it too much," my friend Joey said.

Joey and I were parked at the beach, smoking a joint in his car while metal played on his stereo. Lately he and I had been getting chummier. I liked Joey. He was sweet, simple. He had a funny little mustache and a mullet and he was a passionate kisser. I wasn't about to get serious with him or anything, but he was fun to mess around with and an easy person to talk to.

The problem with Joey though was he was *too* nice. Any time I tried to tell him about Elizabeth, he defended her—not because he knew her or cared for her, but because he was so innocent he couldn't imagine someone would be diabolical enough to do what I accused her of doing.

"Joey, I told her it was the car I wanted and she showed up driving the *exact same one the very next day*."

"Right but, like, she already had it. Her dad collects classic cars. They have an entire building that's just a garage for all his cars."

"How do you know that?" I asked, turning to look at him.

"Because I went over there a couple weeks ago." He handed me the joint, but I waved it away. I'd had enough. "Her family's loaded."

I turned to the windshield where, beyond the parking lot, a black ocean rolled underneath a full-moon sky. "You went to her house?"

"Yeah, everyone did. She had a birthday party."

Maybe it was the weed hitting me, but my heart started

hammering in my chest. My mouth felt sticky, like it was hard to find the words. Finally, I said, "Why wasn't I invited?"

"Because you hate her, I guess?"

He coughed his guts out for a full minute. A stranger would be alarmed, but I knew Joey well enough that I accepted he did this from time to time. He got red in the face and then recovered, taking a deep breath and letting it out.

"You all right, bud?" I asked.

He did a hang ten sign. "All's well."

"I don't hate her," I said, continuing the conversation where we'd dropped off. "But she's an identity thief."

"It's not like you had a patent on vintage clothes and red hair, man."

"Haven't you noticed all the little things?" I smacked his dashboard. "The pumps she bought that look just like my pumps. The purse. She started wearing false eyelashes after she met me, because I did."

"They're false?" Joey asked, blinking at me with a new fascination.

I let out a moan. This was the worst part about Elizabeth —it wasn't even the many things she did, the way she made me feel robbed of myself. It was that no one cared except me. I was ostracized in my own little bubble of paranoia.

"You know what? Never mind," I muttered.

"She showed everyone her closet when we came over," Joey said, never minding my *never mind*. "It's an entire room. Like a vintage store. Wall to wall shoes. Her mom said she'd been collecting vintage clothes all her life and a lot of that stuff was hers, so I really don't think Elizabeth just started buying clothes out of the blue, like, 'cause of you. Their whole house had this *Mad Men* thing going on—"

"Wait." I sat up straighter in my seat. "Wait a second. Did you just say her mom? You met her mom?"

"Yeah. Total MILF." He offered a sheepish smile. "No offense."

My jaw dropped.

Joey squinted at me like I was written in another language. "Was that not—is that not cool, that I called her a MILF?"

"She told me her mom was dead," I said. "That she died of cancer like my mom."

"Whoa." Joey turned down the music. "Your mom died of cancer?"

"When I was young, yeah. Elizabeth told me hers did too, when she was three."

"Maybe you misheard her?"

"I didn't mishear her," I said, annoyed.

"Okay, okay."

Joey rolled down his window and the thick smoke in the car escaped, spinning away into the dark. The sea air hit my face, a relief. The noise of the surf that seemed to match the rhythm of my heart. My head throbbed, stoned and over-whelmed. It was such a weird thing to lie about. Why would you lie that your mom died? Was she trying to steal every-thing from me, even my loss?

"She's a snake," I said.

"Can we talk about something else?"

I rolled my eyes. "Fine."

"What? It's just, like, she's my friend, too. I don't want to get in the middle of this drama."

"Since when are you friends?"

"I mean, we text sometimes. I'm friendly. I'm a friendly guy."

Friendly was one way of putting it. Joey was the type who looked up the word *gullible* in the dictionary. I wondered if he was chummy enough with Elizabeth that he gave her access to the sickening potion that came from props, but I wasn't about to ask.

"Want to make out?" he asked.

"No, Joey."

"Go for a walk on the beach?"

I sighed. "All right."

At the end of the semester, there was a lot going on: senioritis city, the sun blazing in full force and luring us to the beach, the whirlwind of senior brunches and pep rallies and college acceptances and rejections. But through the bustle, I retreated into myself. A gray cloud followed me everywhere. Doubt squirmed—did I make the right choice about going to Northwestern? Did I want to dye my hair another color? Did I even like my bell bottoms? Should I reinvent myself now that I had the chance to start over somewhere? There were times I stopped to look in the mirror and wasn't sure who that person was, the girl-woman with a wide smile and uncertain eyes.

It had all started with Elizabeth, I was sure of it. I had been confident. I had been special. Now that Elizabeth was at school, I faded into the shadows. And finding out that there had been parties—plural, par*ties*—at her fabulous mansion that I wasn't invited to? While she smiled at me and acted like we were cool? While she drove the Karmann Ghia and *beep-beep*ed at me whenever she saw me? Over those last weeks of school, the confusion about her stewed into hatred.

What kind of bitch steals your mom-dying-of-cancer story? Come on.

The final straw was prom. Joey and I had talked about going to prom together, and I'd even told Elizabeth this when she pretended to be my friend and gave me a ride home that one day. And, of course, should have seen it coming—a week before we were going, Elizabeth convinced Joey to go to prom with her. And being the pushover he was, he agreed.

"What the fuck, Joey?" I said when he told me.

He called me on the phone to break the news, stoned and apologetic, heavy metal in the background. Coughing his ass off. There's a special kind of heartbreak when it's a platonic friend dumping you. It stung way more than I thought it should.

"Well, we were just going as friends, you know, and Elizabeth and I kind of, I don't know, we have, like, a thing going—"

"A thing?"

"I mean, like, romantic and shit."

"Romantic and shit." I felt like a parrot. "Dude, I bought my dress and everything."

"You can still go! Just, like, ask someone else."

I drew in a deep breath. "You know the only reason she's doing this is because she knows I was going with you. You know that, right? She doesn't care about you. She just wants to take everything from me."

And then I heard something faint—a girl's voice in the background murmuring, "Tell her to go with someone else as a friend."

The sound of it pricked me like static electricity. It was

Elizabeth. She was sitting there coaching him. She put him up to this, the puppet master.

"Is she there with you right now?" I asked in disbelief.

"Uhhh ..."

I had a *fuck you* ready on my tongue, but I swallowed it and hung up instead. I was sitting on my bed and I went still, letting reality settle in. I stared at my *Girl before a Mirror* painting, wishing I could rip it in half. Wishing I could throw something, break something. Even though Joey was just my friend and prom wasn't supposed to be a big deal, I ached. Once again, Elizabeth Smith got what I wanted. She was, undeniably, a better version of me.

There was a fire behind my face. I sat still as it spread down my throat and found my heart, then moved to my stomach and spread through me, limb to limb. It was rage with a fresh hunger behind it. It was me deciding, then and there, that I would get revenge somehow.

Push, push, push ... at some point, somebody's going to push back.

FIFTY-FOUR
NOW

MARIA LIVES IN MONTCLAIR, a fancy hilltop neighborhood in Oakland. But even for Montclair, the house is stunning—a palatial mid-century masterpiece of architecture behind a private circular driveway. A Lyft driver dropped me off at a nearby shopping center and Maria picked me up like my own private chauffeur, so fashionable in her shiny Tesla, a scarf around her head, oversized sunglasses, nude lipstick. My jaw dropped when I first saw her estate with its tennis court and pond. I'm still in disbelief as she parks and we get out. I start up a lazy spiral of steps toward the front of the house with its gold-lit picture windows and tasteful landscaping, but Maria stops me.

"My office is downstairs," she says, beckoning me to a much less exciting door underneath the house that leads to a basement mother-in-law unit. She hunts through her leather purse for her keys. Won't lie, a teeny part of me is disappointed. I wanted to know what the interior of that dream house looks like. Yet another reminder that this relationship is about one thing and one thing only: my broken brain.

You're walking into hell, the voice warns.

"You're about to die," I whisper.

It isn't until Maria peers back at me over her shoulder with subtle horror on her face that I realize I said it out loud.

"Excuse me?" she asks.

"Nothing, sorry," I say, mortified.

She turns back around and unlocks the door, but not without casting another worried glance over her shoulder. Great. Now my therapist is afraid I'm going to murder her.

The voice cackles.

I bite my tongue, but I really am going to annihilate the voice today. I'm going to have a breakthrough. That's what the voice is so afraid of. It's lashing out in self-preservation. It's a mouse dropped in a snake cage. I was reading on Reddit last night about all these people who had epiphanies that cured their depression when trying psychedelic therapy. I used to be scared, but not anymore. I've been pushed to the edge. I'm ready to ride the roller coaster, ticket in hand.

"Welcome to my home office," Maria says, unwrapping her scarf from her head and tying it around her neck.

"So pretty," I murmur.

It's a cozy room with a wine-colored leather sofa and a daybed in the corner. A partition divides the other part of the room, where a desk sits in the corner with a painted picture of the ocean behind it. Reminds me of Santa Barbara, of the endless assurance of the waves, and I'm immediately relaxed here—a miniature fountain dribbling on a side table and impressive potted palms. A zen sand garden on a coffee table. Fat expensive-looking candles.

Smells like vanilla and sandalwood. A kitchenette, a bath-room. This office is nicer than my apartment.

Get out of this horrible place! hisses the voice.

I smile. Like holy water to a demon—it hates therapy.

I'm going to kill you, I tell it. (Silently this time.)

"This is where I have all my administration sessions," Maria says, taking a seat in a stuffed chair that matches the couch. "How does this space feel to you?"

"Amazing," I say, sitting on the couch.

Maria crosses her ankles, folds her hands on her lap, and patiently rolls through the details with me again so I know what to expect. Today, after drinking some mushroom tea with a low dosage of psilocybin, I'm going to lie down with a sleep mask on and headphones playing relaxing music. My devices get put away. Watches and jewelry and any distrac-tions get put away. This is going to be a mainly internal process, with Maria only here as a guide. I'm to listen to myself, engage with myself, and lean into the experiences that arise. If the voice speaks today, I'm going to listen to it. Engage with it. I'm going to be okay with emotions and discomfort. And Maria will be here to assist me in any way I need.

"Are we ready?" she asks.

"We are," I say.

Maria goes to the kitchenette. As she prepares my magic tincture, I make small talk with her to fill the air, because the voice is relentless in my ear, desperate and repeating itself in a raspy taunting whisper:

Run, bunny. Run away, bunny.

"How long have you had this place?" I ask.

"The house I've lived in for about, oh, eight years now? This extra unit though I built last year for my practice."

Run, bunny.

"You live here with your family?" I ask.

"With my husband. But he's away in Germany on business." She gives me a side-eyed glance and swallows. "He'll be back soon."

Oh God. Is she scared of me? Did she just get scared of being here alone with me because she thinks I said I was going to kill her? I'm not going to kill her. I wouldn't kill her.

Kill her.

My heartbeat goes through the roof and all at once, a cold sweat seeps out of my skin. Oh no. What if this is what it's going to be like when I'm on shrooms? Listening to the voice telling me to kill my therapist? What if I have a psychotic break and I *do* try to kill her? It's too early to be this paranoid. I wish I had a benzo. Should I tell my therapist these thoughts, get them off my chest? That's what therapists are for, right? Or would she report me? Is that considered a threat if you tell your therapist that a voice is telling you to kill them?

"Here we go," Maria says, handing me a steaming cup that smells like lemon and dirt.

"Thank you," I say with a smile.

Run, bunny! RUN AWAY, BUNNY! the voice creaks in demonic despair.

And I drink it. Even though it's so hot it burns my lips and throat, I drink it like I've never been thirstier in all my life.

FIFTY-FIVE

I LIE DOWN on the daybed with a cushy eye mask blackening my vision. Maria places a pair of noise-canceling headphones over my ears and tucks me in with a furry blanket that smells faintly of lavender. For just a second, I'm a child again, this déjà vu poking up like a long-buried seed from the depths of me—of being mothered. The watery drone of new-age music tranquilizes and drowns out the voice. I can barely even hear the voice. Or I can hear it, but I'm not paying attention to it, because I'm so comfy here right now. It doesn't matter. It's like the sound of the blood pounding in my ears or my own breathing or a ticking clock. Always there if I listen to it. But I don't need to listen to it now.

I'm tired. It's been a long day, a long week, a long month. A long thirty years on this planet. I've lived so many lives already, a sampler platter of people and places. As I lie still, they sparkle in flashes like I'm flipping through a glossy photo album. The slanted, flirty stare of my short-lived girlfriend in New Orleans. A riverboat gliding by on muddy water. Doing dishes in the co-op kitchen in Washington. The scent of apple blossoms in the rain. The glimmer of ocean beneath an airplane window. An aching broken heart. Riding a bicycle through a narrow, pebbled street in Amsterdam. A drunken kiss beneath a bridge. The smell of Seoul—car exhaust and kimchi. My father's face. My father's smile. And suddenly, I can feel his smile radiating through me. It's me smiling now. We're the same.

I'm glowing. I'm oozing. My whole life—I could lie here and watch it all again if I wanted, pluck out any memory, or dream whatever dream I want. This is so wonderful. I'm in command of my own mind. It's beautiful in here, why do I fear it? That voice—right now, it sounds far away, distant and tiny, high-pitched.

Run away, bunny!

Wow, I think I'm tripping.

"You're tripping balls," I hear my dad say, and then feel my laugh spilling out of my lips. It's a river of joy gushing out of me, music in the air. Or am I actually just hearing the headphones' music? Is the music the laughter, or did I really laugh? The insides of my eyelids are playing movies, kaleidoscopic patterns shifting into stained glass—freezing, then moving again. I am sunshine. A lit lamp. Jolene.

Jolene. Jolene. Jolene.

My name repeats, repeats, repeats, an iambic copy machine. My smile so big on my face, fire lighting a room.

You criminal, a low voice whispers.

Uh-oh.

Wait.

You guilty piece of shit.

Where did that thought come from? I don't like that thought.

You don't deserve the life you have after what you did to Elizabeth Smith.

Yikes. It's louder now. I can feel it tickling in my ears and my stomach rolls, rolls.

You caused an accident that MAIMED someone and then left her to DIE on the side of the road.

Not now. Not this. I try to think of other things: a moonlit beach. Redwood trees. A Mardi Gras parade. But it's loud. I can actually see it and not just hear it—a convergence of storm clouds. Gray mountainous storm clouds billowing, the horrid puff of smoke from a volcano or an atomic bomb. Rolling in the sky. Lightning flashing.

How dare you go on living your life like a normal human being when you are a CRIMINAL, when you are a STAIN ON THIS GREEN EARTH?

I don't know what to do. This is terrifying. Maria said to listen, but I don't want to listen to this anymore. I'm pinned to the couch though, so heavy, brick lady. I can't move. It's forcing me to listen. So I lie here and take it, my face contorting, invisible hands wrecking my clay.

Anyone who takes the life of a human being is to be put to death. Anyone who injures their neighbor is to be injured in the same manner, fracture for fracture, eye for eye, tooth for tooth. The one who has inflicted the injury must suffer the same injury.

Wait. What? Is my brain reciting Bible verses?

As the words repeat again, I hear two voices. Or three voices. So many voices, overlapping. Or is this just the new age music and I'm so high I can't tell the difference? I didn't expect to be this high, this is really intense. I'm trying to listen like Maria said. For a moment, I come back into my body, moving a finger. I don't know which one to listen to. The one shouting Bible verses is loudest but when I listen, really listen, I can still hear another voice under it—a quiet, high voice that has morphed into one like my own.

Run, bunny. Run away, bunny.

What the fuck is going on? My head is throbbing. The Bible verses keep repeating and then, when I concentrate all my effort into moving my arm, when I can finally get my hand to remember it exists and find where the headphones are, I pull them off my ears and this *whoosh* waterfall of white noise rushes into my ears and I'm so relieved, so relieved, because the overlapping horror chorus ceases and all I can hear is that voice whispering for the bunny to run away.

As if I am made of goo, a jelly human, I shakily push myself up to a seated position and it's like I just rotated the world upside down, a sickening tipping, a hellish carnival ride. I clutch my stomach and wonder if I'm about to puke. I try to adjust my eyes but the room is patterns, endless patterns and nothing else, and I almost panic until I remember *THE MASK* in flashing marquis lights. Right, the mask I'm wearing. It takes way more concentration than it should to lift my hands to my face and pull the softness off my eyelids.

The room. The familiarity of a room, a real-life room. The potted palm in the corner seems to wave hello, as if a breeze blew through it. It's so bright and cheerful.

"Wow," I say, and the word coming out of my mouth echoes. I am a mooing cow. "That was insane."

The room's stillness is striking. I can actually feel the

stillness, the way the furniture waits and the floor waits and the walls wait. My stomach rumbles and I try to burp but can't. Looking over at the other side of the room, the kitchenette is quiet, but there are rustling sounds and whisper sounds coming from the corner where the desk is. I rise on wobbly feet, pudding knees. When I stand, what I see there makes me as still as the furniture.

Maria is behind the desk, looking toward me. I know it's Maria. It has to be Maria, because it's her desk, and she's wearing that scarf I recognize and that wheat-colored pantsuit I recognize, but she has a gorilla head. And sitting across from her at the table, there I am. My back is turned to me, but it's me. My short hair. My jacket. Holy shit, I'm hallucinating. I'm having a psychotic break, just like I was afraid would happen.

"I'm going to be sick," I say.

I stumble into the bathroom on gooey legs and kneel on the tile, tilting myself over the toilet just in time to eject a jetstream of puke into the bowl. Splashy yucky sadness. It's wretched, nightmare stink and stomach spasms. I keep heaving and heaving everything out of my stomach until finally I reach a place of exhausted peace here hugging familiar chilly porcelain. I breathe steadily and ground myself.

"I am tripping balls," I remind myself. "I'm okay. I'm hallucinating but it's okay because I know I'm hallucinating. That's means I'm not psychotic." Puffing out my chest, I say, proudly, "I am not psychotic."

Getting up is an ordeal. I never realized how hard it is to get up off a floor! Wow. Takes so much pushing on the tile and pulling from the counter, and everything is tilty as a ship. Whoa. I go to the sink to wash my hands, the water tickling my fingers.

Run, bunny! Run away, bunny! says a shrill voice that seems to be pouring out of the faucet.

I see myself in the mirror and ... I shouldn't have looked. It's like looking in a mirror in a dream. That's not me. That's not me at all, my face is scarred and burned and one blue eye is duller than the other. And there are two of me. I'm seeing double.

That's when it hits me—no, no. There aren't two of me.

That's Elizabeth Smith standing behind me.

And either I'm having that psychotic break I so feared or that's really her, because she's clear as day. A hundred percent real.

"Hi Jolene," she says, a smile crinkling her face.

Roller coaster drop. My jaw opens, but I don't know what to say.

I told you that you should have run away, the voice says sadly.

FIFTY-SIX

THIS IS BAD.

This is very, very bad.

After a tornado struggle of human limbs I quite honestly don't understand, I am tied to a chair with some kind of long scarf thing. I'm woozy-brained and whacked out on magic mushrooms but I'm pretty sure this might be real and if it is real, then I'm in big trouble. And if it's not real, then I've officially lost it and that also equals big trouble.

Either way: very, very bad.

Sitting in front of me are Maria and Elizabeth, side by side on the couch. I blink and blink and blink to see if I can make them go away, but I can't. They remain.

"What is going on?" I ask, the words slow and goopy in my mouth.

Maria holds a gorilla mask in her lap. A gorilla face puddle. And it's tickling my brain, ringing like a bell, *ding ding*, I saw that mask. I saw it outside my window. Somehow everything makes perfect sense but also it makes no sense at all.

"Go ahead," Maria says to Elizabeth.

"Well." Elizabeth ins and outs a deep breath. "This is my stepmom, Maria," she says, her smile friendly, her eyes knives. "Isn't that spectacular? Sounds like you two have been getting to know each other!"

"How ...?" is the only sound I can manage, like some kind of pitiful cat.

"Well, I guess you took my advice to go to the Healing Oak Therapy Center, which is so fantastic! Isn't that fantastic?"

Elizabeth turns to Maria, reaches out and squeezes her hand.

"Serendipitous," Maria says, squeezing her hand back.

"I totally didn't even mention my stepmom works there!" Elizabeth says.

"What are the chances?" Maria adds.

"You're her stepmom," I repeat.

"Yes. I've raised her since she was six." Maria puts her arm around Elizabeth. "She's my baby."

I swear I can smell the evil in the air, like burned steak, as it hits me how fucking doomed I am.

Oh, bunny, the voice says, low and hoarse but not scary anymore. *Look at you, caught in a trap.*

"When you told me your story," Maria points her gaze at me, eyes aglow. And I see ice in there, crystals in her irises twinkling. A cruel villainess. "I couldn't believe what I was hearing. Some kind of divinity must have led you into my office that day, confessing your *sin* to me. Your *crime* to me."

The words *sin* and *crime* hurt, needles pricking my insides.

"Accident," I whisper.

"You disfigured me," Elizabeth says. The smile is erased from her face. All that's left there now is a blank loathing. "You nearly killed me. You *ruined* me. I lost everything because of you and you just—just kept on living your life!"

"Gallivanting around the globe," Maria says with disgust.

"Feeling sorry for yourself, wallowing in self-pity," spits Elizabeth.

"She's so traumatized, don't you know?" Maria says, looking at Elizabeth and talking like I'm not even here. "She's just carried such a weight around all these years."

Elizabeth sticks her lower lip out and gives me a pitying head shake. "Poor thing."

"Is this real?" I ask. "Or am I having a psychotic break?"

"This is very real, though you'll wish it was a psychotic break after we're through with you," Maria says.

There is a long silence that swells in the room, a silence that breathes on its own, a giant invisible jellyfish that seems to stop time entirely. I am just not understanding this. The facts are laid out for me, yes, but the understanding keeps slipping away from me.

"You got all our texts, right?" Elizabeth asks. "You knew we were coming for you."

Maria straightens her scarf. "We've left you a few presents."

"Mmm, yes," Elizabeth agrees. "And it was so great that I managed to swipe your keys and get them copied—made it so much easier to slip in and out of your apartment. Thanks for that."

"My shoes," I say, looking down at my two mismatched high-heeled Mary Janes.

"Yeah, that was fun," Elizabeth says, grinning.

And then, a house where the lights went out. Her smile vanishes.

"The thing is, Jolene," she says, clapping her hands and leaning in. "I've given you so many chances. So. Many. Chances. In high school, you were constantly on my back. Wouldn't leave me alone. Whatever I did, you had to do. Giving me that weird painting you made of me and then asking for it back. Trying to steal the guy I was into. Poisoning my fucking potion in *Romeo and Juliet*! Admit it, Jolene. Admit you did that. I want to hear you say it."

"*You* poisoned *me*," I say faintly.

"Omigod, even now she's full of shit," Elizabeth says in exasperation, turning to Maria.

"Delusional," Maria says. "Delusional disorder."

Suddenly I think I know what Suzanne meant when she said she could see people's auras, because a ring of fire surrounds these two. They are ablaze. Horror wrinkles through me and I wonder for the first time if I'm going to die.

"Despite everything, I was still nice to you anyway," Elizabeth says to me. "I did nothing but treat you with kindness." She leans forward and enunciates every word. "And then you tried to kill me."

"I didn't try to kill you," I say, my mouth moving automatically, but I'm wavering, dizzy.

"Then I gave you so many chances even after that, Jolene!" Her voice rises. "Like a fool! With no idea what you did to me! I met you in improv class and I was kind to you and tried to be your friend because I felt sorry for you. And you could have tried to make things right at that point. You could have told me, you could have said something. But no. Instead you just ..."

"... went to therapy," Maria says. "Went to therapy thinking it would fix your guilty little secret."

"Not that there was anything you ever could have said that would have made me forgive you," Elizabeth says.

Her eyes are shiny. I think she's crying. Either she's crying or it's raining on her face.

"But it would have shown you had at least a shred of decency inside you," Elizabeth says.

Maria puts her arm around Elizabeth, who buries her face in her shoulder. Maria's face is carved of stone as she watches me. "Do you know what it's like," she says slowly, "watching your daughter scream for hours upon hours because she's covered in third-degree burns? Changing her bandages and cleaning her pus, day after day, as she sobs and begs you to kill her?"

I open my mouth but am unable to make a sound.

"Do you know what it's like to see her horror when she learns she has to lose her leg? When she learns that her gorgeous face is permanently scarred and that she will never be able to do the things she wanted to do with her life?"

My teeth are chattering. I wish the voice would say something, anything. I wish there was somebody here to help me, even if that somebody is imaginary. But as high as I am, as much as the world continues to swirl and the colors are breathing, I'm aware that I'm in very deep and very real shit and no one is going to help me now.

"And do you know what it's like to wake up in the morning every day for years to have to re-remember it all, all over again?" Elizabeth asks, her face contorted as she cries. "In my dreams, I still have my leg. My face is still smooth. Like yours. It's like my unconscious hasn't caught up. And I have to remember it again and again and again."

"And the nightmares."

"Yes! Fire, gasoline, explosions—the sounds of twisted steel. Being trapped in an upside-down car. You don't have a clue what I've been through. And you don't even care!" Elizabeth turns to Maria and cries, "Omigod, she doesn't even *care*."

"You're right, she doesn't know what you've been through," Maria tells her. "But we're going to help her with that, aren't we?"

They clasp hands and share one deep breath. Everything they've said, their storms of words, their chattering cruelty—they swarm around my head like blackbirds. And oddly, it's one of the first times I can remember that I feel no guilt at all, as if the guilt evaporated as soon as this conversation started. Because all I care about is getting the hell out of here.

And that's when I notice what's on the coffee table between us. Did it all just appear? Has it been there, glinting silver all along? The zen sand garden has been replaced. Now it's a saw, frightening as an alligator head with broken-mirror teeth. Next to it, something else—something sharp, pointy, poky. Then there's a block of knives. And finally, a blowtorch.

"Oh no," I say, the words falling out of me.

I dry heave. Maria puts the gorilla mask next to her on the couch and reveals what's under it: a Bible. *Is* that a Bible? She opens it up to a page she has marked with a bookmark with a smiley face on it. My eyes fill with tears. I don't know what's happening, but I'm getting a desperate feeling—a cow in the slaughterhouse feeling. A bird in the cat's claws feeling. I pull my wrists, but they're bound tightly. Like a tic, I start pulling at it with my fingernails. Snagging it on a hangnail and pulling it, pulling it.

Run, bunny, the voice says. *Run away, bunny!*

"I'm a woman of science," Maria says, flipping through the Bible pages. "But I'm also a child of God. Are you familiar with Leviticus?"

"Please," I say.

"Please read it to you?" she asks in a mocking tone. "My pleasure. *Anyone who injures their neighbor is to be injured in the same manner, fracture for fracture, eye for eye, tooth for tooth. The one who has inflicted the injury must suffer the same injury.*"

The room pulsates and reality comes back to me in waves. My brain is working very hard on a puzzle right now. That voice reading it—I heard it in my ears earlier when I was lying on the daybed. And Maria is shapeshifting before my eyes, kind of like those lizard people that Elizabeth was so obsessed with in high school when she was conspiracy theory girl. I thought Maria was so nice. I thought she was on my side, that she wanted to help me. I trusted her and believed her and never once questioned her. But she's a monster. Her face turns scaly and reptilian. She's a *monster.*

"I love that passage," Elizabeth says. "Fracture for fracture. Eye for eye."

"What are you thinking first?" Maria asks Elizabeth, shutting her Bible with a clap. "Are you going to poke out her eye or saw off her leg?"

Elizabeth considers this, as if Maria just gave her a

choice between pancakes and French toast. "I could start off by burning her face?"

"And singeing her ear off, yes," Maria agrees. "Whole left side of her body."

A sound starts coming out of me, rocketing me, and I don't entirely understand it. I think maybe it's something outside us, a natural disaster, a hurricane shaking the windows. But no, it's me. I'm blubbering and crying a string of slobbering gibberish. I really don't want to die right now. Universe, don't let me die this way, tortured to death while tripping on mushrooms. I can't imagine a worse way to die.

But the universe says nothing.

Keep working on that scarf, whispers the voice. *There's a hole where your hangnail caught. Keep pulling at it.*

I do what the voice says, twitching my fingertips, pulling and pulling and pulling. But nothing seems to happen. I don't even understand what I'm feeling. I don't know if I'm feeling the scarf or if I'm crying out loud, I'm having a hard time understanding the difference between what is outside of me and what is inside of me right now.

"I'm feeling generous," Elizabeth chirps, drumming her fingernails on the table as she beholds the array of weaponry like pastries at a pâtisserie. "What would you like to start with first, Jolene? I'll give you first pick."

"You're—you're not—you're—" My mouth is broken. I can't formulate my protest into anything intelligible.

"If you're not going to tell me, I'm picking the eyeball," Elizabeth says, grabbing what appears to be an ice pick and contemplating it in the light. "I think it might be nice to start from the top."

"Go right ahead," Maria says.

Oh my God. Oh my fucking God. Elizabeth is really going to stab my eye with an ice pick and twist out my eyeball. This is not a test. *Mayday! Mayday!* As she looks down at me, ice pick poised mere inches away from my face, I manage to blurt out, "My leg! Start with my leg."

"Interesting," Elizabeth says, exchanging an almost impressed look with Maria.

"She's going to bleed everywhere, you know," Maria says.

"I know," Elizabeth says. "But if that's what she wants, let's give it to her."

"Let me get some sheets from the closet," Maria says with a sigh.

Maria gets up from the couch and crosses the room to a linen closet near the bathroom and, once again, time slows to an ooze. Elizabeth and I watch each other with, I imagine, identically contorted, twisting faces. Her face keeps changing, swirling like water. And I'm lost, drowning in stories— Elizabeth saying that I was the one who poisoned her in high school, that I was the one who took away her boyfriend and painted her and copied her and wouldn't leave her alone. And for a long, eternal moment, I can imagine what she's said is true. That I've had it backwards all along. That I'm delusional. I keep twiddling my fingers and picking at the thin scarf material, picking and picking, and wondering if they're right to do what they're doing to me. If I'm this much of a monster and this is what I deserve. I close my eyes, which throb, and think, I'm sorry, Daddy. I'm sorry this is how it ends for me.

It isn't until Elizabeth bends down to pull up my dress and the sharp teeth of the saw bite my bare thigh that the realization flashes through me with the pain, making me scream as I feel my skin ripping with the first pull and push of the saw, my eyes peeling open again.

That wasn't what happened.

I may be tripping balls, but I know what's real. I know the difference between lies and truth, fiction and non. And I may have caused a terrible accident, but the way Elizabeth tells it is not how it was.

I scream and kick and claw my fingers so tightly that the pain seems to make a superhero of me. Adrenaline surges and I rip a hole through the scarf I've been making secretly behind me and my hands are suddenly gorgeously blood-rushingly free. I thrash my body, kicking Elizabeth backwards, blood a warm gush down my leg. She falls into the coffee table and screams and I don't stop to understand the why or how of anything, I'm not even a woman anymore, I'm a flash of light, I'm a shooting star, I'm a spooked bird and I'm flying out of the room so fast the whole world is nothing but a rainbow blur of spilled-paint color all around me.

FIFTY-SEVEN

IT'S TWILIGHTING OUTSIDE. Is twilighting a word?

I'm still tripping my ass off as I run full speed ahead up the spiral cement stairs that seem to be beckoning me, the blazing gold faux-sunshine picture windows of the mansion-house a beacon saying *come here, in here you're safe!* My leg throbs with my pulse and when I look down, blood is trickling down my left thigh and I can hear Maria shouting somewhere distantly behind me. I get to the front door, thinking, is this my house? Do I live here? What is going on, why is this happening? What a nightmare. This is a living nightmare.

The door is unlocked and I go inside, stunned for a moment as the house seems to breathe all around me. Wow. There's a black-and-white framed photo of a New York City street scene and the cars are moving and the people are actually walking in it and everything. There's a painting of a forest and I can see birds flying in it. But I need to focus. Why am I in here? Am I playing a game of some kind? This suddenly feels ickily familiar. Ickily—is that a word? I touch the blood on my leg, studying its intense dewy redness on my index finger in awe.

I'm an actress in a horror film. The bloody final girl.

I'm running away from monsters.

The stairs I'm climbing seem to play under my feet, each step a note on a xylophone. At the top of the landing, a pressure is mounting in my chest, tightening, and reality hits me in waves. Oh fuck. Oh I need to hide, this blood on my fingers is real, they want to torture me. And I don't know where I am. I don't know what to do, I'm just frozen here in a stranger's house staring at family pictures on the wall. Elizabeth when she was in high school, red-haired, without scars. Her face turns into mine and then it turns back into hers, so subtly it's hard to even notice.

Hide, bunny! the voice says. *Hide somewhere. Don't let them hurt you.*

The voice sounds softer than it used to. Comforting, almost. My chest relaxes a little at the sound of it. There are so many doors up here and I don't know where they lead. I pick the one directly in front of the staircase that's closed and go inside, shutting the door behind me.

It's sparsely furnished, a bed and a dresser with nothing on it, a bookcase half-filled. It's a blank-walled bedroom nobody seems to live in. I can hear bumpy sounds and Maria's voice singing that song, *Jolene? Jolene? Jolene? Jolene?*

They're inside the house looking for you! the voice says. *Quick, get into the closet and hide!*

I do what the voice tells me to do, thanking it with the beating of my heart. Sliding open the closet door as *shhh*-quietly as I can and closing it behind me. It's full in here, so many clothes hanging, long coats smelling like a walk through the woods and plastic-wrapped dresses that crinkle against my cheek. I tuck myself in the corner, a dark musty cave, stepping behind a set of free weights so my feet won't show. I'm hidden. I'm safe here. It's a hundred percent darkness. The mask might as well be back on my eyes. I'm seeing shifting dreamy patterns, living wallpaper.

Time doesn't really exist in here. Nothing exists in here. I'm in a dry upright sensory deprivation tank. And reality keeps lapping at my mind's shore, reminding me that my life is in danger. The pain in my leg is what reminds me—the rhythm of the pain. The facts line themselves up in my mind, me briefing myself in a bullet-pointed list.

- Maria and Elizabeth
- Maria is Elizabeth's stepmom
- Somehow I ended up with her as a therapist. How ...?
- Oh yeah. Elizabeth recommended I go to Healing Oak. Never mentioned her stepmom worked there. Oops.
- They've been harassing me and driving me to the brink this past month
- They are deranged for revenge and want to cut off my leg and burn my face and stab my eyeball out

You'd think I would be horrified, but somehow, it strikes me as very funny right now. I begin giggling into my hands. It's so absurd. Stealing an eyeball and a leg. Why would anyone do that?

You need to focus, the voice says. *This isn't a fucking joke.*

My smile melts at the sound of the voice. The voice has changed today. It's different and yet—so familiar. Kind of sounds like my own voice.

You need to figure out how you're going to get out of this.

Can't I just hide here in the closet forever?

No.

Maybe I could wait here and then sneak out at nighttime. Is it nighttime yet?

No.

The creaking, unmistakable sound of a door opening interrupts my one-woman conversation. I stand so still, so very still. I am a dress hanging in the closet.

"Why don't you go check outside," Maria's voice calls out, jolting me like an electric current. "Check the sauna. Just use the taser on her if you see her."

Taser? Shit, shit, shit.

My pulse gallops. Footsteps.

Oh, she's close. Very close. She's in this room right now, I can feel her presence. I squeeze my eyes shut and reality hits like a drug trip. If they find me, they're going to hurt me. This is actually happening. I can't stop trembling as I hear the *whoosh* of the closet door, golding everything.

There's pressure tickling me. She's moving the coats, the dresses, shifting them to check the corners. She'll see me any second. Taser.

Grab one of the weights in front of you.

"Jolene, Jolene, Jolene, Jolene," Maria sings.

If you don't, she's going to hurt you. I'm telling you. You need to listen.

Gently, I stoop to pick up a weight, just as the coats are moved from in front of me and the light goes from gold to blinding and I see Maria's eyes recognizing me here, the corners of her lips turning up victoriously.

Now hit her as hard as you can.

I'm sure the moment happens fast, but the way I experience it, it takes an hour for my arm to muster up the strength to lift the weight above my head and to come down, gravity pulling it through the air right to the top of Maria's skull. The crunching sound—it's like a smashed melon. I wince as she falls backwards, not wanting to see what I've done. I ache with regret immediately, a phantom sympathetic pain rushing over my skull.

Peeking out, I can see Maria lying on the ground, out cold. Her head is all messed up, caved in; I flinch at the sight of it. My hand flies to my mouth. I did that. Did I do that? I didn't think it would ... I didn't think it would do *that*. Oh my fucking God, did I just kill her?

It was her or you.

I begin crying. The tears aren't just coming from my eyes, they're leaking out of my ears and nose and mouth and hair and skin. I don't like this. I really, really don't like this. This is the worst. I killed my therapist, just like the voice told me to.

It wasn't your fault. It's okay, little one.

A warmth envelops me as I stand here, squeezing my eyes shut. An invisible electric blanket. Or maybe a ghost's embrace. That voice ... I hear it now. It's changed, like someone had a knob they adjusted, the pitch climbing, the mean distortion turned all the way down. It's a voice I haven't heard in years, in so many years. I thought I had forgotten it.

My mother.

Time to open your eyes, it repeats. *Keep moving. Get out of here while you can.*

I blink, wincing at the light of the room, everything still in psychedelic Technicolor. Don't look down. Just don't look down. My thoughts throb in circles: I am tripping on mushrooms. I killed my therapist. I need to get out of here. Don't look down. I am tripping on mushrooms. I killed my therapist. I need to get out of here. Don't look down. I am tripping on mushrooms. I killed my therapist. I need to get out of here. Don't look down. I am tripping on mushrooms. I killed my therapist. I need to get out of here. I need to get out of here. I NEED TO GET THE FUCK OUT OF HERE.

As if moving through liquid, I step over Maria's legs. I can't look at her face, at what I did to her. What I had to do to her. What she gave me no choice but to do to her. I tiptoe to the doorway, beholding the unfamiliar hallway, the dim lighting and stranger house dizzy and buzzing and surreal, and balk when I see Elizabeth approaching, hurrying up the stairs with a lethal gleam in her eye, a knife in one hand, a taser in the other. She reaches the top of the stairs and she's only a few feet away from me now.

"Oh," she says, in soft surprise. "There you are."

She raises the knife in the air and while her smile is saying *hello friend*, her actions are saying *I am going to kill you.* And then, with the knife frozen and raised above her head, she glances behind me and her smile falters. She gasps.

"Omigod, what did you do to Maria?"

Lunge.

I spring forward and thrust my arms out, palms on Elizabeth's shoulders, and push her down the staircase. As she tips backwards, she lashes the knife in the air. The blade slices my forearm. I scream. Is that me screaming, or her? Maybe we're both screaming. She's rolling down the stairs, tumbling like a rag doll, like a rollover car crash, the bumping of bones against wood making me wince.

"Shit," I say. "Fuck. Goddamn it, I didn't want this, I don't want to hurt anyone!"

I know. You just want to live.

"Right?" I say, tears leaking all over my face again.

It's so weird, crying on shrooms. I don't even feel the sadness. It's just dampness on my cheeks, that's all.

I peek around the corner to check if Elizabeth is there. She is. She's at the bottom of the stairs. She's fallen on her side, limp as a puppet.

"Elizabeth?" I ask quietly.

Slowly, step by step, I make my way to the bottom. I stand on the bottom stair for a long time, waiting to see if she'll wake up, nightmarish reality engulfing me like a tsunami. I'm so shocked. I can't move. I can't find the right words to say.

"Elizabeth?" I ask again.

I'm not sure where to go from here. Do I call the police? An ambulance? Do I leave them here and get on a plane and never return? I wish the universe would give me a sign, but I've given up on that.

I'm your universe.

Yes, you are. Thanks for that.

I tiptoe down the last step and stoop in front of where Elizabeth lies. My hand flies to my mouth—she fell on her knife. The knife is in her chest at a horrific angle, straight through her sternum toward her stomach. She's on her side and I push her to her back, gently. Her breaths are horrid to listen to—like how the demon voice used to breathe in my ear, rasping and ragged and wet with blood. Her face is turning an ash gray, her scars pale pink in contrast. She's dying. I don't know what to do. Should I call someone? I don't even have my phone.

"Elizabeth," I whisper.

My eyes sting. The room seethes with something unspeakable. I can almost feel her dying—a vacuum sucking at me. Her eyes search the room as if she can't see, but then they land on my face. She's shaking violently, in shock. Blood reddens her floral dress, the stain growing and growing.

As our gazes meet, there's a strange but intense connection—a warm string that ties my ticking heart to her dying one. It's as if I'm looking in the mirror. As if we're the same person across the universe from one another. I want to hug her. I want to heal her.

"Elizabeth, I'm sorry," I whisper. "For everything. I really am." The words are new, like I just learned them. "I'm so sorry."

Elizabeth struggles through a wet breath, her eyes still locked with mine. Her glass eye is lazy now, pointing in the wrong direction. Her lips start moving, her voice low and nothing but a hiss, full of sludge. She speaks slowly, enunciating every word, every syllable, as if she's savoring it.

"*I*

don't

forgive

you,"

she says.

Those words—they push me off a cliff. She reaches a

limp ragdoll hand to her chest and yelps in pain as she clasps the handle of the knife. Contorting in pain, she pulls it out. She holds it above her head with a trembling grip as if she wants to stab me, and I'm about to let her. I deserve it after what I've done. I cry and nod, but her arm goes limp and falls behind her with a clatter. Suddenly her eyes go still and her limbs go still and everything seems to go still with her for a moment, the room the clock the house the air my heart, as if the whole world paused to die along with her.

FIFTY-EIGHT

A MAGIC MUSHROOM comedown is hard enough, but coming down after a double homicide is just about the worst thing in the world. Though I have to stop using that word and thinking that way—"homicide." It wasn't homicide. It was self-defense.

While I was tripping, reality kept coming in waves. But now that I've come down, I'm lost in the middle of the ocean. This scene is terrible. Blood everywhere. An absolute mess. Now I'm pacing this stranger's house, too stunned to know what to do next. If I call the police ...

... you will be arrested. You will go to prison.

But it was self-defense—

This does not look like self-defense.

I know. My dad's a lawyer though—

He couldn't defend you. Conflict of interest.

Well, what the hell am I supposed to do? Just leave the scene? My blood's all over the place. My blood's probably on Elizabeth and on Maria and they'd trace it to me.

Get rid of the bodies, then.

How the fuck am I supposed to dispose of two bodies? I don't even drive.

I begin crying. I know I shouldn't cry so much, I'm getting my DNA everywhere, but I'm flipping the fuck out right now and it's the only way I can relieve pressure. I didn't want to kill these people. I really am a good person. This is not what I wanted. I look at the crusted cuts on my leg and arm, pinches of pain that remind me I'm not dreaming. I don't want this to be the defining moment of my life, the thing that I'm known for. I don't want to spend my life behind bars. As I'm pacing and biting my nails, I glance out the back window and catch a glimpse of something that sparks an idea. It's twinkling out on the porch.

A hot tub.

Suzanne!

I think of her with a wistful twinge. I'll go further—I think of her with love. She went berserk on me, yes, but she mothered me a little while. She taught me things.

As I drag Elizabeth's body through the house by her cold dead arms, I think, you know, every job I've ever had has taught me something. I might be one inch deep, but I'm also ten miles wide. I had to drag sacks of coffee beans through a shop that felt a lot like dragging this body to the back porch. Had to lift a woman with cerebral palsy in and out of bed when I was an attendant for a few weeks, so I know just how to lift Elizabeth up and dump her in the water. *Kerplunk.* I worked as a hotel maid for a sweltering summer in Denver —I'd forgotten all about that. But I know how to clean the hell out of a scene if I need to. And looks like I'm going to need to.

The only way I can move forward with what I need to do here is to approach it like a job. It's just a job and I need to do a good one. Need to *thump thump thump* Maria down the stairs. Need to lift and lurch her into the hot tub. Need to push the thoughts out of my head, the words from the news article, *human stew*. Shudder. I turn up the jets, close the lid. Need to go to the kitchen and find the mop and the bucket, the ammonia, the hydrogen peroxide, the paper towels. Need to snap plastic gloves on my hands. Need to carefully clean the knife and put it back in the block. Clean the weight and return it to the closet, shutting the door. Mop the floor until it shines, spraying it numerous times to get any trace of blood out of it.

Stepping outside into the cold black night air to start toward Maria's office, I freeze when I see the Ring security sign stabbed in the elegant landscaping. Oh holy fuck. Oh I'm so screwed. Why didn't I think of that? Rich people have security systems, of course they do. I can't breathe. I lean over and dry heave on the lawn. But I'm in this deep, I can't stop now. Maybe if I could get Maria's phone, I could erase the videos—though what if her husband can still see them? What if he's watching all this right now from some hotel room in Germany? The police on their way? I cock my ear to listen for sirens, but all I hear is crickets and the breath of the freeway. I've got to at least give it a shot.

I run around like a chicken with its head cut off for a bit, desperately hunting for her cell phone. Finally, I find it on the kitchen countertop. Facial recognition to open it, you've got to be shitting me. I have to go back to the hot tub, pull her dripping soggy floating corpse head out of the bubbling water, and hold it up to the phone. But bless technology, it works. I'm in now. *Plunk,* her head goes back into the water. I breathe in deeply and find the Ring app. I'm startled to see the entire system's turned off. That makes no sense.

Why would it be off?

Oh yeah, she was planning to kill me. Maybe it was all to protect herself. Well, joke's on you, Maria. Even though I dodged that bullet, I still feel deeply sick, shaky, like the world's never going to be right again.

Time to tiptoe back to Maria's office where this hell all started. Clean down here too. Go through her desk with gloved hands, stealing my phone back, flipping through her schedule. There's nothing slated for today, no record of me. Of course there isn't. She was going to kill me. Gotta leave that schedule wide open on killin' days. I put the torture devices laid out for me in a garbage bag. Shiver. I can't believe this is my life. I check everything again and again. Check until the day's breaking, pink clouds in the sky. And then I walk the long highway down the hill in the bike lane and by the time I get to the bottom, my calves are on fire.

I get on a bus. I'm wearing some sweats I stole from Maria's house and when I look down, I don't recognize myself. I'm a murderer and I'm a nice woman saying hello to the bus driver. I'm still tripping just a tiny bit at the edges of my vision. With a shaking hand, I look out into the early morning whizzing by my window like a long, weird parade. I take out my phone and call my dad.

"You're up early," he says in surprise.

And the sound of his voice—I could melt. I close my eyes and savor that sound, that warm sound that means *home.* He is my home.

"Daddy, something's happened," I whisper. "I need you to come."

"Are you okay?" he asks, his voice seeming to get closer.

"No. I mean yes. Physically yes. I'm okay. But I need you to come."

"What's going on?"

"Well ..." I look around the bus, where everyone seems oblivious to me, in their own bubbles. I turn to the window and whisper, "Hypothetically speaking, what if someone killed someone else in self-defense and then cleaned up the crime scene afterward? They would look pretty guilty, right?" My breath hitches and I fight a sob. "They'd go to prison?"

There's a long, long silence, white noise that tickles my ear.

"Hypothetically speaking, yes." He clears his throat. "Don't say anything more. Not a damn word about this, to anyone. You hear?"

"Yeah."

"Hang tight. I'll be there soon."

He's at my apartment in four and a half hours. He must have driven a hundred miles an hour the whole way to get here that fast. We pack my things into boxes I just unpacked not too long ago. And then, snap of the fingers, Berkeley's in the rearview mirror—just another city on a list of cities where I once lived.

My dad and I don't talk about what happened on the ride home. We don't talk about it when I unpack my things back in my old room again, hanging up my Picasso reprint with thumbtacks.

I don't think we'll ever talk about it.

FIFTY-NINE

IT WASN'T SO LONG AGO I was here, sleeping in my childhood bed in my childhood room in our storybook house hidden in the oak trees. Only a few months ago. And as I lay here staring at the familiar crack in the ceiling that looks like an eye, I accept this won't be the last time I have some kind of breakdown and require rescuing. Everyone needs a touchstone. Everyone needs an oasis. When people offer you help in life, it's a beautiful thing. Take it.

I had mono once in high school and spent a month in bed. Now I have brain-mono, shell-shocked mono. Murder hangover is just another brand of sickness. I sleep long hours of the day, my bones heavy and tired, my brain flat-lined. My dad poking his head in just to bark, "Still in bed? It's after noon for Christ's sake!" if he's in a frustrated mood or, "You okay, bunny? Want to, I don't know, order pizza, go for a walk?" if he's concerned. It's not that different from when I was withdrawing from benzos in this same room.

The vivid memories of the psychedelic murder scene will

haunt me for the rest of my life. I close my eyes and there's Maria's face bashed in. There's the relenting crack of her skull beneath the weight in my hand. I clutch my chest and imagine a knife plunged in there, see Elizabeth's crumpled doll body and the way the dust settled on her eyeball as she died right in front of me. Ugly pictures. I would do anything to erase them. When they bring back lobotomies, I'll be first in line. But for now, I've got to live with these brain stains. What am I supposed to do, go to therapy? I should never have opened Pandora's box. I should have listened to Suzanne.

If I squint my eyes, I can remember just what the walls looked like in high school—a bulletin board with Polaroids of me and my theater crew. A modest shelf of books. Dried flowers and watercolor paintings of sunsets I did in art class. I haven't thought about it in a long time. I spent a lot of my life trying to ignore everything behind me, hurrying as if a monster followed. That's one upside to this whole trauma-tizing murder business—there's a sense of peace and quiet I can't remember ever feeling in my life. Maybe psychedelic therapy did actually work, because that voice and I, we get along now. It's got a motherly ring to it and has lost its witchy edge. And that restlessness is gone.

"What's the plan here?" my dad asks one night as we eat spaghetti at the dinner table. He's got a napkin tucked into his button-up shirt and still wears his shiny dress shoes. I'm in permanent pajamas. "What are we doing? Where we going next?"

"I don't know," I say, twirling around the pasta.

"Flight attendant? That's what you were talking about before. That still the plan?"

"I don't think so."

The thought of bumping a cart up and down an airplane aisle and having to fake-smile all the time and worry about hijackings doesn't sound like fun anymore.

"Okay, then, what? You've always got a plan. Let's hear it."

"I think I'll just stay here."

His mouth is full of meatball. "Here? *Live* here?"

"Yeah."

He swallows. "And do what?"

"Nothing."

"I don't know what to fucking do with you," he says, not meanly. Almost smiling.

SIXTY

ON CHRISTMAS, as I'm staring at the tree in a bourbon-soaked haze, Alice calls me. I should have been the one to break the ice since our rift was all my fault, but I just haven't known what to say. *Sorry, friend! Been busy murdering people and layin' low.* But of course, no spoiler there. Alice is the bigger person. She always will be.

"I'm so sorry I said I hated Sadie," I blurt after we get our hellos out of the way. "I don't hate her."

"It's okay. It's fine."

As if her chiweenie ears are burning, Sadie barks and barks in the background.

"None of that from you, Sade," Alice chides in a baby voice.

I go to my room and shut the door, lie down on my bed. I think I might be bedromantic. I think I might be in love with my bed. Or maybe it's depression. "Sorry I haven't called. I moved back home. I kind of had a breakdown."

"Your dad told me. So sad, babes. I still can't believe

about Elizabeth. That must have been such a shocker for you. How tragic."

"Yeah," I say slowly, my buzzed mind trying to catch up with the conversation. I blink and see brains on paper towels, the slop of the mop head soaking up blood on a hardwood floor. The room seems to swirl for a moment, a funhouse feeling that is in no way fun. I don't know what Alice is referring to, what her version of events are. "Yeah, messed up."

"They think it might have been a serial killer, I was reading. Who knows? You lived right around the corner from her. It could have been someone you knew."

"Could have been," I echo.

"Poor Elizabeth," she says. "I mean, after everything she went through."

"Right. Yeah."

"To then be found that way—by her own *dad*, in their hot tub. Did you hear she and her mom had been in there over a week before they were found?"

"Just terrible," I agree.

My ears are ringing. The thought that I have to keep something this overwhelmingly horrible a secret for the rest of my life arrives like an anvil to the head. A prison cell laughs at me and I imagine the thumping of police at our door.

This conversation requires a numbing agent of some kind. More bourbon is in order.

To the kitchen I go, plucking a new glass out of the cupboard and pouring the amber liquid to the top. I can hear my dad's loud muffled voice from his bedroom. Could be a season's greetings family phone call or an emergency breaking at work, you never know. The intensity's the same. I stand at the sink and gulp down the drink, wincing at the burn.

"What happened with your job? The wacky lady you were working for?" Alice asks.

"Oh, she finished the memoir. She didn't need me anymore anyway."

It's not a lie. She did finish the memoir. I saw an article about it online titled RUMORED MURDERER PENS OUTLANDISH 'MEMOIR' CALLED 'SO WHAT IF I KILLED HIM.'

"Jesus fucking Christ," my dad had said when I showed it to him. "What kind of idiot ..."

"So how are you?" I ask Alice, volleying the conversation back the other way. The last thing I want to talk about is me and everything that went wrong in Berkeley. "I miss you. Tell me all about what's been going on."

Alice chatters about how busy work's been, about how Liam wants to remodel, about how they're thinking about doing IVF this coming year. About a parasite that Sadie has, which I can't help but feel a little shameful joy about. I listen and offer laughter and *uh-huh*s and as I get drunker and drunker listening to details about her faraway suburban life, I have this revelation. I'm a tourist, that's what I am. Other people like Alice have a place in this world, but I'm just a tourist. *A dabbler*, I hear Suzanne's voice say. Nothing wrong with that. I'm the type of person who Alice doesn't say goodbye to—she says *hang in there*.

Alice clears her throat and I can feel we're nearing the end of this conversation. "Can I ask you something, Jo?"

"Shoot."

"You don't ... you don't know anything about what happened to Elizabeth, right?"

The blood stills in my arteries. I swallow hard, too stunned to answer for a second. Then I find my tongue. "What exactly are you implying?"

"I'm just—asking. There was some weird stuff going on between you two—"

"If you have to ask me an ugly question like that," I say sharply, "then you truly don't know me at all."

The line is dead for a moment until I hear a tiny faraway yip, that stinking devil dog. And all at once, I think I would be fine if I never talked to Alice again in my life.

"Merry Christmas, Allie, and thanks for the call," I say icily.

I press *end* and debate blocking her. Instead I just turn the phone off and go back to drinking.

"The fuck? Slow down, you're guzzling my Christmas bourbon," my dad yells at me when he comes out of his room and sees me slumped on the couch, drunkenly gazing at the tree. "I don't want blackout bullshit like last time you were here, come on. Can we learn from our past mistakes?"

He gives me a pointed look. It's rhetorical, but I don't think either of us really knows the answer.

I spend the rest of Christmas day happy and gooey and sloppy from the bourbon. You know what I'm going to do? Decorate my walls just the way they were in high school. Find my old sheets and curtains and books and reconstruct the past like a theater set. I go into the musty, dusty garage, tipsy on my toes, and find a couple boxes that say JO on them. I open them up and sit down on a plastic-covered chair and pluck out a stack of Polaroids with pinholes in them from the thumbtacks that once held them to a bulletin board.

There I am, smiling in the sun: pretty, unspoiled, and young. Not a murderer yet. Not a manslaughterer yet. My eyes prickle, clouds forming in my head. I'd do anything to be her again. Anything. She was perfect, she knew exactly who she was. But I—

My mouth drops as I pull out another picture. It's me and Elizabeth, standing together outside the theater. A pang in the chest. It must have been lunchtime. We're on the steps, smiling like we're sisters. Only ... one of us has red hair. And it's not me.

Elizabeth has long red hair, with long bangs in front. Mine is brown. She's in platform shoes and bell bottoms, but I'm in overalls and hiking boots.

I stare at the picture going in and out of focus in my hand.

I don't understand.

With shaky fingers, I put the pictures back into an envelope and shove them into the box. I pull out our senior yearbook, flipping through the pages, searching for something, an answer. Something to settle this tickling, creeping nausea. Here. This section. The theater arts pages. I breathe a sigh of relief to see myself there, just as I remembered—Juliet onstage gazing dreamily from her balcony.

The caption reads, *Opening night of spring play* Romeo and Juliet, *where (understudy) Jolene Vero plays Juliet.*

Understudy? Wait.

I wasn't the understudy.

No, no. This is backwards. Elizabeth was the understudy. I was home sick on opening night. Unless ...

I put the yearbook back and pull out a rolled-up poster from the same box with a sick feeling, an almost psychic feeling, because somehow I know exactly what I'm going to unfurl. I pick the tape off the side gently and unroll it like a scroll.

A painting. A strange blurry painting of Elizabeth with holes for eyes. Or me? Who painted who and asked for the painting back? I can imagine two stories at once. I can imagine I'm the painter, I can imagine I'm the painted. But it hits me that maybe my retrospect has been a flipped mirror image in some places instead of the real thing.

In high school, you were constantly on my back, Elizabeth's voice says. *Wouldn't leave me alone. Whatever I did, you had to do. Giving me that weird painting you made of me and then asking for it back. Trying to steal the guy I was into. Poisoning my fucking potion in* Romeo and Juliet! *Admit it, Jolene. Admit you did that.*

I put the yearbook into the box in a daze, floating back into the house again. My head is full of toxic smog as I go back into my room, shut the door behind me, and stare at the blank wall. I have such a good imagination I can project anything I want on that blank wall, like it's a movie screen and I'm a film projector. I can imagine covering for Joey backstage while he snuck out to smoke a joint. I can imagine pouring blue Windex into a potion prop bottle. I can imagine that now. But that doesn't mean it's real. I can imagine anything. I can imagine that I was obsessed with her from the moment she transferred to our school. That I wanted to be just like her. That I looked for Elizabeth everywhere I lived, for years and years. That I finally found her again in Berkeley.

Do you really want to know? the voice asks.

Yes. I really do.

Go look at your search history.

With bleary eyes, I turn on the dusty laptop that lives in this room. I haven't used it in a while, not since I was last staying here. I'm drunk and though it's hard to focus, I navigate to the search history. It's from last summer. A long string of searches for Elizabeth Smith.

Elizabeth Smith 29 years old California

Elizabeth Smith Berkeley

Her social media profile.

Her name on the website at the improv school; the class I signed up for.

Her address, somehow.

Searches for sublets in that neighborhood.

"Did I do that?" I ask. "Did I move there—to find her?"

Sometimes the question is the answer. I sit back, shut the laptop. The world seems to spin and I close my eyes.

I can barely remember anything from my last visit home. I got so drunk, I was on those antidepressants that made me black out easily. I must have done it and then forgotten, just completely forgotten.

The horror that I may never know what the fuck is really going on, that I can't be trusted with reality, that memory is nothing but speculation, threatens to swallow me alive. The jaws of the universe are open and ready to devour me. I squeeze my eyes shut and don't know what to do with this nightmarish revelation that I can't be trusted. That I will never in my life be quite sure where Elizabeth Smith ends and I begin.

You've always had a gift for forgetting, the voice says soothingly.

I am transcendently drunk, but you know what? The past is death. The past isn't real. The past is nothing but skeleton and bones.

I lie down on my bed, dizzy-hearted, carousel-brained. I'm good at forgetting. I'm good at life without hindsight. The key is to keep moving. Tomorrow I'll find something new to get excited about. Become a flight attendant or maybe a drama therapist. Move to a new city where I've never been and then another new city where I've never been. Forgetting is pretending. It's an art form. The voice is right, she's always right.

Tomorrow I'll wake up fresh and remember to forget again.

ONE MORE THING ...

WANT to read a bonus epilogue for *Like It Never Was* to see where Jolene goes next? Sign up for my newsletter and download it for free!

If you enjoyed *Like It Never Was,* good news: I have another psychological thriller called **They Are the Hunters** I think you'll like, too.

I also have a collection of psychological thrillers all set in the same universe. They're called **The Jolvix Episodes,** and you can **grab the first three books in this discounted box set** or read them one by one.

NOTE: These standalone novels can be read in whatever order you want, but *Eve in Overdrive* is technically a prequel to *The Slaying Game.*

- **THE PREDICTION:** A newlywed woman's smart device begins offering chilling predictions about her husband.

- **VIOLET IS NOWHERE:** A kidnapped woman and a stranger on the end of a phone line have one week to figure out how they're connected or their lives are over.

- **WHAT JANUARY REMEMBERS:** A dysfunctional family and their sentient companion bot gather for the holidays for the first time since their last Christmas together—which ended in attempted murder.

- **PEARL IN DEEP:** The love of one woman's life turns out to be a psychopath with a disturbing talent for deepfake video.

- **EVE IN OVERDRIVE:** An outspoken journalist buys a cutting-edge car only to find herself at the mercy of a vengeful internet troll.

- **THE SLAYING GAME:** A former Jolvix employee ends up at the center of a serial killer's deadly game.

- Or you can grab the first three Jolvix Episodes in this box set.

READ THE FIRST CHAPTER OF THEY ARE THE HUNTERS

AUGUST

AT TEN PAST MIDNIGHT, on a silent cul-de-sac, a picture-perfect house bursts into flames.

Flames melting the thick carpet. Flames leaping across the drapes. Flames creeping up the grand piano legs and crawling over the floral sofa. They hurry up the wallpaper and blacken the popcorn ceiling. They curl up the photos pinned to the refrigerator with fruit-shaped magnets and turn the grinning family's faces to ash. The boy's chess trophies to plastic puddles. The girl's closet full of sparkling leotards and dance shoes to rubble. The man's tennis rackets and true crime paperbacks swallowed by the blaze. The woman's plant-filled office spun into a mountain of cinders, her wall of accomplishments and degrees that took years to earn erased from this world in a matter of seconds.

It's a very particular flavor of devastation to lose a home, to lose everything you have in an hour's time. Some things are irreplaceable, like baby teeth, childhood drawings, a pageant crown, yearbooks signed with a rainbow of penmanship. But laptops with evidence, a notebook under the bed titled *Notes From a Psychopath*—those are irreplaceable too.

Some might consider themselves lucky to have lost such things.

Police arrive at the scene after the inferno has been extinguished. The firefighters' uniforms are charcoal-streaked, their faces exhausted. One is coughing so hard he's leaning over and puking on the sidewalk. A deputy is currently unrolling the yellow tape around the premises and politely asking the crowd of neighbors to step back. A few are still in slippers and robes. One neighbor, hair in a towel turban, is cradling her Scottish terrier like a baby and crying. The house is skeletal now, windows blown out, roof obliterated, chimney collapsed. The smoke is gone but the stench of it is pollutant. Everyone has a hand over their face to try to hide from it.

The dawn sun is out and the weather already balmy. Despite the morbid circumstances, the birds keep singing. As the firefighters take leave, applauded by the audience of onlookers, police and arson investigators cross the cheerful emerald rectangle of manicured lawn and swarm the house with gas masks and cameras. Within the first hour, the cadaver dog begins barking. It barks and barks and doesn't stop. Curiously, it's not when the dog is inside, sniffing the charred debris in the living room and bedrooms. It's in the backyard, near the fence, a place the flames never touched.

Fifteen minutes and a lot of digging later, the investigators gather around. They crouch to peer in the hole, a hush expanding between them as they understand what they're looking at.

A human head is buried in the rose garden.

———

THEY ARE THE HUNTERS is now available in ebook, audiobook, paperback, and free to read via Kindle Unlimited.

A NOTE FROM THE AUTHOR

If you got this far, I wanted to take a moment to thank you for reading and supporting my work. As an indie author, I put a ton of effort into each book—not just writing, but editing, marketing, and everything else it takes to guide a book through the whole process from a glimmer in the brain to a real, actual thing you can hold in your hands.

If you enjoyed it, please consider leaving a review. Reviews truly make an author's world go round. If you're interested in keeping up with book news, please join my newsletter or follow me on social media. And I love to hear from readers anytime at faith@faithgardner.com.

As always, I tried my damndest to fix every typo, but alas, I am only human. If you spot an error, please let me know! I appreciate every reader who makes me look smarter.

ACKNOWLEDGMENTS

My mom is everything to me. She's the reason I read, the reason I write, the reason my books are polished enough to publish, and the reason I have a career. Without her, none of this would be possible. As always, so much gratitude and love to you, Mom.

My sister Micaela is the absolute best, always dropping whatever she's doing to offer editorial help and encouragement and hilarious cat photos.

So much appreciation to Noelle Ihli and Steph Nelson, writers I deeply admire and who I'm lucky enough to call friends. Thanks to their feedback, I feel better about this book than anything else I've ever written.

Thank you to my family, my favorite people on earth. Big special forever thanks to Jamie for supporting me in every way a partner could.

A heartfelt thanks to readers/reviewers out there who dedicate so much time and passion to reading and boosting authors, all out of sheer love.

And thank you, dear reader, for spending a little time with me and my book.

ALSO BY FAITH GARDNER

ABOUT THE AUTHOR

Faith Gardner is the author of some YA novels and many suspense novels for adults. When she's not writing, she's probably playing music, cooking up a storm, or reading books in the bubble bath. She's also a huge fan of true crime, documentaries, and classic movies—with a special place in her dark little heart for melodrama and anything Hitchcock. She lives in the Bay Area with her family and you can find her at faithgardner.com.

Printed in Great Britain
by Amazon

44913323R00179